PRAISE FOR AMINA AKHTAR

Kismet

"With *Kismet*, Amina Akhtar invites us into the foxhole with Ronnie Khan, a New Yorker stationed in Sedona, just in time for Wellness World War. I loved this book—the claustrophobia of wide 'open' exclusive spaces. Amina teleports us to the passive-aggressive front lines in this dry landscape where caftans and corpses are equally foreboding. You want Ronnie to make a run for it, but she's a real hero—she wants to make a go for it. Lucky for us, she stays. *Kismet* is wicked and smart, a fly-on-the-wall humdinger where a light social gathering spikes your blood pressure. Amina deftly intertwines the earthly with the otherworldly. Read it now so you can be the one telling your friends about *Kismet*."

—Caroline Kepnes, *New York Times* bestselling author of *You*

"Amina Akhtar had me at ravens! Then she kept me turning the pages with her colorful cast of characters, keen insights, and layered, engaging heroine. *Kismet* is darkly funny, sharply observant, and full of surprises. Don't miss this utterly original and wildly entertaining thriller."

—Lisa Unger, *New York Times* bestselling author of *Last Girl Ghosted*

"The twists just keep coming in *Kismet*, Amina Akhtar's dark and delicious thriller. I can't imagine a better companion around these nail-biting curves than the novel's protagonist, Ronnie Khan, who is wide eyed yet smarter than she lets on, naive yet world weary. In a nutshell: she's the perfect heroine. I'd follow her anywhere."

—Jess Lourey, Amazon Charts bestselling author of *Unspeakable Things*

"Dead bodies are turning up in Sedona's upscale wellness community? Sign me up! I loved everything about *Kismet*, Amina Akhtar's sharply observant, funny thriller. Gleeful and gripping, Akhtar has knocked it out of the park with this wickedly entertaining, twisty novel."

—Jennifer Hillier, bestselling author of *Little Secrets*

"*Kismet* is funny, sharp, twisty, and spot on. Whether she's dealing with toxic relationships or everyday racism, Ronnie Khan is a character that you can't help but root for. I can't remember the last time I had this much fun reading a novel. Everyone, and I mean everyone, is going to be talking about those ravens."

—Kellye Garrett, Agatha, Anthony, and Lefty Award–winning author of *Like a Sister*

"Wickedly smart and outrageously entertaining, *Kismet* grabs hold and doesn't let go until a final twist that will have even the savviest readers gasping. Just like the clever, scene-stealing ravens, Akhtar skewers those who deserve it with her trademark wit while also layering in emotional nuance as compelling as the captivating mystery. At once atmospheric, chilling, and thought-provoking, *Kismet* will surely be this summer's must-read thriller."

—Brianna Labuskes, bestselling author of *A Familiar Sight*

"Amina Akhtar yet again brings her wickedly wicked style to this twisty thriller about a woman who's finally taken charge of her life—only to find dead bodies piling up around her in the wellness community where she's starting over. *Kismet* is a page-turner populated by eerie ravens and people who aren't what they seem in a perfectly unsettling desert setting."

—Gigi Pandian, *USA Today* bestselling author of *Under Lock & Skeleton Key*

"*Kismet* is a gleeful (and at times literal) skewering of influencer culture and clout chasing, as well as a deeply relevant look at how easily and often the white wellness world intersects with racism and cultural appropriation—and how blind we can be to that and to the stain it leaves on the world around us. A bold and insightful whodunnit that ensures you'll never look at ravens the same way again."

—Heather Cocks and Jessica Morgan, bestselling authors of *The Royal We* and *The Heir Affair*

"*Kismet* is an unforgettable read, with a fantastic setting and backdrop— sharp, haunting, and loaded with Amina Akhtar's hypnotic, visceral voice. Chilling, surprising, and loaded with biting commentary on the Sedona wellness community, this novel lingered with me for days after I finished it. *Kismet* is mesmerizing—a writer at the peak of her powers."

—Alex Segura, acclaimed author of *Secret Identity*, *Star Wars Poe Dameron: Free Fall*, and *Blackout*

"Unsettling from the very first page, *Kismet* takes its readers on a wild ride set in Sedona's wellness community, featuring a serial killer, crystals, and kick-ass ravens. It's strange and smart and spellbinding, with sharp social commentary and huge surprises. Another eerie gem from Amina Akhtar."

—Megan Collins, author of *The Family Plot*

"A mystery thriller just the way I like them—full of secrets and karma. Amina Akhtar creeps us out and keeps us guessing all the way!"

—Christopher Golden, *New York Times* bestselling author of *Road of Bones* and *Ararat*

Previous Praise

"*#FashionVictim* is sick and vicious and funny and voicey . . . I 'totes' loved this one."
    —Caroline Kepnes, *New York Times* bestselling author

"For those craving a new fashionably vicious read, this book is darkly satisfying."
    —*Martha Stewart Living*

"A diabolical page-turner . . . impossible to put down."
    —*Forbes*

"Darkly funny."
    —Fashionista

"As awesome as it sounds . . . welcome to the cruel world of fashion where women's looks, weight, and youth are the only things to value."
    —*Book Riot*

"Hilariously funny as well as profoundly unsettling . . . will keep readers hooked and laughing, if a bit uncomfortably, from page one until the shocking ending."
    —*Kirkus*

"Full of suspense, social satire, and deliciously dark humor, *#FashionVictim* gives 'killer wardrobe' a whole new meaning. I couldn't put it down."
    —Alison Gaylin, *USA Today* bestselling author of *If I Die Tonight*

"*#FashionVictim* is sharp, stylish, and gleefully sinister; you'll never read *Vogue* the same way again."
    —Jessica Morgan and Heather Cocks, founders of Go Fug Yourself and authors of the national bestseller *The Royal We*

"*#FashionVictim* gives new meaning to the phrase 'dressed to kill' . . . Instead of the devil wearing Prada, she's wearing her victim's blood in a perfect shade of Essie red."

—Aliza Licht, author of *Leave Your Mark*

"Every page of *#FashionVictim* pops with a dark and dishy verve. Fierce in every sense of the word."

—Jessica Tom, author of *Food Whore*

"*#FashionVictim* is a book to not only buy, keep, and read but to inhale from page one. The sense of menace in the prologue will hook readers from the get-go, and Akhtar's sharp as a tack writing will carry you along this entertaining read to a stunning end, um, ending."

—New York Journal of Books

"Gleefully bloodthirsty . . . this dark novel has the energy of *Heathers* gone twentysomething."

—*Publishers Weekly*

"The characters reminded me a great deal of the dark movie *Heathers* . . . a whole lot of sick fun. All I can hope is that the author was not speaking from reality . . . and that another book will be written very, very soon."

—*Suspense Magazine*

"The story's dark humor is one of its best attributes, and while the reader may wonder if Anya will get caught, there's no doubt that whatever happens, she'll be dressed to kill."

—*Mystery Scene*

KISMET

OTHER TITLES BY AMINA AKHTAR

#FashionVictim

KISMET

AMINA AKHTAR

A THRILLER

Text copyright © 2022 by Amina Akhtar
All rights reserved.

Published by Thomas & Mercer, Seattle

www.apub.com

Amazon, the Amazon logo, and Thomas & Mercer are trademarks of Amazon.com, Inc., or its affiliates.

ISBN-13: 9781542034265 (hardcover)
ISBN-10: 1542034264 (hardcover)

ISBN-13: 9781542034258 (paperback)
ISBN-10: 1542034256 (paperback)

Cover design by Shasti O'Leary Soudant

Printed in the United States of America

First edition

For my dad—thanks for moving to this strange place.
And for Bean.

Prologue

The sound of the shovel hitting yet another rock made her shudder. She hated that noise, like nails on a chalkboard but worse. Like the ground was screaming at her for what she'd done. Every time she hit a stone, she winced. *Killer! Murderer!*

"Shut up," she muttered.

Sweat dripped down her face, and she wondered for a moment if anyone could get DNA from it. They could get DNA from anything on TV shows, but out here, they probably wouldn't bother. Her sweat was mixing into the red earth—how would they even know to test it? They wouldn't; she was being paranoid, right? What else was new.

It was night out, and she should have been shivering, but digging was hard work. That, and the slightly cool December night should have been below freezing. But it was warm, too warm for this time of year. Too warm, too dry, and every living plant and tree and brush would soon be kindling for wildfires. She knew why. People had ruined this place. She hated them for that. She didn't even need long sleeves. Sweat dripped down, and she muttered a curse.

"Dammit! I hate sweating!"

Two ravens flew overhead, circling her. She heard them before she saw them. The swoop-swoop of their wings was hard to ignore. She was certain they were the largest ravens anywhere. Everything was different as if she'd stepped into some bizarro world instead of the desert. The spiders were massive and hairy, the hawks would try to attack small dogs, and the larger animals, well, they were big enough to keep you inside.

But the ravens she liked. They knew why this had to be done. They'd told her, in her dreams, in those moments they'd accepted food from her. They looked to her for help. She had to do this. The ravens just wanted to save their home. Every year more houses crept into the wilderness, more people set up their houses, not realizing someone already lived there. Or not caring. And the animals that transgressed on the humans' land, the animals who used old migration patterns that came from their ancestors, were killed.

This was their land. The animals' land. They were here before humans; they'd be here after. Not all of them, but the ones smart enough to adapt, to take what they needed. Like the ravens.

The birds called out, and she nodded at them. Her arms ached, and her hair was pulled into a sweaty ponytail. She wanted this to be over, to finish this. To finally end what she had started. She knew this had to be done. She'd chosen this. She'd chosen to kill, and now she had to bury her victim. Bury this body so deep that no one, not even the snakes and scorpions, would find it. Bury it so that the earth would accept it as its own. Bury it so she could forget her own betrayal.

"I did this. I killed you," she said softly as she worked. The birds cawed in response. They knew why she'd done this: it was for them.

It took another hour of filling before she was satisfied, and then she added rocks on top, not as a marker, but to look less like a grave.

This body would get no gravestone.

"I had to do it," she said. And then got up, wiping the dust off her hands.

She had killed someone. And now the desert held her secret.

Chapter 1

April

"Ooof!" Ronnie Khan stumbled, her hands landing hard on the dirt. The tiny rocks dug into her palms, and she knew that despite her jeans, her knees were going to be scraped. She hated this. Absolutely hated everything about this. Hiking was not her thing. How did anyone enjoy this? There were bugs everywhere and sharp, pointy plants whose only purpose was to maim careless humans like her.

"You okay?" Marley Dewhurst leaned over her, her face full of concern.

"Yeah, but wow, that's gonna leave a mark." Ronnie laughed to show she was okay. That she was willing to do this. Because you didn't change without making an effort. Real, honest-to-god change took work.

Marley held her hand out and yanked her up. "Whoa, a few inches more and you'd have landed on that." She pointed to a scorpion that had been disturbed. It was sitting next to two discarded water bottles and some granola bar wrappers.

Ronnie shrieked, jumping back. "I can do this. I can do this. I can do this," she said through gritted teeth. She was terrified of the desert. Why had she moved here? There were so many ways the desert could kill you. Every new step into the wilderness (or a well-worn trail that was packed with people most days) meant more chances to die.

"You can! You're amazing! You are doing it!" Marley cheered her on.

"Maybe your next project can have better motor skills," Ronnie joked.

"Oh, that's not fair! You're being way too hard on yourself. We've been here for three weeks, and this is the third hike you've been on. That's huge! And you're more than a project to me—you know that."

Huge. Yes it was. Ronnie had moved to Sedona, Arizona, with her friend and wellness fanatic on a whim. And now she was doing what people did out here: hiking. Lots and lots of hiking. Interspersed with yoga. She was doing everything the opposite way the old Ronnie would do things. She was saying yes to life, taking leaps of faith, and trying to be happy. To be well. She hated it.

But this was not what she thought enlightenment would be like. Wellness. All of that shit. If someone had warned her she'd have to hike this much, Ronnie may have just kept her brown butt home in Forest Hills, Queens.

"We're almost done," Marley said.

"You're lying, aren't you?"

"Maybe." Marley stuck her tongue out at her. "But for real, you've got this. You can do it. If you think you can do it, you'll do it."

"I can do it," Ronnie repeated. Like a mantra, like the stupid little engine. She could hike. It was just walking. In the wild. With scary things all around her. But the scariest of all—to Ronnie—were the snakes. Not any snakes, but rattlesnakes. They blended in so well, and it would be so easy to just happen upon one. And then: bam! Life over. How tragic to be out hiking, trying to be well, and then die because of nature.

Ronnie scanned the area around the trail for anything moving. If it moved, it would probably want to kill her. Unless it was a bird. The birds here were something else entirely. Not even remotely related to the pigeons back home. The cardinals were a stunning red, the ravens an inky black. And the size! She'd never seen birds that large just hanging out near humans. They were the third most striking thing about this place. The first two being the red rocks and the color of the sky, respectively. (Fourth was the sheer amount of trash tourists dumped on the trails.)

Overhead, a hawk circled. And larger birds.

"What are those?" She pointed up.

Marley shaded her eyes as she looked. "Huh. Eagles maybe? How cool."

"Or vultures."

"Okay, not as cool." They both laughed. "Ready?"

"Yep! Wait, did I tell you about my dream last night?"

"Let me guess, more ravens?"

Ronnie had been dreaming about the large black birds for weeks, ever since she'd spotted one in Marley's backyard. She couldn't help but be fascinated by them. But she hadn't told Marley exactly what they said to her in her dreams, what they showed her. To be honest, Ronnie didn't quite get what the dreams meant. She saw pictures of things. She'd long ago decided to ignore her dreams, but it was becoming impossible here. Nightly visions of ravens filled her head.

"Yes! And they were talking to me like we were friends, and I could understand them." She didn't say what they talked to her about. The things the dream birds told her made her nervous. They said they'd been waiting for her. And that made her uneasy. She didn't want Marley to think she was weird or crazy.

"You should be writing your dreams down. Maybe they mean something?" Marley suggested.

"Maybe."

Ronnie felt a pain in her knee. She was definitely going to be bruised later. But she was alive, she was here, and that counted for something, right?

It was early in the day, not yet eight o'clock. It was the only way to get some peace on the always-packed trails in Sedona. Come eight or eight thirty and you may as well be back on a crowded sidewalk in Manhattan. It was April, and the trails could get hot. Especially right now, with the temperatures warmer than usual. Ronnie felt sweat run down her face. She wished she'd worn a hat to cover her black hair. Her head felt like it was cooking in the bright Arizona sun.

They walked in silence for the next few minutes. Mainly because Ronnie was trying to keep up without panting and Marley was in the zone. That happy wellness zone. Like a runner's high, only about life. She was the enlightened one. She was the one who'd saved Ronnie, moved her here. Marley was teaching Ronnie to be more empowered. And now she was showing her how to live the perfect, well life. It involved a lot of hikes and smoothies and something called adaptogens. (Ronnie had no idea what adaptogens actually were.)

Just a little more—you can do this. You can!

And then her ankle twisted before she realized it. She went down, again, off to the side of the trail.

"Dammit!" she cursed.

Marley snorted. "You have two left feet today!"

"Ugh, tell me about it."

"Remember, you're just starting your journey. Be kind to yourself."

"Yeah, yeah." Ronnie rolled her eyes but knew her friend was right. She was comparing herself to Marley in her head, and that was a waste of time. Marley had a head start on being well. Ronnie shook her head when Marley offered to help her up. "I got it." She took a deep breath and grimaced. "What's that awful smell?"

"I don't smell anything?"

"Oh god, it smells like something died. That would explain the vultures."

Once she lumbered to her feet, Ronnie looked around. "Over there?" About fifteen feet off the trail, a whole lot of birds surrounded some plants, fighting over whatever they were eating. It was like a writhing mass of feathers.

"What the hell?"

"Let me look." Marley had a hiking stick with her, and she used it to poke the small plants between them and the birds. "What is it?" She leaned forward.

Ronnie scrambled after her. She wasn't going to let her friend face the pile of birds herself. She stood next to Marley and inched forward. "Let me see the stick."

She carefully used it to poke through the feathers even farther. And then she saw it. A glimpse of skin. Human skin.

Ronnie always thought if she found a dead body, she'd scream. Or faint. Or something. But she didn't say a word. She couldn't. She opened her mouth, and nothing came out. Until her mouth watered uncontrollably and she turned to the side and vomited. Loudly.

The sound of her retching sent the birds into the air. And now she could fully see what they were feasting on: A head had been placed on an agave plant. Next to it, on a prickly pear cactus, were human hands and feet.

"Holy shit," Marley whispered, leaning in closer. "Is it real?"

"Don't get close!" Ronnie rinsed her mouth with her water. "Shit, call 911."

"My phone doesn't work out here." Marley held her phone up to the sky in a vain attempt to get service.

"Fuck."

"You stay here, and I'll hike down. It'll be the fastest way."

"What?! No, you can't leave me with that!" She gestured to the head. She was pretty sure it was a man's head. But she didn't want to look too closely. The birds wouldn't let her nearer anyways.

"I can get to someone faster than you."

Ronnie groaned, but her friend was right. She'd only slow things down.

"I'll be fast, I promise. You have enough water? Don't puke anymore, okay?"

Ronnie nodded, miserable. She was going to have to babysit body parts. What stage of enlightenment was this?

She waited for what seemed like hours. Days. "This is hell. Hey, you, shoo!" She tried to keep the birds from feasting on the head but gave up. This was their turf; she had no say. And frankly, she didn't want to upset them. The way some of them looked at her, like they could see through her, was unnerving. A few of them were investigating her puddle of vomit. Gross.

One black raven—which stood over a foot tall—came near her. It pecked her water bottle with its beak.

"Oh, you want water? Okay, hold on." Ronnie slowly poured some out for the bird, who drank it gladly. A few others came to her until she had no water left. "Great, now I'm going to die too." She wasn't mad, though. She marveled that the birds were smart enough to ask her for water. Or were used to begging from humans.

Her backpack had no more bottles but did have more sunblock. Ronnie sprayed it on herself. The sun was so strong out here. Even ten minutes outside would make her tan, and hours would actually make her burn. She wanted neither thing to happen. She could practically hear her aunt's voice saying, "Good desi girls don't get tans."

At least she had a view of the arch here. That was the big draw of this trail. A sandstone arch called Devil's Bridge. The name made her shiver. *What a place to dump a body. Or part of a body.* They weren't on the arch itself. That was too advanced a hike for Ronnie. But normally, there was a line of people waiting to walk on the thin arch, take photos for their 'Gram.

What if the person who left these is still here?

The thought made her nervous. She looked around for anyone. They had beat the rush on the trail, but any minute now it would be teeming with more people than ants. It was blessedly empty now but not for long. *Oh god, what if they're watching me?*

"Over there!" she heard Marley shout. There her friend was, bringing in a couple of park rangers. She ran over and hugged Ronnie. "You okay?"

Ronnie had never been so happy to see anyone in her life. "Just making friends with the birds. You got any water? They drank all mine."

"Ladies, can you stay back while we investigate?"

"With pleasure," Ronnie said, walking back to the trail and as far from the head as she could get. She didn't want to see it. The birds had picked part of the skull clean. At least she didn't know who it was—they were so new to town that they barely knew anybody. Small favors.

Soon, a crowd had formed: the two park rangers, some state troopers, and a sheriff. (The sheriff badge made Ronnie giggle. She didn't know anyone still had sheriffs.) They were all white men.

"Looks like someone was eaten," one of the men said.

Ronnie and Marley stood around, unsure if they could leave.

"Um, excuse me? Do you need us still?" Marley asked. Ronnie was grateful she was there. Her friend knew how to handle things.

"We need a statement from you both."

"Is there somewhere indoors we can do that? I'm about to burn." She smiled widely, and the men nodded. No one said no to Marley. It was one of her many talents. They glanced from her to Ronnie and frowned. It was subtle, but Ronnie saw it. She didn't have Marley's gifts. Or her blonde hair. In Arizona, blonde was the preferred color.

"You can sit in our car."

"That'd be lovely, thank you," Marley purred, and soon they were in an air-conditioned SUV.

Thank god, Ronnie thought. And then felt guilty for being happy. There was a body out there. That was why they were in the car. *But whatever, I didn't know him.*

———

"You girls didn't see anything else, anyone acting strange on the trail?" Sheriff John Reynolds asked.

Marley shook her head, and Ronnie shrugged.

"We tried to beat the crowds," Ronnie said.

"We only saw that because Ronnie fell and said something smelled bad."

"Sensitive nose, eh?" He grinned.

"Yeah." Ronnie hated this. She didn't like being near the police. They could pin things on her on a whim—she saw it happen on the news. And that made her sweat. A lot.

"Ronnie, you need more water," Marley said, concerned. "You're overheating."

"Sorry." She wiped her sweat with a tissue. "I sweat a lot."

"Sweating is healthy," Marley reminded her. "Anyways, that's it: we saw it, I ran to get you while Ronnie stood guard, and now we're here. Anything else you need?"

"Just where you're staying and how long you'll be in town."

"Oh, we live here. We just moved here." Marley grinned.

"Welcome to Sedona," he replied. "Sorry about the . . ."

"Head? Yeah, like, does that happen a lot here?" Ronnie asked.

"No. We don't get random body parts like that."

"Huh. Weird." She wanted to say that this place seemed a good spot to dump things. That the desert was vast, the climate harsh, and the ability to find a body slim. If she were murdering someone—not that she would—she'd totally use the desert to hide things. Or a pig farm. Pigs ate anything. A pig farm in the desert? Now that would work wonders—

"Ronnie, hello?" Marley snapped her fingers in front of her face.

"Sorry, I zoned out. All the heat." Ronnie smiled weakly.

"Let's get you home."

———

Home was a two-bedroom house nestled in a small development in Sedona. They were renting, for now. Marley wanted a larger house, but the prices were astronomical, even for her. (She'd moved out West with her trust fund and Ronnie.) The better the view of the red rocks, the higher the price tag.

"Jesus, what a freaky morning. How are you feeling?"

"Okay. That was scary."

"But you did it! You made it through! We should celebrate." Everything was a reason to celebrate with Marley. Ronnie didn't quite understand the concept. Celebrate getting through the day? Why?

"I don't know, feels weird to celebrate when someone died." She grimaced. *Please don't let me hurl again.*

"Right. You're right." Marley nodded. "One hundred percent. But we didn't know him. Or her. Did you maybe take a photo of it while I was gone?"

"What?! No! Oh my god, I would never."

Marley made a face. "Damn. Was kind of hoping to post it to Instagram."

Ronnie stared at her in shock. There were things about her friend she didn't understand. Like wanting to post a picture of a severed head on social media. But then, she didn't know Marley that well. In fact, she'd only met her a few months earlier, in January.

"Let's meditate and maybe pray for the victim. How's that?"

They sat on the floor, pillows all around them. And Marley intoned, "Take a deep breath. And exhale everything you're holding in. And inhale happy, positive thoughts. Exhale creepy, bad ones." This went on for thirty minutes. All the while Ronnie couldn't stop thinking about that head. She'd felt like it could see her. Which was stupid—it was dead. But still.

And then she thought of the ravens she'd given water to. She'd read that ravens and crows remembered faces and those that were kind (or unkind) to them. *God, I hope they remember me as nice. And don't come into my dreams anymore.*

———

Living here had not been a goal of Ronnie's. She hadn't even known Sedona existed before she'd met Marley. But now she was a person who meditated, did yoga, hiked, and drank smoothies. A far cry from her life in Queens with her aunt. But then, she also had never stumbled over a body in Queens.

This was week three of Life with Marley. Like, actually living with her. And Ronnie often felt like she was an anthropologist living among a strange people. White people. Marley was different from any person she'd ever known. She was thoughtful and sweet and for some reason wanted Ronnie to thrive. Actually thrive. It was fascinating and alien to Ronnie. She was used to living with her Pakistani family and Pakistani friends and Pakistani boss.

Though both she and Marley had been born and raised in New York, they'd grown up in vastly different worlds. Ronnie's revolved around her aunt and keeping their house clean, while Marley was doing step-and-repeat poses since she was a toddler with her socialite mother, Joan. Yet here they both were, living together. In Arizona.

Ronnie still wasn't sure if she'd made a giant mistake in moving across the country with a woman she barely knew. She couldn't go back to Queens if this fell through—she'd sold her house. Her parents' house. It was all gone. Everything was gone. She had to move forward, face the unknown, all that fun stuff.

Life was here now, with the ravens and scorpions and stray human heads.

———

Before

Ronnie had started six weeks of empowerment lessons with Marley in January. It was part of a "new year, new you" challenge. She felt strange needing lessons on standing up for herself, but the truth was, they were helping. She was standing taller, saying no to things—at work. And she was starting to see that maybe the reason she was so miserable was because of her homelife. That perhaps she didn't need to endure everything her aunt Shameem threw at her.

But Farrah—her boss, who had insisted she needed the lessons and paid for them—had only covered six weeks of Marley. And that was coming to an end. Marley had promised she'd be a new person, someone unrecognizable. But after six weeks, Ronnie felt the exact same.

"Um, do you think we can do another six weeks?" Ronnie asked Marley after they finished her final lesson. "I'm just getting so much out of this."

"Oh, I'd love to. But I'm moving. To Arizona. Didn't I tell you?"

Ronnie stared at the blonde woman in front of her. "Oh. No, but that's so cool." Arizona. The one person who believed in her—besides Farrah—was leaving. Figured.

"You should come," Marley said, nodding her head. "Oh my god, you should. It would be huge for you! Don't say no, okay? Just think about it."

For the next twenty minutes, Marley went on and on about her recent visit over the holidays to Sedona. "Oh my god, the hiking! And the rocks! It's just the most magical place, and I swear, being there makes you automatically happy."

"It sounds amazing." And it did.

"It is! You'd love it," Marley said, an authority now on what Ronnie would and wouldn't like.

"I wish. I could never leave like that."

"Why not? I mean, you're an empowered woman. You can do whatever you want. And isn't it your house? Like, you can sell it and be free. Shoot, with the market being what it is, you can sell by tomorrow."

"Haha! That's funny." Marley made good jokes.

"I'm serious! You don't have to stay here. You can go anywhere you want in the world. Just say yes to life."

Say yes to life.

Just say yes.

Marley had said at the beginning of classes that this was going to help Ronnie be a new person. "New year, new you." And now she had a shot at leaving and starting fresh, away from her aunt's prying and abuse. It was one of those aha moments when a lightbulb went off. Ronnie suddenly saw the rest of her life laid out before her. If she didn't leave now, she never would. She'd be Shameem Khala's servant for the rest of her life. She'd never know a moment's happiness. Or what love was. She would be here. Day in, day out.

"I'm in. Take me with you," Ronnie said.

Marley looked at her with surprise. "Really? Because that would be amazing."

"Yeah, if you don't mind a tagalong."

"You're anything but. Oh my goddess, get ready because your new life is waiting for you!"

———

Meditation time was over. "Let's get lunch!" Marley chirped. She was completely unfazed by the human body parts they'd seen just that morning. Ronnie tried to shake it off too. But she couldn't help it. She felt sad for the person and terrified that things like that happened in this cheerful tourist town.

"Sounds great!" *Please don't be salads. I want a burger.* "I'll go change into something more appropriate."

"Sounds good. Oh, and Ron? I'm proud of you." Marley said that a lot. It made Ronnie feel strange. Uncomfortable and awkward but still a bit warm? Whatever, it was nice to hear. For once.

Ronnie had never had friends before. Not real ones, not like Marley. And she had no idea how to be a friend, except to do whatever Marley wanted. Her aunt never let her have friends or a social life. No one from outside the community at least.

When she was little, she had had friends. She'd made some in preschool and kindergarten. But then everything changed. Her parents died, leaving Ronnie—and their house—in the care of her mother's sister, Shameem. Ronnie was six and barely remembered those years. (She tried not to. No sense wanting something that no longer existed.) She only remembered when everything changed and she was left alone. Shameem was different from Ronnie's mother. Nusreen Khan used to play with Ronnie's hair, oil it, braid it. She'd taught her daughter how to cook and read and delighted in everything Ronnie did. Shameem could barely stand the sight of Ronnie. But her aunt loved the four-bedroom house that came with her niece.

Ronnie sighed and picked up her phone to call her aunt. They hadn't spoken since Ronnie had moved out West. She knew her aunt wouldn't answer; she wanted to hear her voice on the voice mail. It was both comforting and enraging, and that kept her going. No point in leaving a message. Her aunt would never call her back. Not after what Ronnie did, leaving like that. Selling the house. *Her* house. It had always been Ronnie's house.

Ronnie put on a sleeveless tank top and tight yoga leggings. These were Marley clothes. Marley had bought them for her. In the four months she had known her, Marley had made Ronnie over into the perfect image of wellness. Her hair was medium length now, and Marley told her to leave it wavy and curly. Before, it had been an untamed mass that was cut maybe once every two years—if Shameem allowed it. Ronnie's skin was radiant, her mustache waxed into oblivion. Her teeth were as white as Marley's, and Ronnie added tinted moisturizer and mascara as she got ready for some lunch. Because, like Marley said, looking good was a big part of feeling good. Ronnie still wasn't used to going sleeveless. It was a desi thing. Good Pakistani girls didn't show off their skin.

Until now.

"How do I look?" She stood for Marley's critical examination. She watched as Marley tilted her head, narrowed her eyes.

"Good, but you need at least one crystal necklace. I mean, we have to look the part."

"Oh, totally!"

The café was one of Marley's favorite new spots. Well, everything was new to them. But this one was her favorite. Because everyone went there: the Tree of Life Café.

Marley strode in and smiled at everyone. When she ordered, she asked for a healer's discount. "I'm a life coach and healer," she said.

"No way! I'm a clairvoyant!" the waitress said. "Our chef is a medium and a Reiki healer."

The table next to them chimed in as well. "We're pet psychics."

Everyone was something in this town. Everyone except Ronnie. When the waitress and the table near turned to look at her, she just shrugged.

"I'm, uh, nothing?"

Chapter 2

The Town

The police had found her body. *Her* body. Her gift to the universe. Matt Ford had been special, and he hadn't even known it. He was evil. That he had known—he'd admitted it when he'd begged for his life.

"Please, you can't kill me! I'm sorry. I didn't mean to hurt anyone!" He'd begged and cried. But it was too late; the universe demanded retribution. Matt had taken advantage of people wanting to better themselves. He'd even caused at least one death that she knew of. She was certain there were more bodies linked to him. There was nothing redeeming about Matt, not one thing. He may have been kind to people when he needed to be, but it was a facade. And she saw through it.

She'd wanted his body to be found—it was why she'd left him in a well-trafficked hiking area. It would be packed with people come sunup. Sedona's trails always were. You couldn't hike anywhere without running into tourists, their trash strewn about. Often, if you weren't lucky, you'd step in a pile of shit, and it was human shit at that.

If she could, she'd rid the area of all these people. But what was a tourist town without tourists? No, this would do. Perhaps it would scare away the shittier folks. That's what nature wanted. It wanted to be left alone. She could hear it screaming for help. But no one was paying attention.

"Why?" he'd asked.

"Because the ravens," she'd replied. The birds. They'd started all of this. They were the ones who came to her in her dreams, telling her how to heal herself, the land. How to make things better. They'd wanted Matt to die for his crimes. She'd had no choice, really. You couldn't say no to nature like that. It would find a way to kill him if she didn't. So she'd promised the birds she'd do it. She'd take on their quest, such as it was. In return, they'd help her. Guide her.

She'd killed Matt on a full moon. It was a release. A gift to everyone. *I did this for all of us,* she thought. He'd deserved it. They all did. They weren't the real deal—they were frauds. They were worse than frauds: they were scammers with bad karma, taking advantage of desperate people. And there was a body count because of them. She was the hand of fate, guiding them to the next dimension. Or hell, whatever.

The hikers—she'd heard—had puked when they'd found her gift. That made her laugh. This was definitely her calling.

It takes a woman to get things done right.

Matt had never known he was being followed; that's how clueless he'd been. He hadn't known she'd trailed him for weeks, day in and day out. Men rarely noticed anything. She could have dressed up as a scary clown everywhere he went, and nothing. Absolutely nothing. She laughed again, this time a giggle. Men *did* notice a woman's laugh. But not Matt.

Sometimes, she'd tried to get him to spot her. She'd inch closer, touch his hand. Inhale his scent. He'd smelled like tobacco, patchouli, and sweat when he was alive. Now he smelled like dead flesh. One time she'd even almost reached over and moved his brown hair out of his eyes.

The desert held a lot of secrets, and one of them was the location of Matt's torso, arms, and legs. They were her puzzle pieces, and maybe she'd let them be found. She had left his head near Devil's Bridge Trail, and she found that fitting. Matt belonged in hell, and this was the closest she could get him. The trail had a sandstone arch, and she'd wanted to put him up there, but truthfully, she'd been exhausted. Dismembering a body took work, and her muscles had been aching already. Add to that a hike, and she had been ready to dump him in a parking lot.

So instead, she'd put him with a view of the arch. She wasn't a monster. He may as well have something to look at while he rotted. She'd placed his head on the top of an agave plant as if it were growing out of the thick spikes, and his hands had been stuck on a prickly pear cactus next to it.

"There. See? You wanted to be one with nature." It was more than he deserved. He hadn't been that kind to his victims, hadn't afforded them a beautiful view in death. He deserved to have his face eaten off by fire ants while alive or be stung by hundreds of scorpions. But his screams would have alerted someone. There was always a hiker around, even when you found the most deserted spot you could. Or, in this case, one of the most crowded spots. But no one would hit the trail until the sun came out.

The universe needed her to do this. The animals and the trees, the tarantulas and the scorpions. Even the coyotes and javelinas were begging her to make this effort, to sacrifice those who had wronged her—and everyone else. The ones who made things worse here.

"The universe requires retribution," she'd said. "This will help us heal, to be well." That was all she wanted, for the land, the birds, herself, for all of them to be well again.

Matt deserved this and every other evil she could wish upon him. It was his karma, not hers. This was what happened when you did what he had done.

A raven had swooped over her head, the wings so large they made noise. It had cawed once it got to the top of a pine tree.

She'd glanced at it, and for a moment, they'd gazed at each other. The raven was pleased. She was certain. She'd smiled and waved to it. "I did this for you," she'd whispered. It knew. She had made her vow to them not too long ago. Once they'd come into her dreams. She'd clear this area, their home, of evil. They just had to let her.

Now for my next one. Matt wasn't the only person she'd have to take care of. She was following others, writing down their names and actions and where they went each day. They all deserved what was ahead. She was a Fury, righting the wrongs of the world, spurred on by the energy of nature around her.

"I'm coming for you." And then she let loose another bone-chilling laugh.

Chapter 3

Before

Shameem Khala stared at her.

"You cannot be serious." Her accent was heavier than Ronnie's mother's. Or what Ronnie remembered of her mother, which wasn't much. Snippets. Fragments. Like how her mother's hands smelled like garlic but were so soft; Ronnie loved touching them. Or how she would hand-feed Ronnie and gently comb her hair.

Nusreen had been in the US longer than her sister. Shameem had come to find an American husband and lived with her sister's family. Instead, she'd ended up raising her niece and stayed single. Not exactly what she'd planned for her life.

"I'm selling the house," Ronnie said. Her voice squeaked. She could do this. Marley told her she should do this. *Be empowered. This is what you need to do. This is your life.*

"It's my home!" her aunt yelled, her eyes wide.

Ronnie knew that look. But she wasn't going to back down. "No, it's my house. They left it to me." She was about to add that she would split the proceeds of the sale with her aunt, when she felt the sting on her face.

Slap!

Shameem Khala had put her whole palm into that. Ronnie rubbed her sore face.

"You zaleel larki! I raised you here and now you throw me out! Like I'm garbage? You're a disgrace to your parents. I gave up my life for you. I did everything and this is how you treat me?"

Ronnie remained stone faced. Her aunt loved to slap her. Hit her when she talked back. It wasn't abuse; it was just how things were. You didn't talk back to your elders. Every desi knew that. And maybe if Shameem hadn't given up everything to stay on the sofa in Ronnie's house all day long, she'd have found love. Or someone who could tolerate her. But Ronnie could never say that to her aunt.

"You have sixty days to move." Her voice was steady—she wasn't sure how.

"You would do this to family? Desi girls do not behave so disrespectfully! Shame on you!" Her aunt spit on the floor. "You're Amrikan now," she hissed. "Just put me in a nursing home and leave me to die." Amrikan was an insult thrown at the ABCDs: American-born confused desis. That's what her cousins called her back in Pakistan. Ronnie was just another desi with an identity crisis. She was Amrikan now. Any instance of her having a backbone was dismissed with that insult.

Ronnie shrugged though inside she was terrified. She'd never stood up to her aunt before. Not like this. Only over small things. Like cutting her hair or wanting to wear a shorter dress. Or even just going out after work. Shameem disapproved of everything.

"That's not how we behave in Pakistan." She clucked at her niece.

Then go back there, Ronnie wanted to say. But she held her tongue. She was an expert at keeping her mouth shut and her face blank. She'd be lying if she said a part of her didn't enjoy sticking it to her aunt just a little. Shameem Khala deserved it. But Ronnie would never admit it out loud.

Word spread in the local community that Ronnie was throwing her aunt out on her ass. And soon, other aunties came over to chastise her. The backup, as she thought of them. Her aunt's flying monkeys.

"Behti, how can you do this after all she's done for you?"

"Your parents wanted her to live here. She's your khala!" *Khala* meant your mother's sister.

"This is bad behavior."

Ronnie didn't argue. There was no point. She'd never be right. Only they, the aunties, were right. Only their approval mattered. When one of them was threatened, they swarmed together, breaking the will of anyone who tried to go up against them.

"How's Preethi?" she asked Savita Auntie. Hindus, Muslims, and Sikhs mixed in her neighborhood as if the fighting in their home countries didn't exist. Preethi had run off and married a white man. She had been excommunicated. Nothing as official as the church, but she was no longer welcome in Forest Hills.

Savita Auntie spit on the ground at the mention of her daughter.

They would do the same when her own name came up. Ronnie knew that.

Chapter 4

"Now take a deep inhale and hold it for three . . . two . . . one. And release." The yoga instructor was smiling that empty look that said she'd hit nirvana. Ronnie envied her. At least this woman had a goal, a purpose. She had neither. Her entire purpose in life had been to survive her aunt. And now that she had, she had no idea what the hell to do with herself.

"Now shift into downward dog. Make your transitions as important as your poses."

Sweat was running down every part of Ronnie's body. Pooling on her mat. This wasn't one of those sweaty yoga classes—this was just Ronnie. Her left hand started to slide, too slick to grip the mat. *Don't fall, please don't fall.*

"Ooof!" Down she went, landing on her face. *Dammit.* She heard a soft giggle—Marley was laughing.

"Sorry," her friend mouthed. She was in a perfect downward dog. And not sweating at all. In fact, Marley was pristine. God, sometimes Ronnie hated her.

Take that back. You do not. Marley is a good person and good to you.
Fine, I take it back.

When class finally ended, with a *nah-mah-stay* that made Ronnie flinch, she was relieved. And starving. Brunch was next. Who didn't enjoy brunch?

Part of trying to get the lay of the land involved going to the most crowded classes and meals, something Ronnie would prefer to avoid. Marley insisted, though. Marley had a plan. She wanted to insinuate herself into this community of healers, hippies, and New Agers. She wanted to be the big fish in a small pond full of crystals. And she'd spend whatever it took to make that happen. And Ronnie was along for the ride.

She wiped herself with a towel. How did these women not sweat? How was she the only person who looked like she'd been caught in a downpour? Was there some yogi secret she wasn't entitled to yet? She turned to ask her friend, but Marley was already at the front of the room talking to the instructor. Two happy white women laughing at life. That was Sedona in a nutshell.

Ronnie begrudgingly joined her.

"That was a brilliant class, thank you!" Marley said.

"My pleasure. Your form is perfect." The instructor was tall, thin, blonde. Her skin was too tan, not from the sun but from bronzer. "I'm Caroline." She looked closer to her late forties and she had a slight British accent.

"Marley. And this is Ronnie. We just moved here."

"Well, welcome!"

"I'm a healer. But wow, it's hard to meet people here." Marley was so good at this.

"It is. But I'm always down to grab some matcha if you are!" Caroline grinned at her, and Ronnie, for a brief moment, saw their friendship laid out. Marley and Caroline would become the best of buds. They'd be a match made in heaven. Marley would start to push Ronnie out, and then one day, she wouldn't want her around at all.

The idea of that froze her stomach. She hadn't settled in, and already she was seeing the writing on the wall.

"Marley, we should go." She nudged her friend.

"Oh right. Food!" Marley laughed. Caroline laughed with her. They were already mirroring each other. Though, Ronnie thought, Marley was the more attractive one. Caroline had years on her.

"Just be careful out there. I heard they found a body."

"We found it!" Marley squealed before lowering her voice. "We found it. Oh my goddess, it was terrifying—right, Ron?"

"So scary."

"We were hiking and there it was!"

"You should really talk to a friend of mine at the news station in Phoenix. They wanted more details," Caroline said.

"Oh, I don't know."

"I mean, you'd be a natural on TV. I can have them call you both."

"No. Not me," Ronnie interrupted. "I mean, I don't want to be on TV. But, uh, Marley, you could do it."

"Oh, do it with me, come on! It'll be fun!"

"No, I'm good. This is your moment."

TV. No, she didn't want to be on TV. She didn't want attention. Ronnie wanted to sort herself out without prying eyes. She'd been raised being watched closely by every auntie around. Now she wanted to move in anonymity.

"Well, here's my info. Text me and I'll pass your info along." Caroline smiled as she said it. Ronnie hated her. She couldn't help it. She felt a deep revulsion for the woman. She wanted to wipe that stupid grin off her face. Mainly, she wanted to keep her away from Marley, her only friend. *You can't have her.*

"Let's go," she urged again. And this time, Marley followed her.

"Wow, how nice was she? I told you people here are lovely."

"Uh-huh."

"You don't like her?"

"Honestly, you're way better and cooler than her."

Marley laughed. "You're so sweet and good to me. Come on, I'm famished."

she learned to keep to herself and, eventually, stop having altogether—Shameem wouldn't look at her. Or go near her. If her aunt could despise her more, Ronnie wasn't sure how.

To a young child, it didn't take much to see monsters. And Shameem hid any abuse from anyone except Ronnie. She slapped, she hit with flyswatters, she threw shoes. She would beat the weirdness out of this child. She put Ronnie to work in the kitchen, hitting her with wooden spoons when she couldn't get things right.

"You live in my house, you live by my rules," Shameem was fond of saying. Ronnie didn't find out it was, in fact, *her* house for decades. "If you don't like it, leave. Go to the foster care. Or I can send you to Pakistan." That threat was enough to make Ronnie behave. Pakistan, where she knew no one. Barely spoke the language. She wouldn't be able to make it.

"Sorry, Khala. I'll do better." *Always do better. I must be good.*

———

"Shhh, it's on!" Marley tucked her long legs underneath her on the gray sofa. She turned the volume up on the TV. Ronnie joined her, handing her friend a glass of wine to match the one for herself.

Another new thing for her: drinking alcohol. She'd never really drunk before. Not because of religion. Shameem only went to the mosque to keep up appearances. Ronnie had never had the opportunity to drink before she met Marley. She had had no social life and no one to drink with. And certainly not someone who would show her how to drink. (Was she supposed to just order something at a bar? She didn't know.)

"Body parts were found on a popular hiking trail in Sedona, Arizona." The news cut to Marley, looking stunning. She had on a white caftan and wore two crystals around her neck. "I was hiking with my friend Ronnie, and we smelled something awful. There were vultures everywhere, it was like a scene in a movie!"

"Oh wow, you look amazing!" Ronnie said, her tongue already heavy from half a glass of wine. "You're a natural for TV."

"I still wish you'd joined me."

Ronnie didn't say anything, just drank her wine. Not everyone was meant to live in the spotlight.

Caroline texted as they were watching. Marley clapped with glee and narrated the texts for Ronnie.

"Oh my goddess, she wants to hang out! Finally! A friend here!"

A friend here. A friend who wasn't Ronnie.

"She wants to celebrate. Want to come?"

"Uh, no, I'm good."

Ronnie watched her friend jump for joy. She never inspired such joy in Marley. And she hated that about herself. Well, she hated a lot about herself.

It's fine, I can have fun by myself. Sure. Why not.

Chapter 5

The Town

The ravens were curious. There was a new human in town. Two, actually, but only one was worthy of their attention. She was leaving them bits of food. Fish, meat, water. And she wanted nothing in return. They weren't sure they could trust her. But for now, they feasted while she watched.

Humans could rarely be trusted. But every so often one came along who wasn't awful. They weren't sure where this one stood on their scale, but for now, food was food.

They ate and left, not lingering. Though they kept watch over her. To see what she'd do next. The ravens kept watch over everything here. Like they were sentinels of nature.

They had seen that body get left. The pieces. Hell, they'd tried to eat some of it. But humans tasted funny. Not at all as good as other meat. Evil humans tasted worse, and they weren't sure why exactly. But one was dead. And that was reason to celebrate. Their human—not the one feeding them but the one who had promised to help them—had done what she'd said she would. She had killed him to make them happy, to right the wrongs that had happened.

As a test, they left a shiny piece of metal for the human feeding them. See if she accepted the offering. Nothing was free; everything was a transaction. In nature, with humans. Symbiosis. That's how it worked.

They watched as the human picked up the metal and held it in awe.

"Thank you!" she called to them.

Maybe this one wouldn't be too bad.

Chapter 6

Ronnie stood on the trail where she'd found that head. The skull was down to the bone in some places. She felt panicked and glanced down at her bare feet. Why would she be out here without shoes? Any number of things could sting or bite her.

She didn't want to see this. She knew it was bad. But the ravens told her to keep watching, so she did. She saw a woman; the face wasn't clear. Just that she had dark hair, like Ronnie. She was the one who had left the head. She turned to face Ronnie, and she found herself staring at herself.

Ronnie woke up screaming. Another freaky dream. That's all it was. *Just a dream. Nothing to worry about. Just ignore it and it'll go away.* She curled up with her pillow, keeping it close enough to her mouth that should she scream again, she could muffle the sound.

———

"I have a surprise for you!" Marley grinned at her. Marley loved to surprise her. It was something Ronnie had to adjust to. Surprises, in her limited experience, were never good.

"Oh?"

"Yes, we are getting massages! My treat! You've been working so hard getting us settled." Ronnie had been too. She'd helped get things moved; she'd sorted out furniture delivery; she'd even dealt with the local propane people, who would come fill giant tanks of gas the size of small cars for the houses to use. The propane tanks were outside every home. There were no gas lines put in. If there were ever a fire, they'd all go up in one giant fireball.

"I am a little tense," she admitted.

"See! Go get ready! Let me pamper you! Caroline told me about this amazing spa."

Caroline. Ever since their night out, all Marley talked about was Caroline. Ronnie hated the woman. It was an immediate dislike. If she examined her feelings more, she'd probably realize she was jealous.

Ronnie ran to her room. This room was nothing like her room at home. After Ronnie's parents passed, Shameem had put Ronnie in a smaller room in the basement. The windows were too high for her to reach, and the floor needed to be fixed with new concrete. Her parents had planned on redoing the basement but never got to it. Ronnie's old room upstairs was fit for a little princess, full of toys and a canopy bed. Her new room held a plain twin-size bed and not much else. "So you can be closer to the kitchen." Her room at Marley's was large enough for a king-size bed (though she only had a queen). And the lighting was beautiful. The walls were painted a blinding white, and Marley had insisted on pale pink and light gray everything for the furniture.

"I want you to feel at home," she insisted.

Ronnie wasn't fond of massages. Touching was strange to her. She felt herself freeze and tense up whenever someone hugged her or patted her hand. Something Marley loved to do. It was just one of the many ways Ronnie felt she was deficient. Who didn't like hugs? Weirdos, like her. But with Marley's help, she was learning to like these new things. The only time Shameem touched her was to hit her.

"You're like an alien," Marley had once joked. "How have you never tried sushi? Or a massage?" Or insert whatever normal thing Marley had had growing up. "It's like you were raised on another planet."

"Well, thank god I have you to guide me now, right?" And Ronnie meant it. Having a friend like Marley was life changing.

———

"Are you happy here?" Marley asked after their rubdowns, as they sat in bathrobes and sipped cucumber-flavored water.

"I am. It's an adjustment." Ronnie had been so tense that the massage therapist had asked if she needed a Xanax. She'd already taken one that morning.

"And you've had such huge life changes. I worry that it's too much for you."

Ronnie looked at her friend and nodded. Marley meant it. Sometimes, she wasn't sure if people did mean what they said. Her aunt said a lot of things but meant so little of it. Especially when they were in public and she had to act like a loving aunt.

"Yes, but we have to make changes, right?"

"Right. But if you're overwhelmed, you'll tell me, right? I don't want you to hit a wall with all this stuff."

"I will, I promise."

"Okay, good. You're home now, you know. You're with me. We're family." She put her hand out and grabbed Ronnie's and squeezed. "We can tell each other anything."

And then Marley laughed. "Do you remember that first night? When you came to my empowerment session?"

Ronnie grinned but didn't know what was so funny.

"You were such a mess!" Marley giggled. "Your hair, that hideous blouse you wore that gapped at your boobs. I mean, just look at you now! My first success story."

"All thanks to you." It rolled off Ronnie's tongue so easily. The empowerment class had been the first step toward her new life. Marley was starting her new wellness empire, and Ronnie had walked in. A blank slate. Someone she could mold. And Ronnie didn't mind being formed into someone else's image. Her current one wasn't that great. Clearly, Marley knew what was good and well because she was happy. She was rich. She enjoyed her life.

"Because of us." Marley corrected her. "You've worked so hard. Don't underestimate yourself. Manifesting really works wonders," she went on. "I mean, look at me!" Marley had manifested becoming a life coach and moving to Sedona. She'd manifested finding the one student who would help her. And soon, if she had her way, she'd manifest herself into being the most successful healer in all of Sedona.

"Hey, after this, let's go shopping. I need more crystals."

Ronnie murmured a yes. She knew exactly where they were going too.

———

BritStar Crystals was Marley's favorite store in town. It was also the only store where the proprietors wanted nothing to do with her friend. Ronnie found Marley's insistence on going there fascinating. She didn't let them not liking her stop her. So far, she had bought at least $5,000 worth of crystals for the house. And still, the owner never cracked a smile at her. Her name was Star, and she was utterly unimpressed by everything Marley said and did. And it drove Marley insane.

All Ronnie knew about the woman was that she was a twin, her sister was the Brit from the store name, and they had been born and raised right here in town. They were beloved by almost everyone. And Star couldn't stand Marley but liked Ronnie. It was utterly bizarre to her. How could anyone not like Marley?

"They'll all love me eventually," Marley said each time they went. The twins somehow had pull at the Kismet Center, the wellness spot that Marley wanted to be a part of. It was like a one-stop wellness-o-rama place, and Marley wanted to belong there. She wanted them to want her. Ronnie felt that on a level she couldn't explain to her friend. Wanting to be loved. Wanting someone who would never care about her to accept her. Wanting someone to want her to exist. She had to help her friend. That's what friends did, right?

The bell made a tinkling noise over the door whenever it was opened. Ronnie liked the sound. It was pretty. Soothing.

"Welcome! Let me know if I can help you with anything," Star called out.

YOU BREAK IT, YOU BUY IT signs were all over the shop. Ronnie knew they meant it. In the few times she'd been to the shop, she'd seen someone drop a crystal and have to fork over money for it. This was not a store to play around in.

"Hello!" Marley grinned.

Star stared at her. "Hello." She said it without a smile.

"Ronnie, look at this amethyst! It's divine!"

Ronnie felt Star watching her. Every time she came, Star's eyes were on her but not in a menacing way. Star didn't seem to be watching her out of fear of stealing. Rather, the woman seemed curious about her. *Why? Why would anyone be curious about me?*

"Everything is so pretty here," Ronnie said quietly. She had never been one for crystals, but seeing them here, displayed and shiny, made her want one. Each crystal promised to make her whole, well. Make her into a perfect person.

"They've all been shamanically blessed," Star said as Marley handled the giant amethyst rock.

"Oh really?" That hooked her.

"Yes, my sister is a shaman."

Ronnie saw her friend's eyes light up at that. "Wow! I'd love to work with her! See, Ronnie! I told you this place was beyond."

Marley brought the crystal to the counter. Ronnie felt Star's gaze more intensely now.

"How are you settling in?" the shop owner asked.

"Fine, we're great actually," Marley replied.

"I was asking her," Star said, pointing at Ronnie.

"What, oh, uh, good. Yeah, good." She could tell her face was turning red.

"You two are quite a pair. How did you meet?"

"Oh, it was divine intervention! I was teaching an empowerment class and in walked Ronnie and I knew, I just knew, she was going to be a huge part of my life. We were like instantaneous sisters, right, Ronnie?"

"She changed my life," Ronnie said, hoping she'd hit the right amount of gusto.

"I'm a healer," Marley added.

"I see. Well, this may help with whatever's bugging you," Star said and handed Ronnie a black tourmaline. "It repels negative energy. A gift."

Ronnie stared at her. What negative energy? Why did she need this?

"Ronnie, say thank you." Marley elbowed her.

"Oh, uh, thanks. I wasn't expecting it." She smiled shyly.

"There's weird energy around lately. You should always protect yourselves." Star stared at Marley as she said it. Ronnie wanted to ask her what her deal was but refrained.

"Maybe it'll repel finding any more bodies," Ronnie joked. The silence that answered her told her she'd messed up. "Um, I mean—"

"You found a body?" Star asked her, an eyebrow raised.

"We both did. On the trail leading to Devil's Bridge," Marley said, waiting for Star to ask them all about it. But she didn't.

"Oh. Matt. Matt Ford. That's the body you found." A name to go with the head. "The sheriff mentioned it. That had to be scary for you both."

"Was he a friend of yours?" Ronnie asked softly. She'd have to really apologize for her quip if so.

"Nope. Couldn't stand the guy. Just another scammer around here. You have to be careful who you get mixed up with." Star said it while staring at Marley pointedly.

"Any crystals for me?" Marley joked.

Star just kept staring. "That'll be five hundred, please."

Marley handed over her credit card. "Is your sister available for a session?"

Star pointed her to the bulletin board near the entrance. "I can't speak for my sister, but her info's up there. Look for Brit."

Ronnie stayed silent. She didn't need to be part of this conversation. Sometimes, she felt if she spoke too much, people would know she didn't belong here.

"Wow, so many services! And what's up with all the missing-person flyers?" Marley motioned to the flyers on the board. Some were so old they were yellowed and frayed. She read the names of the ones she could see. "Sasha Bryant. Jennifer Marsh. Linda Adams. There's a lot!"

Star shrugged. "In a tourist town, people come and go. Some get lost hiking. You know how it is." Lost hikers were a nightly thing on the news, Ronnie had noticed. Hikers went up a mountain and didn't come down or fell off a cliff or, worse, slipped and plummeted into the Grand Canyon. (Those unlucky enough to see the canyon that up close were only ever recovered after death, their smashed bodies hidden from news cameras.)

"Did anyone find them?"

"If they had, the flyers wouldn't be up there." There was no flyer for Matt Ford, Ronnie noticed. No one cared that he was missing. Or maybe they'd taken it down already.

"Oh! The Center! Do you work with them?" Marley pointed to another posting.

Star nodded. "Yep. Lorraine is awesome." Lorraine was the founder.

"I'm dying to work with her." Marley looked as if she wanted to say more, but Star didn't ask. She didn't care.

"Good for you," Star deadpanned, and this time Ronnie caught her eye. Star winked at her, and Ronnie couldn't help but smile at her. "Thanks for shopping with us. Have a blessed day."

"Thank you! See you soon!"

"I'm telling you, she's warming up to me!" Marley said as they got into her red Mercedes SUV. "It's only a matter of time before we're the toast of the town."

Ronnie agreed, rubbing the smooth edges of her new rock in her hand.

Chapter 7

The Town

"Oh come on, it couldn't have been that bad!" Brit laughed as her sister told her about Marley and the Great Bad Funk around Her.

"Whatever, she's not good. There's just something so dark about her."

"You worry far too much. She's perfectly nice. You just don't like her."

Star shrugged. "I'm telling you, she's a bad person."

They were identical, but you could still tell them apart. Star's hair was dark brown—nearly black—and she was less likely to smile at you. Brit had lighter hair than her sister—a gorgeous brown mane—and somehow, just being near her made you feel happier. They dressed differently too. Star wore jeans and a T-shirt almost exclusively, and Brit was fond of dresses and caftans, all made from organic cotton. Beyond that, everything from their height (five foot six) to their expressions and mannerisms were the exact same.

"She's the angel—I'm something else," Star would joke.

Two sides of a coin. Star was envious of Brit's penchant for loving people, for embracing their goodness. But she had her own talents that she kept to herself. No one liked hearing that bad things were about to happen or that they were on the road to hell. So she stopped telling them. She focused now on ridding people of negative energy.

"Are you healing someone tonight?" Brit asked. Brit knew the answer, but they'd long ago learned that people freaked out if they didn't talk out loud. They weren't telepathic by any means. They simply had that closeness that only twins knew. They were in the living room of the three-bedroom house they shared. They'd grown up in that house. The walls were a faded off-white, and paintings by the twins covered nearly every inch. It gave off a chaotic vibe, but they loved it. The furniture was older than they were, and they didn't replace things until necessary. On the outside, everything was clay colored and stucco, and the trees around the property made them feel they were far from civilization. But they weren't.

"Yes, I hope it doesn't take long. I could use a night off."

"Just be safe out there."

"Always." Star paused. "That Marley lady and her friend are the ones who found Matt's body."

Her sister shuddered. Brit hated violence of all kinds. "I still can't believe there was an actual murder here. And someone we knew! Wasn't she on TV about it?"

———

Star's client tonight was via the Kismet Center. Supposedly the customers were vetted as much as the healers, but Star wasn't too sure. This one kept giggling at inappropriate moments. She wanted to walk out to make a point, but she knew Lorraine would flip her lid.

"We have to do the work" was Lorraine's favorite refrain. So Star did. Maybe it was half-assed tonight, but this woman was closer to healed than before. (She claimed her dead ex was haunting her, but Star was certain that wasn't the case. The woman wouldn't take that for an answer.)

"You're clean and free now," she said and took the cash and left.

They really needed to get better clients at the Center. Lorraine had to do something. Star knew they needed the money—the Center wasn't making enough. Lorraine was funding everything thanks to money her dead husband had left her. (Make that several dead husbands. Nothing alarming—old folks died all the time, and Sedona was full of them. Lorraine had been smart and swooped in on a few lonely widowers.) But still, Star preferred to choose her clients with care.

When she parked her old Subaru in the garage that night, Star felt eyes on her. Her neck prickled, and she shivered. Someone was watching her. She turned to peer into the darkness. There were no lights on her street, besides the house lights. Normally, Star liked it that way. She could see the stars without anything getting in the way. But tonight it felt sinister. Whoever was out there wanted to harm her. It wasn't the same eerie feeling of a large animal watching you at night. They had the occasional bear come their way, and there was a bobcat family living somewhere behind the twins' home. But this was different. It felt menacing. Evil.

"I know you're there." She said it loud enough for the person to hear. "I'm not scared of you." She wasn't scared. Not for herself, at least. But the thought of anything happening to her sister made her stomach turn. Brit had already dealt with too much. After that incident in the desert. *Stop.* She wasn't going to dwell on it.

Star instead flipped the finger to the darkness and went inside. Then she locked all the doors and made sure the windows were shut. She had never had to worry about this stuff before.

Chapter 8

Ronnie held the shiny black rock in her hand. A gift, Star had said. She had given her a gift. Ronnie couldn't remember the last time a stranger had done something like that for her.

Now, you know that's not true. She sighed. Marley did nice things for her. In ways that really counted. When Ronnie needed her, Marley was there. Ronnie couldn't forget that. She didn't want to take her friend for granted.

She had shown up at Marley's door right before they'd moved here. Ronnie had had a huge blowout with her aunt after finalizing the sale of the house. She was forbidden from leaving. But she had to go. She hadn't told her aunt, but she'd been dreaming again. Ever since Marley had come into her life, Ronnie had been seeing strange new places she had to go. She couldn't stop her dreams from happening. And usually, they made so little sense there was no way she could.

"You don't even know this Marley-Sharley person!" Shameem Khala bellowed.

It wasn't that her aunt was worried about her. Rather, she didn't want to lose the free house and maid.

The night she left, Ronnie took her mother's gold jewelry—which her aunt had hidden from her. Ronnie had always suspected Shameem had kept her mother's things. Her kupra, her jewelry. Her purses. But Shameem denied it, claiming she'd sold everything to pay bills. (Ronnie found photos of her mother wearing the same orange-gold choker and earrings that Shameem would wear. Her aunt had lied about selling them.) Anything that reminded her of her mother, she took. Shameem had kept it all from her.

On the way out the door, she picked up the flyswatter. The one her aunt hit her with. And she threw it out in a random trash can outside.

When she buzzed Marley's apartment that night, she said the only thing she could: "I have nowhere to go." The truth. She didn't. Her house wasn't hers anymore, and she could go to a hotel but didn't want to be alone. And Marley welcomed her with a hug.

"You're so brave. I am so proud of you," her friend said, softly brushing Ronnie's hair for her. "You will always have a home with me." She gave her a room to sleep in and tea to drink. She told her she was better off and then bought her a plane ticket to come with Marley to Sedona. "You deserve so much." Ronnie didn't believe her, but she held on to this moment of kindness.

She owed Marley for her help. More than anyone knew. Marley had saved her, taken her in. Given her shelter, kindness. And she'd paid for Ronnie's beauty treatments, waving her hand when Ronnie tried to pay her back. "I love doing this for you. You're going to be so well soon." For the first time, Ronnie felt wanted. She felt loved.

If her friend were at all less kind now and then, it was from the stress of moving. It wasn't easy to pack up and leave and start somewhere new. It would make anyone grumpy.

"I love my new amethyst, don't you?" Marley sang, and Ronnie nodded automatically.

"It's gorgeous."

"What did she give you again?"

"Oh, just this black rock." She held it in her hand, palm open.

"Oh."

Ronnie saw her friend's face and smiled. "Would you like it? She should have given it to you."

"Really? Are you sure?"

"Of course, I'd love you to have it. We can keep it in the house to repel negativity for both of us."

Marley snatched it so quickly out of her hand that Ronnie barely registered the motion.

———

Marley's stint on the news made just enough waves for people to start talking to her. Whenever the two went anywhere, someone would stop to talk to them about the body. Ronnie hated it. This was what being small-town famous was like.

"Did you ever meet Matt before he died? Let's just say his enemy list was long."

"Did you see anything else?"

"This town's turning to shit. It's all the new folks coming in."

Marley soaked up the spotlight like a sponge. It worked for her. Ronnie would stand a bit behind her friend whenever these interactions occurred. No one wanted to talk to her anyways. And this way, she could watch everyone.

"You know, that Caroline is a genius. She said this would happen. You really need to spend time with her," Marley said. "I want my friends to be friends!"

"Oh."

"What?"

"Nothing, just something seems weird about her. Vibes, you know?"

"You just need to get to know her. I haven't steered you wrong yet, have I?"

No, Marley hadn't. "Fine, let's hang out with her."

"That's my girl!"

———

Ronnie found nothing about Caroline online. Granted, she didn't know her last name. But she googled *Caroline + Sedona + bad vibes* and . . . didn't get much. Just page after page about the vortexes and whether they were real.

She knew something was off about Caroline though. As unenlightened as Ronnie was, she saw it, like a sign hanging over the woman's head. Ronnie recognized something in her that she found in herself: hunger. And hungry people would do anything. When Marley left to have dinner with her new friend, Ronnie stewed. She was the one who'd moved here for Marley, who'd given up everything. *Did you, though?* Marley should be spending her time with Ronnie.

On a whim, Ronnie googled her dreams. Not her specific ones. Just that she had them and they came true. The results were all about precognition, which she was certain she didn't have. Ronnie wasn't special enough to have any kind of psychic abilities. She scoffed and closed her laptop.

I should go make new friends. She thought it like it was the easiest thing in the world, to make friends. Ronnie had never been good at it. And whenever she did make friends, Shameem would forbid her from seeing them.

Well, she's not here, is she?

She paced the house until she decided to screw it and go to the only place she knew anyone. She got into her Honda Accord—not nearly as nice a car as Marley's, but Ronnie didn't want to waste money on her first car. She'd been raised to live as frugally as possible, and despite having money from the house sale, Ronnie lived like she was broke. It wasn't intentional; it was just how she was raised.

She'd bought the car their first week in Arizona, at her friend's urging. "We both need cars here." Ronnie, thankfully, had her license. But only because she hadn't told her aunt she was taking driving lessons. One of the many things she'd hidden. Living a double life was all she knew. Ronnie could have nice things if she kept their existence entirely to herself.

She started driving, her hands holding the wheel so tightly her knuckles turned white. Driving was terrifying. She had never enjoyed it. But she had known she'd need it one day. It was part of her escape plan. Save money, hide all her documents, learn to drive. One day, run and be free.

It took all of five minutes to get to her destination: the crystal shop.

She parked out front and walked in, letting the door chime sound wash through her. Now this place had good vibes.

Ronnie smiled and waved at Star.

"Hi, again!"

"Hello. Oh, you think I'm Star. I'm the other twin—Brit."

Ronnie felt stupid. *I should leave.* "Oh, wow, you two look identical." She stood, awkwardly. She'd already messed up her first attempt at making friends. *So stupid, Ron.*

"Ha, right?"

"Um, I'm Ronnie."

"You're new in town, right? Star mentioned you."

"Oh." Was that good or bad to be mentioned?

"What can I help you with?"

"Um . . ." Shit. What did she want help with? Before she could answer, Brit stood directly in front of her, staring at her face.

"Oh, I know what you need. Come." She winked. And gently took Ronnie's arm to guide her to the counter. "I don't think you came here for crystals."

"I . . . just thought maybe Star was around so I could say hi. I don't want to bug you." *This was a bad idea. I am an idiot.*

Brit held her hand up. "None of that talk. Let me pull cards for you."

Ronnie said nothing, just watched the woman shuffle a deck of tarot cards. She really looked so much like her sister. Ronnie had so many questions for her. She'd always wanted a sister. Someone she could confide in. Someone who would be with her against the world (Shameem) forever. She'd always imagined moments when she and her sister would flee and live together in a house, just the two of them.

"You've just left something really dark. See this." Brit pointed to the card. "Tower. Big changes happened. Guess that's your move."

"Oh, yes." What would the cards tell this woman? That Ronnie was weird and a loser and didn't know what she wanted out of her life? Would they tell Brit not to be friends with her?

"See this? Three of Swords."

"Oh, I get that a lot."

"You do tarot?"

"No, Marley does."

"Right, I've heard of Marley. Saw her on TV. Anyways, you have to heal your heart. So many wounds—things were done to you that weren't your fault. You know, you have so much love in you, but first you need to love yourself."

How? How did anyone do that?

"Yes, you're in the right place. Empress. Embrace your feminine side. But also, immerse yourself in nature. It will help heal you." Brit paused a moment. "Are you a seer? A psychic?"

"Me? No." Ronnie laughed. "I'm nothing."

The way the twin looked at her made her squirm. "Well, maybe just be open. And be in nature."

"The ravens will love that," Ronnie quipped. "I've been trying to make friends with them."

Brit laughed. "How's that going?"

"Okay. I feed them. But I also dream about them." Why was she telling this stranger this? *Stop talking!*

"Oooh, that's cool. You'll find that they're very magical birds." Brit leaned in toward her. "Sometimes I dream about them too."

Brit smiled at her, and it was dazzling. Like a real smile, the kind actors on TV or movies had. And for a brief moment, Ronnie felt something amazing. She felt like she belonged.

That feeling didn't last.

"Cool. Okay, well, um, thanks."

"Hey, you don't have to go. Hang out with me. It's a quiet evening. Let me show you around the shop."

For the next hour, Brit talked about every stone, every rock—she even let Ronnie hold them.

"You know, you could use this." She took out a rose quartz. "Keep it under your pillow. It's to help bring love into your life."

"Does it work?"

"If you believe and are open, it will."

Be open—I can do that.

"Hey, you aren't looking for a job, are you?" Brit asked.

Ronnie was certain she'd misheard. "A job? Me?"

"We could use extra help here. For when we both have clients. That's where Star is now. Think about it, don't say no."

A job. An actual place to go to. "But I know nothing about crystals." *And I'm not good with people and will probably fail at this.*

"You know that rose quartz is good for love." Brit grinned at her.

Ronnie couldn't help it; she loved being near this woman. "Okay, yeah, that'd be fun!" Ronnie paused. "Uh, did Star tell you we found that body out there?"

Brit's face paled. "She did." Her voice sounded different now. Like she was upset.

Shit. I shouldn't have said anything. What if she liked him and he was dead? "I'm sorry, I didn't mean to bring up something awful. It's just . . . does that sort of thing happen a lot here?"

Brit shook her head. "No. Matt was an anomaly. An abhorrence. Don't worry about being safe, I'm sure you'll do fine here. So want to start next week?"

"Okay." Ronnie gave Brit her info.

She didn't even think to talk to Marley about it. No, she would do this without needing approval. Maybe. She could do this. Empowerment!

When she got home, Marley was on the phone with Joan, her mother. These calls never went well.

"Mother, I'm not chasing a fad. I really love it out here. No, I am not in a cult."

Ronnie tiptoed by, waving.

Chapter 9

The Town

The ravens circled each other, playing tag. They whooped and warbled and swooped their wings. This was fun.

The new dark-haired woman was below, watching them. They should tell her what they wanted, see if it worked. She was new here but had already taken to offering them food and water. That was the sign of a good human. The other one with her, the one with the light hair, never gave them anything.

They cawed again and again until it almost sounded human. Their ability to mimic was the stuff of legends, and so often, when strange sounds were heard out here, it was the ravens making fun of things. They particularly loved doing coyote screams, scaring off other animals so they could eat all they wanted.

They circled over the woman's head, and she watched them with awe. Good, they thought. We should be revered.

The other human called to Ronnie, and she turned. That must be her name, the ravens thought. And as they watched her walk back into the house, they called her name. At first it came out garbled, but they got it close enough that she paused.

"Ronnie!"

Her mouth fell open. "Oh my god, did you hear that? They said my name!"

"No, they didn't! You're being silly," the other one said. The ravens didn't like her.

They watched as the humans went back inside, and then Ronnie came back out with some ground meat for them. Yes, she was a good human. They needed to keep her around.

The ravens went back to playing games and tricks on each other after eating. For fun, one of the birds shit on the red car in the driveway.

———

The ravens weren't the only ones watching Ronnie. *She* was too. Their person. The one who'd murdered Matt, the one who would get rid of everyone ruining this little slice of paradise. Would Ronnie pass muster? The ravens thought so, but they couldn't keep an eye on everyone, see every person's aura. Like when Brit had asked them if she should go on a quest in the less populated part of the desert and the ravens had said yes, not knowing who would be accompanying her. They'd seen what happened to her. They'd tried to help, but they hadn't been able to do much except let Star know where her sister was.

That was why this had to happen, they reasoned. If someone could get to Brit, then no one was safe here, especially not the wildlife.

They watched as their human watched Ronnie. She'd take care of it. If Ronnie were evil, she'd find out. That was her job. She was going to clean up Sedona.

This playground for the well and wealthy had become nothing more than a garbage dump. Trash littered every trail. Some areas had had to be closed down due to human feces being all over the place. They came here, shit everywhere, and went off to the next great wellness destination—Tulum.

The ravens were sick of it.

Chapter 10

May

"Wake up! Ronnie, wake up!" She was sound asleep in her bed when the covers were ripped off of her. She was dreaming about home, about Shameem. Ronnie threw her hands up instinctively, covering her head from blows that weren't coming.

"You were having a bad dream." Marley frowned. She gently pushed Ronnie's hands down. "I wasn't going to hit you." She looked sad at the idea. As if her friend being scared of being hit hurt her.

Huh, Ronnie thought. *Maybe she does care?* It wasn't easy to believe that anyone cared for her. "Oh, sorry." Ronnie lowered her arms. "I guess I was having a crazy dream," she said and laughed to cover her mistake. The last thing she wanted was anyone asking what she dreamed about.

"Well, wake up. We have things to do today! We are going hiking again!" Marley chirped.

"What time is it?"

"Six thirty. Come on, chop-chop!"

Six thirty? That was inhumane. Ronnie watched Marley leave her room before sighing and getting out of bed. She wanted to curl back up, hide under the covers while the air conditioner blasted.

Hiking. That was something white people did. Ronnie didn't get hiking. No one she knew back home hiked. Back home—she shook her head. Back home no longer existed. This was home. And the last time they'd gone hiking, well, there was the whole decapitated head thing.

She stumbled into the kitchen in jeans and a gray T-shirt. It was the best hiking outfit she had. She had already doused herself in SPF spray.

"Here." Marley handed Ronnie a coffee. Followed by a smoothie. "I know going back out there is scary, but we need to do it. Reclaim what's ours! Don't let one bad thing ruin the outdoors for you."

"Of course. I need something for my headache." They had had too much wine last night. Ronnie didn't even like wine, but she drank it because it was Marley's preferred drink.

"Try the smoothie. I want you to be well. Feel good. No saying no!" That was Marley's new mantra with her roommate. No saying no. Go along with things until they became second nature. A new-and-improved Ronnie would be born; she simply had to do what she was told. And then everyone would see how amazing Marley was, how she'd turned Ronnie's life around.

"Don't forget the SPF!" she added.

"Already on." Ronnie religiously slathered on SPF 50 if she even went out to check the mailbox. It was ingrained in her. Once, when Ronnie was little, Shameem had rubbed suntan lotion onto her by mistake. She wouldn't look at Ronnie all summer. "You're too kala." Too black. Too dark. Not good enough, never good enough. As if a darker skin tone reflected character. Ronnie hated how much her aunt was in her head. Marley said a good fuck-you would be to get a nice deep tan, but Ronnie wasn't ready for that yet.

"Grab your backpack and let's go!"

They were going to hike to Cathedral Rock, a vortex spot. The parking lot was full of cars. Marley cursed. She drove around and around until she found a bit of dirt to park on.

"Won't we get a ticket?" Ronnie asked.

"So what? People park their cars on 89A all the time." The traffic in Sedona and the neighboring Village of Oak Creek was pure hell. The closer you got to trails and waterfalls, the more tourists left their cars along the road while they wandered the highway in bathing suits like it was a beach boardwalk.

Ronnie was deep in thought as they walked. She had to find her own place here. Not like a house—though that would probably be good—but more metaphorically. *I can't glom on to Marley forever. I need to have my own life.*

"Hello? Anyone there?" Marley stopped walking, and Ronnie collided with her backpack. "Ron, you have to pay attention where you're hiking because if you get hurt, I am not carrying you out of here." She laughed as she said it. "I'll leave you on an agave plant like that head."

"Sorry, I was zoned out." She paused. "It's so pretty here!"

The hike wasn't long, but there were steep inclines they had to scramble up. Once they reached the first plateau, Ronnie hoped they'd turn back. No such luck.

"Keep moving, we're almost there!"

They got to the base, which, admittedly, was stunning. Even Ronnie was moved by what stood before her, red rocks rising up in a formation, surrounded by green plants and trees. A treasure created by nature. Brit said to be with nature. Well, here she was.

She paused to rest before they turned back. Except Marley kept walking.

"Wait, where are you going?"

"We have more to do," her friend called back as she started the harder climb. Ronnie stared before running after her.

"Fuck," she muttered.

"I heard that. This will be good for you. I promise!"

Ronnie would have replied, but she was out of breath, climbing over rocks as the ground inclined upward.

Please let us stop before the super hard part. She caught up to Marley and stood at the bottom of a crevice.

"We have to go up," Marley said. Not a question. A demand. The climb was five feet at first and then leveled a bit. Then another ledge. And another. Ronnie thought she was going to die here and Marley would have to leave her body wedged into a crevice. Marley shouted out encouragement but didn't lend a hand. Finally, Ronnie pulled herself up, her arms shaking from exertion. This had to be it, right?

It wasn't. They had another plateau to get to, another climb. Sweat stung her eyes, and she cursed her dark hair for making her hotter.

"We're here," Marley said. "See? You did it. You pushed yourself. And now look at you. I'm proud of you." And her smile said she was being truthful.

"Thank you for making me get up. This is awesome." Ronnie gasped the words out, so out of breath she barely made a sound. She was trying to sound positive and life affirming. And she meant it. The view was something else. Red and green, like Christmas but in nature. Just a few months earlier she hadn't known places like this were real.

"Feel that?"

"No?" Ronnie saw Marley's face change and quickly added, "What is it you're feeling? Maybe I'm just not recognizing it."

"It's like the ground is talking to me. The rocks, the bushes, everything is telling me yes. 'Yes, Marley, this is all for you. Yes, you're doing it. You will get everything you want.' Don't you feel that?" She closed her eyes, and her mouth was open. Ronnie hoped a bug wouldn't fly in there, but the thought made her giggle.

"Is this the vortex?" Ronnie thought it would be something more. Like a sign saying, ENERGY HOT SPOT: YOU ARE HERE with a big red arrow. FEEL ENLIGHTENED! But it was just part of the hike, though it was filled with other hikers.

"Yes!" Marley breathed. "Can you feel it?"

"What is a vortex?" She should have paid more attention to the stories she'd googled about them. But all they had said was "Energy! Vibes!" Not the most helpful research.

Marley swiveled her head to look at her. "Well, everything has energy, right? Some places have more energy. And it all comes together here. It all converges here. It's like the energy at Stonehenge and Machu Picchu, but it's here, and we get to feel it."

Ronnie nodded as if it made sense to her. But she felt nothing. Absolutely nothing. "So that's what I'm feeling? Wow!" Ronnie lied, laughing to sound light. If you grew up with strict parents (or an insane aunt), you became adept at lying. Lying was how you got through life, how you fit in. Lying was what you did to survive. She looked around. It *was* stunning up here. They weren't at the very top—that would involve gear and probably permits. But this was as high as she could go. The view surrounded them, and Ronnie inhaled it all.

"Isn't it everything?" Marley unrolled her yoga mat from her pack and sat down. Ronnie followed suit. "Now, really open yourself up. Let go of the blocks." She said it as if it were the easiest thing in the world. Ronnie did as instructed, minus the blocks thing. This would be over soon. She could go back to bed after and never hike again. Until the next time Marley wanted to go out.

"Feel that?"

"Yessss," she breathed. Her lies flowed easier now.

"Good."

Ronnie didn't feel shit. Not a damn thing. No wave of energy, no rocks whispering to her. She was empty and didn't understand what the fuss was about. She glanced around, and everyone—there were at least thirty other hikers here—was enthralled. Some were clutching each other's arms. *Am I broken? I'm the only one who doesn't feel anything. Was it that she was empty or just not in tune enough?* Both options freaked her out, if she was being honest. Because she had no idea how to fix either.

Ronnie sat on her mat and started to sway ever so slightly. She knew this was what her friend wanted, and disappointing her was not an option. She'd already disappointed too many people in her life. She had to be better. You didn't become a happy, well, loved person by disappointing the world. She never wanted to let Marley down.

After thirty minutes, Marley was ready to go.

"See? Don't you feel incredible? The energy here is otherworldly. Oh, fuck." She slapped her arms, killing an ant that had crawled on her. "I really hate the bugs. Fucking nature, right?"

Ronnie nodded.

"Look! How funny!" Marley pointed to a raven on the ground. It was attempting to pick up a coin. "What a silly bird." She walked over and snatched the quarter away.

"You shouldn't do that," Ronnie warned.

"Well, it's not like the bird can use it." Marley laughed.

Ronnie saw the way the bird looked at her friend, then at her. For a moment, she met its dark eyes. She couldn't look away, as if the bird were mesmerizing her. She felt a chill so deep in her bones she didn't think it would ever stop. Marley was already walking back on the trail when Ronnie took a coin out of her backpack, put it near the glaring bird, and whispered, "I'm sorry." The ravens knew her name. Her face. She didn't want them to hold a grudge.

"Let's go get a treat now!" Marley called as she continued back down the trail.

The treat was an oat-milk-matcha chai latte at the Tree of Life Café. They sat at a scratched-up wooden table and sipped their drinks while Marley chatted about the body they'd found and the vortex loud enough for everyone to overhear. A few patrons glanced their way, and on the counter was a jar with a handful of coins, a memorial fund for Matt Ford. (Ronnie dropped a dollar in it.)

"I'm glad you felt something today. Because honestly, you're the least spiritual person ever. We need you to open. Open open open!" Marley laughed, but Ronnie could tell she was annoyed with her.

"I'm sorry, I'll be more open."

Marley elbowed Ronnie. "Look."

It was one of the twins though Ronnie wasn't sure which. She was still working on telling them apart.

"Hi!"

"Hey. How are you guys?" It was Star—no smile.

"Good, want to join us?" Marley asked.

"Sure." She grabbed her drink and sat down. "How are you two settling in?"

"Great, we just had a fabulous hike!"

"Oh fun!" Star turned to Ronnie. "How's that black tourmaline treating you?"

"Oh, um—"

"She loves it! She uses it constantly, right?"

Ronnie glanced at her sharply. "Uh, we share it. It's just such a powerful crystal." That was as close to the truth as she could get. She didn't know why Marley wanted to lie to Star.

"I heard you came by the other night—sorry I wasn't there."

Ronnie felt Marley's eyes on her. She hadn't told her friend about visiting the store. About the job offer or meeting Brit. Not for any reason. She just wanted to feel it out first. See how she felt about the offer.

"I did. Brit is so nice!"

"Well, I love the idea of you working with us. You're starting next week? Week after?"

"Uh, I think so." Ronnie knew she was blushing. Attention did that to her.

"Ronnie, you didn't tell me you were getting a job?" Marley said, her eyes darting between the two women.

"I didn't want to jinx it. You know, if anything went wrong."

Star laughed. "Nothing will go wrong, you'll see. Anyways, gotta run. Brit's waiting for me." She waved as she left.

"So . . . ," Marley said.

"You were out with Caroline, and I wanted to take initiative. You know, try to make inroads for you. It's hard to find my own place here, you know? Like, where do I belong, besides with you? I'm sorry, I should have told you."

Ronnie closed her eyes for a moment. *Shit, I fucked up. Why can't I ever do anything right?*

"Hey, it's cool! I'm glad you did that. You need to make friends here too." Marley's smile was gentle. "Deep breaths, you don't need my permission to do things. I'm not like a tyrant."

Ronnie let out a breath. "Whew, okay." She smiled back at her friend, but her heart was racing.

"Besides, if you work for them, it would help me a ton. Let's go buy new journals. Mine's full. And you need to be writing everything down. That's how you know you've changed."

Chapter 11

The Town

The ravens were talking about Marley. That's not what they called her. But they didn't like her. She'd stolen their shiny coin. They hated her for that. They hated all the pretenders, all the mean ones.

It wasn't that they were against healers. But the ravens knew who was real. They could see it, just like they could see colors humans couldn't. The real healers had a purple glow to them. Marley did not. She had no glow. That's how they knew. By watching.

If you didn't have a purple glow—or white, in the case of Ronnie—the ravens knew you were going to do something bad. It was a fact of life for them. They knew who to trust, who not to. Though they rarely saw the white auras. Most people were red, or blue, or a pretty purple. But Ronnie's was white; she was special. In fact, some of the ravens weren't sure what white meant, as they'd never seen it before.

And they were almost always right about humans. Like about Matt Ford. He had no glow. He was nothing, empty, soulless. He'd tried to get to Brit. He and his friends. All glowless and soulless. Just like Marley. Who had just dropped her empty cup on the ground because she thought no one was watching. But they were watching; they were always watching.

Some humans were just selfish. Others were pure evil. Wanted everything for themselves. They needed Marley to leave. To be one of the people their human ran off. They had to make this happen, somehow.

They'd keep an eye on her. At least her friend was nice.

"Ronnie," they trilled. "Ronnniiieeee."

Chapter 12

Before

"Where are you going?" Shameem asked from the sofa, where she was picking up gulab jamuns and eating them like candy, her thumb and index finger covered in the sticky rose-flavored syrup.

"To see a friend," Ronnie mumbled. She had an appointment with Marley. She couldn't call her a friend just yet, but explaining to her aunt that she was taking empowerment lessons would be a disaster.

"What friend? You don't have friends. Is it a boy? Are you going out with a boy?"

Ronnie was in her thirties, yet her aunt still worried she was going to go on a date and become the talk of the aunties. The aunties had tried to set Ronnie up to be married, but no one was interested in her. The few meetings with men she'd had had ended with them pawing at her breasts and then telling lies to everyone about her. Ronnie didn't want a husband, at least not one like that. No, she wanted to only ever take care of herself.

She couldn't help it—she rolled her eyes. Like anyone would even want to date her?

"Don't make those faces at me! Bathameez!" Her aunt picked up a shoe and threw it at her. It missed, barely.

"Sorry, Khala. It's just a friend. From work. A woman. I promise."

"What friend? You don't have friends," she repeated, rubbing it in that Ronnie had no one close to her in her life.

"It's just for a work project. I won't be long."

"You'd better not be. You need to clean the house. You're the laziest girl. I should move us back to Pakistan." That was always the threat hanging in the air. It had been years before Ronnie realized there wasn't anything behind the threat. That her aunt knew if they sold the house, Ronnie would get all the money. So Shameem stayed where she was, on the sofa, eating more sweets.

Sometimes, Ronnie imagined her life without her aunt. Without this presence around her that only took, never gave. Shameem would hang on to Ronnie her entire life if she let her—and the community expected Ronnie to care for her aunt forever. The thought made her shudder.

Extended families weren't just the norm for the desi community; they were expected. It was just how things were done. You lived with your folks, or they lived with you or your husband's family, and no complaining because we all had to endure it. When she was a child, Ronnie remembered her mother telling her to marry an orphan.

"Never marry a man with a large family," Nusreen had told the then-five-year-old Ronnie. Ronnie had made the appropriate grossed-out face, and she and her mother had laughed. But now she got it. She understood. *Don't chain yourself to someone's family—you'll have to take care of them forever.* She held that advice deep in her heart.

The commute to Manhattan gave her enough time to pull herself together, to smile and be cheerful. She wanted Marley to see that she was making an effort. She was trying.

And that had to count for something, right?

One day I'll be free. I know I will. And then, well, she'd have to figure the next part out. With Marley.

Marley had life made. Her mother—though overbearing from what Ronnie could see—was nothing like the faux mother she had. Marley's mother even named her dogs after her daughter. Shameem wouldn't let Ronnie have a pet, even a fish.

"Why? So I can do all the cleanup? You need to focus on taking care of me," her aunt would mutter. Ronnie had once rescued a bird that had flown into one of the windows. She'd carefully placed it in a shoebox and bought birdseed to nurse it back to health.

Until Shameem had found it.

"You brought this unclean thing into my house?! Throw it away. Now." And she'd forced Ronnie to dump the injured bird outside, where a cat would no doubt eat it.

"I'm sorry," Ronnie had whispered to the creature. "I'm so sorry."

Ronnie closed her eyes, took three deep breaths, and then walked in to face Marley at her apartment. That's where the sessions were held now that Marley knew she wasn't a "lunatic." Marley's word.

"You're here!" Marley gave her a huge, tight hug, and for a moment, Ronnie felt at peace. This was love. Right here. This was more love than she'd felt in her entire life.

Chapter 13

Shameem was screaming at her. Ronnie stared at her mouth. It was so wide open she could count all her aunt's teeth, and she could see the dark fillings inside. She wasn't listening to what her aunt was saying; she could only stare at her teeth and then the void behind them. If she let her, her aunt would swallow her alive, and there'd be nothing left of her.

"You never listen!" Shameem yelled.

Ronnie remained fixated. She didn't move, she didn't scream, she didn't wince. Her dream self should have flinched, and she thought it was strange she didn't. In real life she would have. "I'm watching you!" And the yelling got louder, more deafening, and filled her ears until it was the sound of a raven cawing loudly.

And then it got quiet. Eerily silent. The raven stared at her and motioned for her to follow. Ronnie didn't question; she just did as asked. She saw a large crystal, larger than any she'd ever seen, and it was covered in blood. It was being brought down over and over onto a woman's head. A woman she'd never seen before.

The ravens insisted she watch, but she couldn't. She needed to wake up, get away from this horror, from the sound the crystal made every time it hit the poor woman's head.

Ronnie sat up, gasping for air. Another freaky dream. She tried to shrug it off, but there was a difference between her regular dreams and these. It was like she was there. Like it had actually happened. She shivered. Ronnie hoped it wasn't real. She didn't need to see things like that.

She was still shivering when she realized her window was open. Ronnie tried to keep the air conditioner off at night, and the temperature after sundown was so nice. Sleeping with a window open was such a strange sensation. Anyone could come in even though she was on the second floor. That was partially why she did it: to show she could conquer her fears.

Ronnie was about to get up to close the window when she saw it watching her. Sitting on her dresser opposite her bed. Its eyes were black; all of it was a shiny black, the moonlight reflecting off it even in the darkness. The raven watched her. Up close, it was even larger than she'd thought. Over a foot tall. How had it gotten inside the screen? She looked, and the screen wasn't on her window anymore.

How was she supposed to make it leave? She didn't want to scare it. Frankly, the thing scared *her*. Ronnie stared at the bird. "You have to go," she whispered. And pulled the covers to her chin. *Please let this work. Please let it listen to me.*

The raven watched her. It tilted its head as if appraising her. She felt like it could see into her soul, and that terrified her. What if it didn't like what it saw? The raven let out a loud caw before flapping its wings and flying back out the way it had come. Ronnie jumped up and closed the window in case it decided to come back.

Was this part of her dream? She was sure it was. Her brain unraveling her fears while she slept. Maybe Marley knew a way to make bad dreams go away. She bet Marley never had bad dreams.

In the morning, when she woke again, a raven feather sat on her dresser, placed just so, as if a present to her. A warning. An omen. Something, it had to mean something—she just wasn't sure what.

Ronnie didn't tell Marley about her dream or the feather. Any of it. She didn't want her friend to think she was crazy.

———

The air smelled like burning. The heat and smoke were overpowering. It was fire season, and any place that had a season where everything burned was a little frightening to Ronnie. (Fire season used to be just the premonsoon months, but now it was year round.) She sat at her computer looking at Google Maps, trying to find exit routes in case they needed one. The thought of being trapped inside, burned alive, filled her with a terror she'd never had before coming here.

"You're being ridiculous, it's fine. They know how to handle the fires here," Marley said.

"I know logically you're right, but I still want to be prepared. I'm going to make us go bags just in case."

"God, don't become one of those crazy preppers, please!" Marley laughed at her. Of course she did; she didn't have to worry about such mundane things as burning alive. Ronnie envied her for that.

Every time she stepped outside, she smelled it. Like a barbecue the entire area was having, and the smoke hurt her eyes. It was from the controlled burns in Flagstaff. Fires to prevent fires. She imagined doing that every day, setting fires and digging trenches to keep people safe. What about the animals? Surely they didn't want their homes burning. But what did she know? She wasn't from this place; she wasn't used to life here. Everything was so different.

Overhead the ravens flew, and Ronnie was certain they were there for her. She didn't know why, but the idea of birds waiting on her made her feel powerful—and terrified.

Ronnie was on a walk. Not a hike. Not a trek. But a walk. There weren't a ton of sidewalks here, but she was determined to walk just as much as she had back in New York. Driving everywhere made her feel lazy. So she walked, taking in the sights. Learning the turns of the streets and stopping now and then to take in the view. Red rocks would loom up from behind a house, and it was breathtaking.

This was when she felt like herself. Whoever that was. But she didn't feel like she was pretending when she was walking. She was just her. For better or worse.

———

"So, Ronnie, I hear you're going to go work for the twins." Caroline was dipping her sushi into soy sauce.

Ronnie fiddled with her chopsticks. She was terrible at using them, but she was trying. The first time she'd eaten sushi was with Marley. Shameem never let her go out to eat. ("Our khana isn't good enough for you anymore?")

"Uh, yes, I start next week!"

"Fun! What's Ronnie short for?"

"Pardon?"

"Your name?"

"Uh, Rania."

"But she hates being called that," Marley interrupted. "So we go with Ronnie."

"Pity, it's a beautiful name."

Rania was what Shameem called her. What her aunt bellowed when she needed something. Rania was not someone Ronnie wanted to be anymore.

"Why did you leave New York?" Caroline asked. Ronnie squirmed. This felt like an interrogation.

"To be with Marley, of course." She smiled.

"Your family is Muslim?"

Ronnie nodded.

"Interesting. Were they planning an arranged marriage for you?"

"Caroline!" Marley interrupted. "That's not appropriate to ask."

"Why not? Well, were they?"

"Of course not," Ronnie scoffed. "That's not how my family is." That was a lie. If someone "eligible" had shown any interest in her, Ronnie was sure her aunt would have married her off. But no one wanted Ronnie, and that was fine by her. It wasn't something Caroline or Marley would understand, though. Everything was viewed through their white Western lens, and arranged marriages were up there with niqabs and burkas as bad Muslim things.

"Anyways, how fabulous is it that she's working with the twins?" Marley said, changing the subject.

"Amazing. Just, you know, be careful," Caroline warned. "They're not always what they seem. But I bet you'll do fine. Just fine."

If Ronnie had been nervous about starting her new job before tonight, now she was petrified. What did Caroline even mean?

"How so? How are they not what they seem, I mean?"

"Brit . . . well, what happened to her was tragic. I frankly don't know how she survived." Caroline dipped another piece of sushi in soy sauce and opened her mouth wide to eat it.

"What happened to her?" Marley asked.

"A horrible vision quest in the desert gone awry. Honestly, if you ask me, she hasn't been the same since Star found her. She was much more outgoing, nice, fun. Now, well, she's a lot like her sister."

Ronnie hated hearing them gossip about the twins. Brit and Star had been the nicest to her of anyone she'd met here so far. Not that she'd met a lot of people. But still.

"How long have you lived here?" she asked Caroline.

"Oh, a few years. It all bleeds together, huh? Oh, Marley, darling, I was thinking: We should get you on TV more. To help you make a splash. What if you spearheaded a safety thing? Like making sure you always have a buddy while hiking. I bet the news would love that."

Ronnie sat back and let the two women talk. They were more suited to each other than to her. And though she didn't quite like Caroline, the

71

woman had good ideas. Ideas that could help Marley, which was way more than Ronnie had done.

"Ron?"

"Sorry? I zoned out."

"Caroline thinks you should join me on a TV segment."

Ronnie felt her face pale as the blood drained. Shit. TV? No. That meant bad things. "I can't. I'm sorry."

"Oh, come on, it'll be fun—" Caroline began to say.

"No. I am not interested." Ronnie said it quietly, but it was enough to end the discussion. No TV. Never again. They couldn't make her do it.

She went home after dinner while Caroline and Marley went out. For a girls' night that didn't include her. Whatever, she didn't want to go anyways. (A lie. She wanted to be invited so badly it made her want to scream.)

She sat home with her glass of wine and picked up the phone to call her aunt. And then thought better of it.

"Pull yourself together. You don't need her. You don't need the past. Let it go. Let it go," she whispered. Her eyes settled on Marley's laptop. And Ronnie did something she never thought she'd do: she opened it and went through Marley's emails.

Nothing weird, nothing about Caroline. Ronnie wasn't sure what she was looking for. She knew she needed to know what Marley was doing these days. Her friend spent more time with Caroline than with her.

The emails were about more TV appearances for Marley. More moments to talk about the head they'd found. All anyone wanted to hear was how scary it was. But why wasn't anyone talking about why Matt Ford's head had been found? Why had he been killed like that? The town seemed to care a little, but no one cared enough to find out.

"It's just weird," Ronnie muttered to herself. If she died, she'd want people to find out why.

Chapter 14

The Town

The ravens had a new target. They were watching her now. Only she had no idea they were there. Or that they would be the ones to finish her off.

The big house wasn't Fiona's. She didn't own it. Fiona owned nothing. She had stolen it and everything else that was hers. The ravens marveled at her trickery. Somehow, this human managed to get housing and food without putting in any work.

Was stealing work? Maybe, they thought. They sometimes stole meat from the coyotes when they had a kill. But they also helped the coyotes find prey, so it was even. Fiona did no such thing. She helped only herself.

The birds liked peeking in through her windows. There was so much to look at! The old woman who'd lived there before was gone. No one remembered her. Fiona had taken her house and left the woman's name on everything so the pension checks would still come.

"What did it matter," she'd say to herself, out loud. That old bitch was dead.

The old bitch was Fiona's aunt. She'd ripped off her own family, taking the house and anything else she could. Nothing had been given to her; she'd stolen it.

Her aunt Linda used to feed the ravens every day. All the birds, actually. And left water and fruit out for the deer and visiting javelinas. Fiona did no such thing. She despised having the animals around. "Filthy, dirty, and covered in germs" was her usual refrain.

Fiona especially hated having the ravens visit. They came for Linda but found Fiona. And then they lingered, staring at her with their beady eyes. They could feel the revulsion in her. Fiona despised them because they could see her. They knew what she was. Soulless and glowless.

They knew she wasn't worthy of living there. In that house, in this part of the world. She was a taker, and you couldn't live in nature being a taker. There had to be a giving, a symbiosis. Fiona was nothing but a parasite.

Every so often the birds would rile her up. Swoop in too close to Fiona's head, shit on her car, throw rocks at the windows. If they pestered her enough, she'd leave. Instead, she tried to kill them. She shot at them until the men in uniforms came.

The ravens knew she had to go. She had to leave this place. One way or another and if they had to, they'd do it themselves.

They flew to their human. She'd take care of Fiona. They knew she would. The ravens stood outside her house until she let them in. And they told her everything. She listened. She understood.

"I must kill Fiona."

She was evil, the ravens said. Just like Matt. Her blood could wash things clean.

She nodded. "She deserves it. You're right."

Fiona was on her list already. But the ravens wanted her to be next. There was no arguing with them. It was what had to be done. It was too late to appease the birds; they wanted blood. And who could blame them? Certainly not her.

Fiona Healer (real name Lawrence) was about to face death, and death always won.

Chapter 15

Before

Ronnie had walked into a hornet's nest. She'd run to the store for her aunt. "We're out of milk." And had stupidly left her phone behind.

She came home to her aunt scrolling through it. Ronnie had a passcode, but it wasn't an original one. Her aunt had guessed it: her mother's birthday.

"Who is this Marley?" Shameem asked, her voice quiet. But that's when it was dangerous. When she grew quiet. The yelling Ronnie could deal with. The soft voice, that's when things got scary.

"A friend from work." A lie. Sort of.

"If I ask Farrah, she'll tell me the truth." Farrah was Ronnie's boss and a daughter of Shameem's friends. That's how Ronnie got the job, which involved making spreadsheets. That was all she did. Spreadsheets and order office supplies.

"She'll tell you that she asked me to meet with Marley." Half-truths. Farrah was the one who'd found Marley on Instagram. She was the one who'd insisted that Ronnie meet with her so she'd be "less of a doormat."

"Don't lie to me."

"I'm not lying. Can I have my phone back?"

"Why was it locked?"

So you wouldn't snoop through it. "In case I lost it."

"Why are you talking back to me? With that smart mouth. Here's your damn phone." Shameem threw it at Ronnie. It hit her right shoulder, and Ronnie yelped. "You can't sneak around and hide from me. Ever."

Ronnie didn't say a word. There was no point. Any trying, any explanation, was talking back. She had to stay silent except for when she said, "Yes, Khala. Of course, Khala. Anything you want, Khala."

She picked up her phone and went to the kitchen, where she made her aunt tea. She hated that woman. All Ronnie knew is she'd never do to anyone what her aunt did to her. Ever.

Chapter 16

"And here is our calendar, so if anyone wants to book anything, they can. Though honestly, we like to meet them first. You know, for vibes." Brit was training Ronnie on her first day of work.

"Oh, okay."

"Is this your first retail job?"

"No, I used to work in my aunt's friend's shop. But then I switched to an office job." She'd switched because Shameem's friend had treated her just like family.

"Oh, cool. Well, I hope this isn't too boring for you? I mean, we want you to be happy here."

Ronnie blinked. They wanted her to be happy? "I am happy," she said, smiling. Not a lie, she was enjoying herself. To her surprise, Brit leaned over and hugged her.

"Good. We think of this store as our home, so that makes you family. And what you like and want matters. Now, let's go over the various stones, but don't worry—I won't leave you with the tourists by yourself just yet."

Ronnie dutifully took notes, writing down what each rock was for. She'd make a little cheat sheet to help because no way could she remember all of this.

In between learning about rocks and the twins' calendar, Ronnie got to watch Brit charm everyone who came in. Customers would come in for one rock, only to leave with five more.

"How do you do that?" she asked after watching Brit size someone up and give them the perfect crystal.

"I just get a feel for people, you know? Like with you. I get a loneliness and sadness. You can always talk to me if you want, by the way."

"Oh." Ronnie thought she had done a good job of hiding how she felt. Hiding those feelings that popped up no matter what. The past was the past; she had to put it behind her. "Is that all you see with me?"

Brit shook her head. "No, but those are just what you're focusing on. There's a light in you, but you need to let it shine."

The door chimed, interrupting them. Ronnie wanted to ask what the light inside her was. What it meant.

"Well, hello, Ronnie!" Caroline and Marley came in together, arms linked. "We were out to lunch and simply had to stop by to say hello."

"Look at you! Oh, I'm Marley. I think you're—"

"Brit," Caroline said with a smirk. "How wonderful to see you, and back on your feet."

Brit's face paled. "I'm going to the back," she said quietly. They watched her leave the room.

"Yikes, doesn't like you much, does she?" Marley laughed.

"We have a history," Caroline replied. "Now, Ronnie, I need a crystal. What do you suggest?"

"Um." She grabbed her notes. "We have this new quartz that's beautiful and works for most things." It had just arrived and been blessed. It was also a couple hundred bucks.

"Sold! You're a natural at this."

"Ha, uh, thanks."

"See you for dinner?" Marley asked.

"Sure thing!"

After they paid and left, Ronnie went to the back to check on Brit. Her new boss was sitting with her legs crossed, eyes closed, surrounded by black crystals.

"I'm fine, don't worry," Brit said without opening her eyes. "Want to join me?"

Ronnie sat down and tried to mimic her as best she could.

"I find that some people's energy is so dark I have to shield myself."

"Caroline?"

Brit opened her eyes. "Yes. Stay away from her if you can. She's not good people."

"Oh. Marley loves her."

"Well, she will have to make up her own mind, but trust me when I say that Caroline is evil incarnate."

"Can I tell you something?" Ronnie bit her lip. "I can't stand Caroline." She giggled nervously. "I don't know what it is, but I've hated her since we met. She's been perfectly nice. It's just, yeah."

Brit nodded. "That's your intuition. You need to trust it. Listen to it. It'll guide you. Want a tea?"

The rest of the day went without anything exciting happening. Brit didn't mention Caroline again or warn Ronnie away from anyone else. How strange. What had Caroline done to be so disliked? *But then, I don't like her either.*

She'd have to talk to Marley about it later.

———

"I'm home!" Ronnie called out. She'd brought a present for Marley. Two, actually: a bottle of wine and a crystal.

"Hellllllo!" Caroline was perched on the sofa. "Our working girl is home."

Fuck. "Hi, Caroline. Where's Marley?"

"Taking a bath, I think. She had a call with Joan and had to soak it off." Joan's life revolved around Joan. Ronnie was usually the ear for Marley after one of their calls.

"Oh. And you're just sitting here?"

"As good a place as any!"

Ronnie went upstairs to look for Marley. She wasn't sure she liked Caroline sitting in the house. Like she lived there. Like she was the new Ronnie.

"You're home!" Marley said, her head and knees the only parts not submerged. Ronnie blushed. She was no prude, just inexperienced. Seeing any naked body was a strange sensation. A thrill, though not sexual (not always, at least). She felt like she was doing something she shouldn't. And that made her feel dizzy.

"Yep! I brought you a gift. Caroline's here?"

"I know. Tell me everything?"

"Later, okay?" Ronnie didn't want to talk about work. Or the twins—though it was just Brit today. She didn't want Caroline to know anything about them. Why give her more gossip? She may not know a lot about the woman, but if Brit hated her, there had to be a reason, right? And Ronnie needed to find out what it was.

She went back downstairs and offered Caroline some wine before sitting on the sofa with her. This wasn't betraying Brit. She was digging for info. Besides, how could she betray someone she barely knew?

"Aren't you a delight?" Caroline grinned at her.

"So how do you know the twins?"

"Oh, we go way back. But they're not my biggest fans. My methods are too out there for them. But they run an excellent store."

Ronnie nodded, taking a sip.

"My turn to ask you a question. Marley said you had a very traumatic upbringing. How are you coping?"

Marley said what? Ronnie choked on her wine, coughing so hard her eyes watered.

"Oh dear, sorry. That wasn't tactful of me, was it?"

"No, I'm fine. Sorry, let me get some water."

She ran into the kitchen, where she stayed for as long as she could. She wasn't entirely sure how she felt about Caroline knowing anything about her, but she did know she didn't like Marley talking about her. It was irrational—she knew that. But her story was hers and not for anyone else. This was not okay. Not in the least bit.

That night, Ronnie dreamed she was lost in the desert. It wasn't her, but in the dream it was. She was confused and delirious and stumbling. All while Caroline was laughing. Dream Ronnie fell to the ground, and a raven came by. "This is how you die."

———

Before

"Rania got her period today." Shameem said it with an eye roll. Her friend Savita giggled.

"Uh, better watch out, Rania. You can get pregnant now."

Ronnie hated anyone knowing her business. If her aunt knew it, the whole community did. There were no secrets. She was eleven, and now the aunties would look at her differently. Because of a period. So stupid.

"I'm not worried about that," Ronnie mumbled.

"Hey! Do not disrespect your aunties this way. Apologize!" Shameem ordered.

"Sorry, Savita Auntie."

"Now bring us chai."

"Yes, Khala."

"I swear, hiring a nokari would be easier than getting her perfectly trained," her aunt complained.

"But you've done such a good job with her. She'll make a good daughter-in-law someday."

"Who would want to marry her?" They both laughed.

Chapter 17

"Ugh, I'm so frustrated." Marley stared at her email while running her hands through her hair. It was a day off for Ronnie, who was now working three days a week at the crystal store.

"What's up? Can I help?" The chance to help Marley with something was always a good moment. It made Ronnie feel useful. And when you were useful, people wanted to keep you around.

"I just, okay, I mean, I sometimes wonder if it was a mistake to come out here?" Marley lay on the floor as she said it. "It's just so hard to make inroads here."

"But you're doing it! This is a small town, everyone knows each other. It'll just take time."

Marley rolled her eyes. "Sure, Jan," she joked.

"I'm serious! Look what you've done for me. You can do that for so many other people." Ronnie wouldn't admit it, but being the one to give the pep talk, instead of needing one, was a great feeling.

"I know you're right, but still. I didn't expect it to be so hard. Every time I've come here, everything was so easy." Marley had visited Sedona several times before she'd decided to move there. She loved it. She loved the vibes, the energy vortexes, the hiking. She loved that everyone wore crystals and you could buy dream catchers just about everywhere, including the grocery store. She loved the Kismet Center, which had been recommended to her by the hotel concierge. It was the ultimate place to be healed—and harder to get into than some Ivy League schools. You could visit as a nonmember and pay extra and only go to a set number of classes and healing sessions. Marley was dying to become a member, to get that approval. It would go so far in launching her as a healer. But every time she tried, she was told no.

Marley had never had to really work for anything besides her mother's attention and love. But everything else in her life had been handed to her on a Tiffany & Co. silver platter. She was part of the upper echelons of Manhattan society. Whether she liked it or not. Marley had decided to take her bank account and go at it alone. And coming up against an obstacle—any obstacle—felt overwhelming to her.

"Maybe," Ronnie began slowly. "Maybe it's because you're not used to being told no? Like, this is the universe's way of making sure you really want this?"

Marley stared at her. "Huh. You might be right. Like, if I give up, then I didn't really want this." She sat up. "Ronnie, you're a freaking genius! Oh my goddess, what would I do without you?"

Being useful meant longevity. It meant survival.

"I bet there's just one person you need to charm to make it all happen," Ronnie added. She had no idea if it was true or not, but she wanted it to be. "Make that person your project."

"Oh my god, yes. *Yes!* And I know just who. The bitch who won't let me past the desk at the Kismet Center. Fiona what's her name! She didn't even care that I was on TV."

"I bet if you booked a session with her, that'll make her more open."

Marley stared at her before nodding. "I swear, I could kiss you. My little genius!"

Ronnie grinned. This felt good. She was good. She was making things happen for them. Just like it was meant to be. "And maybe do more TV."

"You sound like Caroline. She wants me to be the local expert for the news. I'm going to pull a card." Marley was getting into tarot, and that meant reading Ronnie and herself daily. "Oh look! The Fool! A new journey for me! Oh yes. For sure. You're so right."

"And for me?"

"Three of Swords. You have to heal some old heartache. Is it your aunt? I bet it is. Have you talked to her recently?" Just like Brit.

Ronnie shook her head. "She hasn't forgiven me for selling the house."

"But it was your house."

"That doesn't matter. You just, I don't know, you don't do that to family where we come from."

"Well, she should have been nicer to you. Ugh. If it helps, Joan's dog died." Marley called her mom by her first name, something Ronnie would never do. "But she's had it cloned, so whatever."

Ronnie laughed. "Your mom cloned her dog?"

"Yep. And is naming the new one Marley. So see? All of our parents suck. Come on, let me take you to lunch. My treat because you're so awesome."

It was over salads that Marley got the news she wanted. "Oh my goddess, Ronnie, you were so right. Fiona wants to do a session with me!"

"See? It just takes time."

"Well, now I have to go shopping. I need the perfect caftan for this. Something that says I'm so healed I don't need her sessions."

"Yessss!"

"And one for you too!"

"Oh. Okay!" Ugh, not more caftans. They looked god awful on her. Ronnie didn't want to wear anything that looked like something Shameem would approve of. She preferred her jeans and tees.

When Ronnie started buying new clothes after meeting Marley in New York, Shameem had taken scissors to her new jeans and shirts. "These are not appropriate clothes for you," she'd muttered. "You're not Amrikan. You don't need to dress like them."

Them. Like they, too, weren't from here now. Ronnie watched helplessly as her aunt cut through hundreds of dollars of clothes. She and Marley had picked them out so carefully. And now they were all ruined.

"Go put on a salwar kameez like a good girl," her aunt ordered.

Kameezes were just caftans. And Ronnie hated them now.

———

The next morning, Ronnie read the local paper while Marley went to her appointment with Fiona. The paper said another body had been found. Some woman, possibly just a lost hiker. Ronnie hoped that's all it was, a hiker who was lost. Someone who'd stepped in the wrong place and fallen. That was easier to stomach than murder. *Please don't be another dismembered body.*

"What the fuck," Ronnie muttered. It was one thing to have murder in the big city, but in a smaller town, it all felt too close for comfort. The murderer could be anybody.

She'd have to show it to Marley. Ronnie already wanted to put up cameras just in case, but Marley didn't want to live in a surveillance state. "We don't need them! We could sleep with our doors unlocked."

"No! We can't. Please don't do that," Ronnie had begged.

"I won't, I promise. I'm sorry, I didn't mean to upset you."

She wasn't sure what time Marley would be back. "I should do something," she said to the empty house. Ronnie hated how her voice echoed. It reminded her she was all alone. She didn't want to be lazy sitting around the house. So she got up and went outside, where she tidied up the yard. It didn't take long for her to start sweating.

The ravens were near, and they watched her. Ronnie waved, then felt self-conscious for waving at birds.

"You look like a crazy person," she muttered, laughing at herself. Her mirth died down when Marley came revving up in her car and slammed the door. The birds took off flying.

"That fucking bitch!" Marley yelled. Her front windshield had a large hole in it with a circular crack radiating around it as if something had hit it. Flown into it.

"Oh no."

The session, as told by Marley, didn't go well. At all.

"She's a scam artist. Oh my god, such a freaking scammer!" Marley paced around the room, her colorful red, pink, and white caftan taking all of Ronnie's attention.

"I hate her!" Marley continued. Ronnie had never seen her so worked up.

"What happened?"

Marley stopped pacing. "Can you pour me some wine?"

"Sure." Ronnie poured a glass for each of them because she knew her friend hated drinking alone.

"First, and thanks." Marley took a big sip. "Her house is huge. Like, either she's raking it in or she's stealing, because no way. She had crystals bigger than my head!"

"Wow."

"Right? And in this giant, gorgeous house, she made me sit outside, on her shitty lawn, on a gross blanket, and drink sugar water that she called tea. That was it. The whole session was about tea. Can you believe that? She charged me two hundred bucks for shitty tea!"

Ronnie couldn't help it—she let a laugh loose. She couldn't stop herself.

Marley glared at her.

Ronnie snorted, her eyes watering. "Oh come on, that's kind of funny. If it was anyone else, you'd say it was hilarious."

"Ugh, you're right. I just wish I knew who was the real deal here, because that's who I want to align with. Oh and then, she said some bullshit about having potential and wanted me to pay her to work with me. Ugh. I feel so stupid."

"What did she say about the Center?"

"She said, 'We can't let just anyone in.' Can you believe that? I hate her. And I rarely hate anyone. I hope she gets what's coming to her."

Ronnie felt a chill as Marley said that. Karma was real; she knew that.

"The best revenge is living well, isn't that what you tell me?"

"It is. God, you're right. And then, as I was leaving, a bird hit my car! Like the bird just flew into my windshield. How does that even happen?"

"Oh no! Is it okay?"

"Oh yeah, it flew off. I need more wine. Let's just drink and wallow and then I can move beyond this. And you know, this is a lesson in what not to do." She smiled, as beatific a smile as she could muster. "The universe is full of lessons for us."

"I'm sorry, I know you were looking forward to it."

"It's fine, I think I need to go cleanse myself from that negative energy. It was all over her. I feel like it's clinging to me. I'm going to take a bath."

"I'll bring you some wine."

"You're such a dream."

As Ronnie left the chardonnay on the side of the tub, she heard Marley talking to herself. "No one does that to me and gets away with it. No one. I'll get her. I will."

Chapter 18

THE TOWN

The ravens were incensed. They had followed Marley home. They'd heard her lie. Marley hadn't told the entire truth. She had about Fiona. But she'd left out the part about the bird dying on the side of the road, where Marley had thrown it out the window. As she'd pulled out, she'd felt the thump, saw the glass break. And there it was: a raven, its feathers bloody, sticking out of her windshield.

"That's bad luck, you know," Fiona had said. She'd watched the whole thing. So had the ravens. They'd seen their family member die because of this woman.

"Poor thing! Is there a vet near?" Marley had made a show of picking it up and putting it carefully on the passenger seat. "I'll save you!" she'd promised. It was a lie.

Once she had pulled away, she'd chucked it out the window.

The ravens were gathered around their dead friend. Birds could mourn; they had their funeral rites. And right now, they were cawing into the wind to let others know what had happened.

They would avenge this. They would. They'd get that woman for killing their friend. They had to. If they didn't push back against humans, the entire world would be lost. The big dumb apes did whatever they wanted. She was glowless; they'd known she was evil. But they hadn't known she was evil enough to kill one of their own.

They huddled together and began forming a plan.

Chapter 19

The Town

June

Blood was quite literally everywhere. On the walls, on the lush tapestry hanging on the wall. Even on her own arm.

What did she expect? She'd been a bit wild. Careless even. She couldn't help herself. This had been fun.

She glanced down at the lifeless eyes of Fiona. They were a pretty hazel color.

"Don't even think of haunting me, you bitch."

This one had felt good. Fiona was a scam artist of the worst kind. She'd convince people their departed loved ones had messages for them and then spit out bland platitudes about crossing them over and how you had to go on with your life. And the ravens had really wanted her dead. So she'd done what she had to.

It was all too easy to murder someone here. People were so trusting. Fiona had let her into her house. Sat her down, offered her disgusting-tasting tea. Granted, Fiona had thought this was a paying session. As if she'd pay that bitch anything.

"You must release what you're holding," Fiona had said.

And she'd shrugged. "Okay." And brought the heavy quartz crystal down again and again onto Fiona's head. The rock was ten inches tall, a real beauty. Each time it had struck Fiona's skull, it had made a sucking wet noise as if the crystal hadn't wanted to let go. She'd hit her at least eight times. She hated Fiona; she'd wanted her to suffer. The crystal now sat on the coffee table, covered in blood. And maybe bone and brain matter. She didn't want to look too closely, to be honest.

"I'm not done yet." She was talking to the body. And she wasn't done. She had to finish up with Fiona. She washed the blood off her hands and arms and found rubber gloves in the kitchen. As she pulled them on, she surveyed the mess. She yanked the tapestry off the wall. The blood was all over it so no saving that. After moving the coffee table out of the way, she placed the tapestry in front of Fiona, who was still sitting in her chair.

She shoved, harder than she needed to. And with a thud Fiona fell onto the tapestry. It wasn't as bad a noise as when she'd hit her. That wet sound would be with her for eternity.

She rolled Fiona's body up and left it on the floor. And then she cleaned up as much as she could. In case any trace of her was there. And she deleted her info from Fiona's calendar and phone. No one would know she'd been here. Her car wasn't even parked out front.

The rest of her plan would have to wait till later, but she dragged the wrapped body to the garage and shoved it in the back of Fiona's Jeep Cherokee. And she took the blood-covered crystal with her. No sense in wasting it.

———

Night came agonizingly slow. But it was here, and she could do what she'd planned. She grabbed the three jars of manuka honey from Fiona's kitchen—that stuff was forty bucks a pop! Fiona was raking it in. And then she drove the Jeep on State Route 89A toward Cottonwood.

There, behind a church where the earth mother statue used to stand (the church had had it torn down), she turned onto a dirt road.

No one but joyriders came on this road and certainly not at night. She drove awhile, far away from the main road so that no one would see her. She stepped out of the car and felt eyes on her. This was what Sedona was. Natural and fierce and not at all human. The coyotes or bobcats or bears watching her would have to chill. She wasn't in the mood for dealing with them right now.

Dragging Fiona out of the back took some work; the body was stiff. But she made it happen. And then pulled it into the tall, dry grass next to the dirt road. It was a foot high, and no one would see the body from the road five feet away.

"Snakes, don't bite me, please," she implored. She was doing this for them, after all. All of them.

Once she got Fiona in place, she unrolled the tapestry. She grabbed the three jars of honey from the car and opened them, pouring each one onto the body.

"Returning you to nature so the world can devour you."

She knew that the smaller bugs, the ants and the wasps, would come for the honey. And then the larger ones would come for them. And so on and so forth, until nature had a feast.

Later, she'd leave the Jeep back in Fiona's garage and sneak out to where her car was hidden, down the road a way in a clearing of trees. She took a breath. That had taken so much work. She hoped the next one was easier.

Because there would always be a next one. Always someone she had to take care of. People didn't understand that there was a balance here, a need to keep things in check. And if anyone got out of line, disrupted things, they'd have to die. It was nature's way. And she knew a lot about nature. She knew what was needed. Because the ravens told her. And they never lied.

She got home and washed her hair, soaking in a bath, a glass of wine near. She had cleansed things. She had made it better.

Chapter 20

There was blood on the floor in Marley's bathroom. Ronnie recoiled in disgust. She had never lived with someone like Marley. Someone who cared so little for the sanctity of her space, beyond making it Instagram worthy.

Ronnie hated seeing blood. Just a drop was enough for her to get dizzy. Blood reminded her of things best kept secret. Blood could tell the world everything she'd done to get here.

So much of Ronnie's life now was different and confusing to her. Like how Marley threw out food so quickly. Or went through bedding, tossing out what she didn't want anymore. (Ronnie took the sheets out of the trash, washed them, and put them in her room.) And then there was the bathroom. She'd never seen anything like it. Marley would make a mess and leave it there. Period blood on the tile floor, toothpaste stuck to the sink. Floss tossed wherever. It was horrifying.

This was how rich white people lived, she thought. People who never had to scrub their own toilets. Ronnie had grown up very differently from Marley, and at times, she felt the expanse between them to be too large for her to cross. She closed her eyes.

She could have set up a cleaning lady, but she had a day off and wanted to be helpful. So she cleaned. She was good at that. Cleaning was like second nature to Ronnie.

The strangeness she felt here wasn't just because of Marley. It wasn't fair of her to put this on her only friend in the world. Sedona was weird. It wasn't what she'd expected. She didn't belong here, and she knew it. Everyone here wore caftans and crystals, and they looked like Marley: tanned darker than Ronnie, with bleach-blonde hair. Everyone was white. All of them.

Ronnie had imagined Arizona to be more diverse, and parts of it farther south were. But everywhere Ronnie went here, she was the lone person of color. She knew there was a local indigenous tribe around, but the healing circles in Sedona were kept almost exclusively white. Except for Ronnie. It was unnerving. But she could never say that out loud to her only friend. She'd take it the wrong way. (She'd seen two Black women in a café and had wanted to run to them, but Marley had told her she was being weird.) Sedona was a white person's idea of an idyllic, scenic, healing town, complete with guns and signs for ultraconservative politicians everywhere.

Ronnie finished cleaning, washing her hands several times to make sure no blood was on them. She went to her room and picked up a book to read, something Marley had assigned her on learning to love yourself. Maybe that would help. Marley was meditating somewhere in the house.

Instead of reading, though, she lay down on her bed. She closed her eyes, and images of her aunt flashed in front of her eyes. Her aunt, her only family. She didn't exactly miss her. How could she? But she missed having a place that was really hers, even if it was so small only a twin bed could fit there. She didn't even miss that bed—her new one here was far more comfortable. But the pretending was getting to her. Pretending to be normal and happy and well. That took effort. With Shameem, she only had to keep her mouth shut and head down, and she'd avoid a slap. But with Marley, she had to act like someone she wasn't. She had to act well. And that was harder than anything Ronnie had done yet.

If Marley ever saw who she really was, she'd throw her out of the house. Ronnie was certain of it. And then she bet Caroline would move in. And the two would live happily ever after—without her.

"Ugh, stupid, evil Caroline," she muttered. "You're acting jealous and possessive. That's beneath you," she reminded herself. She'd read that in one of the many books Marley had given her. "Marley loves you, but she needs more people around her. It's fine. You're fine. Let it go." She tried to shrug off her dream where she died in the desert, with Caroline watching and laughing. The dreams weren't real. They couldn't hurt her.

She pushed that feeling as far down as she could. She was happy for Marley. It was fine. Everything was fine. And her secrets would never get out.

To be sure, Ronnie did her usual ritual when she got anxious. She called her aunt and listened to her voice mail greeting before hanging up. One day she'd leave a message. Today wasn't that day.

———

Every time Marley went out with Caroline, she came back with some new idea. Some new mission. Something that would be just the thing to win everyone over and make her the fabulous hot shit healer in town.

This time, it was videos. Caroline had convinced Marley she had to do YouTube and TikTok videos about what was happening.

"People look to you for guidance in these matters."

"They do?"

"Sure, they saw you on TV. You're an expert now."

"An expert. I like that!"

Ronnie didn't say a word, just let the two of them chitchat until Marley declared she was going to make a video.

"That's what people do now—they don't need TV stations," Caroline stated. "And you'll reach the youth."

"Do you think it's good to link yourself to a grisly murder?" Ronnie asked.

"She has a point," Marley agreed.

"No. Listen. What's happening now is bad. It's terrible. And we need someone to pull us all together. That someone is you. And if it's not you, well, you'll miss your moment. Opportunity is knocking. Are you answering?"

Shit, she was good. She even had Ronnie nodding along.

"Let's do it in the backyard. Ronnie, be a dear and help us set it up," Caroline asked. Ronnie didn't want to say yes to anything Caroline asked. But she did it because Marley wanted her to.

"Wait a minute!" Caroline shrieked, looking at her phone.

"What?" Marley asked.

"They found another body! That's it. You have to do this video now."

"Shit. Another one?"

"And this one was even worse." Caroline grinned, and it was gruesome, Ronnie thought. *How can she revel in someone being killed? That's just wrong.*

"We're a small, tight-knit community. But evil is here. And we need to stop it before more of our people die. I want all of you to be safe, to be well. We must work together now."

Marley smiled solemnly at the camera. "We cannot let them scare us, let them win. We have to work together to be safe. Join me—let's be safe together."

"And . . . cut!" Caroline yelled before clapping. "That was perfect. Let's edit and post it."

Ronnie only watched. She didn't know how to help anyone be safe, but if Marley said she knew how, she'd trust her.

"So what's the plan?" she asked.

"The plan for what?" Marley looked confused.

"To keep people safe? You said for folks to join you?"

"I don't actually mean join me. It's hyperbole! Right, C?"

"Right!"

Right.

Chapter 21

The Town

The ravens watched at dawn as the animals ran to the body, to the sweet honey covering it, to the smaller critters who'd gotten there first. Everyone devoured each other, and it was a sight to behold.

The ravens didn't feast. They stood perched in the lone juniper tree that grew out here. They knew this body, of all bodies, was tainted, and no amount of honey could fix that. She'd had no glow. None at all. Sometimes there was a faint glow, a glimmer of hope that this person could be good. But no. Not this one.

They'd tried to warn their fellow animals, but no one listened, not when an easy meal was right there. And while they couldn't blame them, the ravens still tutted.

Fools.

Human meat was never good. But this one, especially, had a funk to it.

Vultures circled. This meat would make them ill, the ravens said. They should leave it—it was evil, the ravens warned. But vultures were vultures, and they'd take the risk. Vultures could eat anything, but evil flesh was evil flesh.

The other animals ignored them. They weren't as bright as the ravens.

Maybe the human should have buried her, they wondered. But no, evil had to rot away. And not in the ground. Burial was for loved ones. This body, this human, was evil through and through. She had no loved ones.

At least their human had kept her promise. That was something new to them. Humans, in general, didn't keep their word. But theirs did. (She glowed so brightly that the ravens didn't need the moonlight to see her at night.)

For days, other animals feasted on the body. Some animals got sick; others went crazy and attacked their friends. Some didn't feel a thing, but the ravens saw it. Their glow diminished. You could never eat evil flesh. It would infect you.

The ravens stood off to the side in their juniper tree, watching it all unfold.

It took over a week for the humans to arrive. This was a spot where the humans rode funny vehicles, driving fast and shouting. It was fun for them. The birds didn't quite get it. Fun for the ravens was chasing other birds.

From the dirt road, the humans couldn't see Fiona. They couldn't see the smaller bugs and the birds and lizards feasting. But once the larger animals came out, the humans noticed.

The people screamed—they were male, yet their voices went so high. The carnage in front of them shocked them. They hadn't expected it. Why would they? They were at the top of the food chain, the ultimate predator, with tools that killed from afar. But now they were being hunted. That fear would make anyone scream.

They trod through the grass to get closer to what was happening, not paying attention to the snakes. Careful, the ravens wanted to say. The three men held up their rectangles again and again before leaving. They ran so quickly and sped away in their buggies.

Soon more humans followed, this time the ones in matching clothing. And the snakes were taken off the body with poles. They had come to feast on the smaller animals who were eating the body. A veritable smorgasbord for nature, only the main dish was human. The larger animals were scared off with noise. The ravens took flight, too, but stayed circling overhead. Eventually, the body was covered and taken away, and the humans trampled into the dry prairie grass that was a foot high, looking for things. Clues. Shiny things. The birds didn't know what they were after.

They'd better be careful, the ravens said to each other. There were far more snakes there than they realized. And there were far worse humans around them. The humans didn't know, but they would.

Chapter 22

Another murder. Caroline and Marley rode the attention wave as much as they could. More videos, more being stopped by locals to talk about it.

The body found this time was intact, mostly. Or so the newspaper said. Of course it was, Ronnie thought. Whoever had dumped it had covered it in honey. That couldn't possibly have been an accident. That made two murders since she'd come to town. At least. That was two too many. It was one thing to have murders in a big city but a small town?

She was reading the paper at the store. Today, she was with Star, and her training method was so different from Brit's. Brit was gentle, patient. Star knew everything and made fun of people after they left. Ronnie couldn't decide who she liked better. Did she have to choose?

Ronnie stared at the photo of the victim. She knew that face. She'd dreamed about her. She'd known Fiona would die and hadn't been able to stop it. Fiona Healer. Marley had gone to her. She should have gone too—said something to her. But what? "Sorry, Fiona, you don't know me, but the ravens came to me in my dreams and showed me you were going to die." That was a one-way ticket to the nuthouse. Fiona had died from blunt force trauma. And Ronnie knew what the weapon had been. Could she tell the sheriff? No, he'd think she'd done it.

"Did you see this? They found another body," Ronnie said.

"They did?! Where?" Star was next to her and reading the paper faster than she thought possible. "Holy shit. Fiona."

"You knew her?"

"Yeah. She worked for Lorraine. She was . . . well, she thought of herself as a healer, but . . . I wonder how she died."

"She was hit with a crystal over and over." Ronnie said it automatically before covering her mouth in shock. "I mean, that's what I heard." *Shit, don't tell anyone about your dreams.*

Star ran her hand through her hair, agitated. "We need to figure out what's going on. One body is bad but two?"

"Two is scary," Ronnie agreed. "I just want to know why they're being killed. You know. In case they deserved it."

Star stared at her. "Even if they did deserve it, we should make sure they have a good send-off. It's the right thing to do."

"Oh, yes, of course. I didn't mean it like that. Just, you know, if it weren't a good person, then I'd feel less bad about it." *Then when I see her in my dreams, I can feel okay about it all.*

"I get that. But people are complicated. Some love others, some hate them."

"Like Caroline."

"Right." Star's voice had changed. Her syllables were more clipped. That's how Ronnie knew she was angry.

"Shit, I'm sorry. I didn't mean to say that this person deserved it. No one does." She put her hand on Star's arm. *Please don't be mad at me. Please please.*

"No, it's not that. I just . . . Caroline isn't what she seems. So be careful around her, okay?"

"She says the same about you guys." Ronnie watched to see if there was any reaction. When would the twins tell her what Caroline had done?

"Interesting."

"Anyways, she's always with Marley. I try to avoid her, but . . ."

"Oh, and what does she have Marley doing? That's her thing. She tries to help prop people up, thinking it'll help her own standing."

"Uh, they're doing videos or something. About the murders."

Star's face looked grim. "Of course they are."

"Can I ask? What did Caroline do that makes you dislike her so much?"

"You can, but I'm not ready to answer that. It's not my story to tell."

"Oh. Fair enough."

"Now, let's talk about you. What's your story? We know so little about you."

Ronnie froze. Why would anyone want to know about her? "Oh, there's not much to tell. Shitty upbringing, orphaned, met Marley, here I am." She did a little flash of her hands as if to say, *Ta-da!*

"That's not all. But when you're ready to open up, let me know. We accept you as you are."

Star got distracted by a customer, and Ronnie took it upon herself to dust everything. She didn't want to tell anyone anything. Because dirty laundry shouldn't be aired to outsiders. Ever.

Before

"Sit." Shameem was furious. Ronnie could tell. Just by the way she spoke. *Oh no, what did I do now.*

"How was school?" her aunt asked.

"Okay." Ronnie was sixteen. A junior in high school.

"Did anything happen today?"

Fuck. Her aunt knew. Her aunt knew what she'd done.

"I'm sorry, Khala. The counselor made me talk to her. I tried to get out of it." The school counselor had taken an interest in Ronnie. She wanted to help the girl, so she had asked prying questions about her homelife. Like, did she enjoy living with her aunt? (No.) Was she treated well? (No comment.) Was there anything they needed to know? (Silence.)

"Because of you, we now have this children services coming by. Do you see what you've done? You're an idiot. Now they'll take you and put you in a home. They'll rape you. That's what happens."

Ronnie couldn't help it—she cried. She fell to her knees and begged forgiveness. "Mafi, please, Khala. I'm so sorry. I tried to not say a thing. I promise."

"We do not talk to outsiders. They don't know our lives. Remember that. And when the social worker comes, you had better behave. If they find out about your dreams, they'll lock you up. Now, go cook dinner."

The social worker did come. A few times. But Ronnie's smiling-till-it-hurt performance assured her everything was fine. Shameem was charming, smiling, and doting. It was all an act. Because you never ever told anyone your secrets. Ever.

———

The house was empty when Ronnie got home. No one around, just her and the birds. Because they were always there. Always watching, perched up in a pine tree. Ronnie didn't mind them. At least she didn't have to pretend to be whole and good when they were around.

She took meat from the fridge and chopped it up before taking it outside for them. It was supposed to be her dinner, but Ronnie would rather give it to the birds. She'd eat a yogurt or a sandwich instead.

She stood back and watched first one large raven explore her offering, and then it called for another. Soon, four birds were eating away. Good, they were easier to befriend than humans.

Ronnie made sure there was water out before turning back inside. As she walked to the back door, a shiny coin landed at her feet. A thank-you.

"You're welcome," she said, waving the coin.

The ravens, she decided, were friends. They expected nothing from her except a little kindness. A little food, some water, making sure they had plenty when it was too hot out. In exchange, well, sure, they left her coins. Shiny bits of metal they found. But mostly, she hoped this meant they were her friends too. Because Ronnie needed friends even if they weren't human.

Chapter 23

THE TOWN

Fiona's body had been found; she'd made sure of that. She'd dumped it on Bill Gray Road, where joyriders on ATVs were bound to come across it eventually. The honey had been serendipity. Nothing destroyed forensics like animals. She'd been relishing the panic since the body's ID had been released.

That's how she knew she was on the right path. That this was a mission from the gods. She had to do this. She was the chosen one.

"My, my, my Fiona!" she sang to herself and then laughed. Oh, but she was hers now. In death, Fiona had become something she'd never been before: one with nature.

But now she had to start planning more. Because her work had only started. She had no choice but to carry on. It was the only way to save this place.

———

The ravens were outside the store again, perched on juniper trees and buildings. They sat, watching. They liked to be there, Star noticed. It was like they were keeping guard.

But still, she shivered.

"What is it?" Brit asked.

"Just the usual feeling of impending doom," Star replied.

"Wow, there must be twenty birds out there."

"At least."

Star thought it was probably an omen. Brit, she knew, would disagree. Something about the ravens being the lifeblood of the town. Star respected the birds. They'd helped her find her sister when she was lost. And since then, they'd kept watch over Brit. But seeing so many large black birds was unnerving.

"Do we really need so many cameras?" Brit asked.

"We do." Star was up on a ladder, adjusting the floodlight cam that would go over the doorway. There were cameras inside the store as well.

"I want us to be safe. This is the best way, trust me," Star said, getting down from the ladder and admiring her handiwork. "If a fly gets near us, we'll know."

"I don't like this," Brit muttered and went inside. Star followed her.

"Look, I don't like it either, but we have to protect ourselves. Some bad shit is happening, and we need to stay safe." She didn't add that she'd found footprints outside their house, prints that weren't theirs. Someone was getting too close to the twins.

Brit had her back to her sister, but Star knew what she was doing. She was pulling tarot cards. Star stood next to her.

"What's the word?"

"Nothing good. Look." She pointed to the Tower card. Followed by Death and the Three of Swords. "Change, drastic change, endings, and heartbreak. I'm officially freaked out."

"Or maybe we need to deal with change to have a new beginning."

"Can't have a beginning without an ending first."

Star rubbed her sister's back. "Maybe we can go away soon? To the cabin?" They had a cabin deep in the woods outside Flagstaff that was their hidden hideout. They could get away from everyone and breathe.

"Maybe. I don't know, I feel like we have to stay here. Just in case. Keep people safe."

"Whatever you decide."

Star went back outside to finish installing her cameras.

Chapter 24

"You know what would be simply incredible?" Caroline picked up a green olive and held it with her thumb and index finger. She dipped it into her mouth, where she sucked on it, pulling the red pimento out. Ronnie watched, fascinated. *That's how you're supposed to eat olives?*

"More olives?"

"No, Ron, but thank you. I think we should do something in person. Like, a rally. Marley, don't say no! Just think about it."

A rally. They wanted to have an event. But what kind of rally? And for what? Rally for safety? Ronnie thought the idea was stupid. Which must have been written all over her face.

"I don't know—" Marley started to say.

"Nope, you're not saying no. Listen, we need to motivate people beyond videos. Interact with them. Show your followers you care what happens, that you're in this together. It would do wonders for your credibility, your reputation. Just think about it."

Marley nodded. "My followers." She said it slowly as if savoring how the words felt in her mouth. Then she smiled.

"They need you," Caroline said.

"They do."

Ronnie watched without saying a word. The more Caroline said something to Marley, the more her friend was swayed. Caroline was like a devil whispering into her ear. A Svengali. Ronnie both hated her for that and admired her. Imagine people doing what you said. Could she get people to do what she wanted?

"How do you do that?" she asked. She hadn't even meant to say anything. But Caroline's ability was fascinating.

"Do what?"

"Convince people to do what you want?"

Caroline laughed, shrugging her shoulders. "I just give suggestions! It's up to everyone else to do what they want."

Suggestions. She could do suggestions, right?

"So where would we do the rally?" Marley asked, getting them back on topic.

"Leave that to me. We may have to start small, but we can work up."

Ronnie picked up an olive and tried to eat it like Caroline. But instead of looking at all cool, she started choking as the pepper flew into her throat.

"Oh god!" Marley jumped up to hit her on the back while Ronnie coughed, her eyes full of tears.

"I'm okay!" Ronnie rasped. She wiped her eyes. "I need water."

"Careful, Ron, eating olives is a learned skill," Caroline said with a laugh. Ronnie smiled as she poured more water, chugging it until she didn't feel like dying anymore.

"Apparently!" She coughed. "Maybe you should suggest to me how to eat them?" She laughed at her own joke. No one else did.

"Oh, did you hear about the body? They identified it." Caroline leaned forward, eager to share her bit of gossip. "It was Fiona from the Center." She said it like she was excited, as if the news was the best bit of dirt ever in their town.

Ronnie nodded. "I know, I read the paper. She was left for animals to eat."

Marley avoided her gaze and acted like she was deep into what Caroline was saying. Ronnie didn't ask any more questions, but there was an uncomfortable gnawing sensation in her belly. Something had happened to that woman, something bad. Was her friend involved? She'd vowed revenge. Had she gotten it?

That's crazy. It's Marley. Your Marley. She would never.

Would she?

"That's weird," Ronnie said, trying to get her friend to talk. *Suggest it.* "Don't you think so, Marley?"

"So bizarre!" Marley grimaced. "But let's be real: this was karma. She got what she deserved."

———

"That'll be fifty dollars even." Ronnie said it with a smile. Ronnie was getting good at working in the store. She was friendly and funny, and the customers liked her. She kept her cheat sheet of crystals next to the register so she could pretend to answer their questions.

"What's that?" Star asked.

"Oh, um, I couldn't remember everything about every rock, so I made a little cheat sheet."

Star picked it up and read it.

God, I'm stupid. I can't even remember some rocks.

"This is really good," Star said.

"Really?!"

"Yes. I wonder—maybe you can make little cards to put under each display? That way people know what they're for?"

"That's a great idea! I can do that!"

"Good work, Ronnie. You're really a godsend."

A godsend. Her? That had never been said to her before. Not once in her life had anyone been grateful for her presence. The twins said please and thank you; they told her she was great. And she had no idea how to respond to that.

Ronnie shrugged. "Just trying to learn everything."

Star nodded. "You're doing amazing, you know that, right?"

"I am? Well, I had another idea." *Suggest it. Like Caroline does.* "What do you think about rearranging things. By need. So all the protection crystals are together and the love ones and the money ones. And the overlapping ones can be near each other, almost like a gradient."

Star nodded while she spoke. Ronnie waited for her to reply no. It was too much work.

"Interesting. And we could have your cheat sheets up. That would cut down on stupid questions from people. Let's try it!"

It worked! Her suggestion worked! Or at least, Star was into it. Ronnie still had to actually follow through on her idea.

Ronnie waited for closing before she began. Star left her with the keys and showed her how to lock up. Each section would have a sign stating intentions: healing, manifesting, love, protection. And under each basket of crystals, she included her little cheat sheet with info on each and every single one.

It took hours, and it was close to midnight when she finally locked up the store. It was eerily dark at this hour. Not too many streetlights on, no crazy nightlife. Just her and her car, which was parked at the back of the lot.

"Shit." Midnight in Queens, hell, even four in the morning in Queens, was different. Not that she was ever out that late. But someone was always around. Not here. The sky was so dark the stars could be seen, and Ronnie paused to look up.

"Wow." She breathed it all in. She tried to pick out the various constellations, but she barely remembered any from school. It wasn't like she could see anything in a city.

Ronnie would have stood there forever had the high-pitched squealing howl of coyotes not made her run. She dashed to her car, got in, and locked the door as if coyotes could get in. She felt eyes on her.

She laughed at herself. She was being crazy; she knew it. But there was something so beautiful and so terrifying about this place. Ronnie started the car, unable to shake the feeling that she was being watched. "Probably the coyotes," she said, driving right by the person in black who had been watching her. She didn't even see them.

Chapter 25

Before

Ronnie had fucked up. She set the tea tray down for Shameem and her friend—Mahnaz Auntie. When no one acknowledged it, she let annoyance get the better of her.

"You're welcome," she muttered.

"What was that?" Shameem Khala asked, her eyes narrow. "Did you say something?"

"Of course not. Please enjoy." *Fuck. Fuck fuck fuck. I need to keep my mouth shut.* She didn't know what had gotten into her. Yes, she did. Marley. Marley had gotten into her. Ever since she'd been meeting with that woman, she'd been feeling strangely good. Almost . . . worthy of things. But she couldn't behave like that with her aunt. All entitled and wanting validation.

"Sheedah should give you lessons on how to behave," Mahnaz Auntie said. The two older women erupted in laughter.

Sheedah. Mahnaz's daughter-in-law. Straight from Pakistan because no one raised in America would marry her son. *Shit, don't let them know I thought that.* Sheedah was so busy caring for her mother-in-law that she barely had time to breathe. And that's how everyone expected it to go. You didn't marry a person—you married a family.

Sheedah had been in the US all of six months, and Ronnie had tried to befriend her. She saw her as a kindred spirit. Someone who would relate to her.

But it hadn't gone well.

They had been at Mahnaz Auntie's house.

"Sheedah!" Mahnaz Auntie bellowed. "Sheeeeeedahhhhhh!" she yelled again.

Sheedah came running.

"Ji, Ammi-ji?" She called her *Mother dear* as if Mahnaz were now her mother. That bugged Ronnie. She'd never call anyone Mother.

"Chai." An order. A statement. Ronnie jumped up to help the woman.

"Sit," Mahnaz Auntie ordered her. "She can manage."

Ronnie sat as still as she could on the plastic-covered sofa. Rarely was she invited over; she had to make sure she didn't screw this up. Shameem Khala loved her best friend. Ronnie had to impress her.

"Rania, tell me, are you dating anyone?" Mahnaz asked as Sheedah brought them tea and rusk.

"No, Auntie. I don't date."

"Waiting for your khala to find you a husband. Like a good girl."

"Uh, yeah." God, the idea of her aunt lining up someone for her to marry was hellish.

"You are a very pretty girl, you know," Mahnaz continued. "If you put a little effort, I bet we could find you someone." She bobbed her head side to side as she said it.

"Thank you, Auntie. Sheedah, do you need help? I'm better in the kitchen." If she stayed on the sofa, Mahnaz Auntie would try to set her up with her youngest son. And the idea of being Mahnaz Auntie's servant for the rest of her life made Ronnie want to vomit.

"Fine, go help her," Shameem said with a wave, dismissing her.

Ronnie smiled and ran to the other room. She didn't want to help Sheedah so much as hide from her aunt's view.

"You good in here?"

"Oh, hi, Rania." Sheedah was wiping the kitchen down. "Can I get you something? You hungry?" Her accent reminded Ronnie of her mother. It was light and musical, and she loved hearing it.

"No, I just wanted to hang out with you."

"Oh."

They had never been close. Ronnie didn't even know if Sheedah liked her. But surely, a woman in a similar position as Ronnie had to feel like she did?

"So, um . . ."

Ronnie had no idea what to say to her. *Hey, Sheedah, do you want to make a pact to escape? Do you want to help each other?*

"Just spit it out, I don't have all day."

"Sorry. Just wanted to see if you wanted help."

"I'm fine."

"Yes. Of course. Are you . . . okay? I mean, with everything and the changes in your life?" *What are you doing? Shut your mouth. Don't say more.*

"Of course I am! I love my new family."

"But the way they treat you—"

"Is customary. It's my duty to take care of them. Maybe if you did your duties, you'd be in less trouble all the time."

"Oh." Mahnaz had clearly talked about Ronnie.

"You know, if you ever need something—" Ronnie began.

"I don't. But thank you."

Ronnie hadn't known at the time what had gotten into her. But it was Marley. Always Marley, urging her to stand taller, keep her head up, voice what she wanted. And here she was trying to help Sheedah—when the woman obviously didn't want her help.

When she and Shameem Khala got home later, the first thing Shameem did was grab her by the hair. "You think I don't know what you said to Sheedah? She tells Mahnaz everything. Like she's supposed to. Stop infecting people with your Amrikan disease."

Ronnie whimpered. "Mafi, Khala, I just wanted to help her in the kitchen. Maybe make a friend. I'm terrible at it, I'm sorry."

"You will be. You better be more like Sheedah, or else."

Sheedah had betrayed her. Such a small thing, to ask how someone was. Yet it had caused a disaster. Ronnie ignored her after that. And every time Mahnaz Auntie came over, Ronnie quieted that part of her that was waking up, that was wanting love and attention. And instead, she smiled like a Stepford wife and asked, "More chai, Auntie-ji?"

Chapter 26

"Jeez, which one is it?" All the houses looked the same. Arizona was full of these identical houses, each neighborhood given some vague name that made you uncertain if it was a nursing home or housing development: Sedona Views, Red Rock Living, Desert Mountain, Vista Trails. Identical houses next to more identical houses, each one so similar you could be forgiven for going to the wrong one. Peach walls with coral accents and landscaped yards full of rocks and cacti, maybe a pool in the back. The land here was a developer's dream, and new housing developments cropped up like prickly pear. Blink, and a new one showed up.

"Up ahead, I think." Marley checked the map. They were headed to Caroline's house, where they were planning to film a new video. Ronnie didn't know why she had to join in, but Marley had asked her to. It was one of her days off, and she had nothing better to do.

The houses had American flags outside; some had Blue Lives Matter flags. The occasional house had an old Trump flag. Ronnie made a note to avoid those people.

"On the left, number 1210," Marley said.

Ronnie parked in the driveway. Maybe she could just drop Marley off and wouldn't have to spend any time with Caroline. That would be ideal. But she couldn't figure out how to do that, how to say, "I'm good, thanks! Have fun!"

"You're here! Welcome, goddess." Caroline stood in the doorway. "Come!" She kissed both of them on the cheek. "Oooh, I love pinot noir." She nodded to the bottle in Ronnie's hands.

The house smelled like incense. Not just incense but incense burned on top of incense, on top of even more incense. Ronnie's nose itched, and she coughed. "Your house is so gorgeous," she managed to say.

"Please, it's a cookie-cutter house. But real estate here is so pricey these days. Come, let's crack this bottle open!" Caroline laughed.

The house wasn't decorated like Ronnie had expected. She'd imagined something glamorous, bold. Like Caroline was. She didn't like the woman, but she was also slightly in awe of her. What must it feel like to go through life without any doubts? Without that voice saying *you're wrong* all the time? But that's not what the house looked like at all. It was bland and dull. Gray walls and sconces and art that wouldn't draw you in. A LIVE, LAUGH, LOVE sign hung in the hallway. Bags of clothes were piled here and there as if Caroline had put them down to unpack and then left them.

"Did you just move in?"

"Oh, this isn't my house. I mean, I'm living here. But it's been vacant forever."

"You're squatting?" Marley couldn't keep the shock out of her voice.

"Yep. Listen, we have to take what's ours. The patriarchy will keep us down if we let it." Caroline opened the wine and poured three glasses while the other two women exchanged shocked glances.

"Wow. I've never met a squatter before," Ronnie admitted.

"You'd be surprised. There are a lot of us here. The snowbirds buy up the houses, and they sit empty for ages. Or they turn into Airbnbs. I'll probably get booted soon—they usually start rolling in by September. Now, I think our next video should be something more."

Ronnie noted how Caroline spoke. Just steamrolled toward what she wanted until you had to give in. She had to try it. Not that she could ever pull it off herself.

"More?" Marley asked.

"Yep. More. I want tears. I want real fucking emotion. How are you going to inspire someone if you look like a news anchor?"

"I—"

"I mean, where's the passion? You have got to reach out and grab what you want!" Caroline pantomimed reaching out with her fist and grabbing the air. "Think you can do that?"

This was it. This was going to be the moment that Marley told Caroline to fuck off. This was when her friend came back to her and stopped letting Caroline run things. Ronnie was sure of it.

Marley grinned. "I absolutely can."

Ronnie blinked a few times before forcing a smile onto her face.

The backyard view of the red rocks made it clear why Caroline had chosen this house. It would be a perfect setting for this video. Ronnie helped set things up and waited with water in case Marley needed it. That was her job today: water girl.

Caroline had printed a script and was going over it with Marley. Ronnie waited.

"Okay, ready? Let's do this!"

"Hello, my fellow travelers and healers. I'm Marley Dewhurst. I live in Sedona. I work here. I'm one of you. But now, I'm terrified of dying here.

"Another body was found. A murder happened on our trails. Someone we all knew and loved." Marley had to say that line a few times to make sure she didn't laugh. "Fiona Healer's body was found covered in honey in the desert, off Bill Gray Road. She was one of us. She lived with us, and now she's dead." (Fiona's real last name was Lawrence, but she went by Healer to everyone who knew her.)

"Who will be next? Me? You? We must do something before they come for us all.

"Join me as we fight this invading evil and keep it out of our lives. I am setting up citizen patrols to help keep an eye on our people, to keep us safe. Sign up for my mailing list for more information. This is for the good of Sedona, for the good of all of us. We won't let the Sedona Slasher win. Join me at a rally at the Whole Foods parking lot tomorrow at eleven in the morning." Toward the end, Marley's lip trembled. But she didn't cry.

"Bravo!" Caroline called. "The restraint was perfect this time. Just a little shake, no sobbing. No being hysterical. I'd follow you into war! What did you think, Ron?"

"Oh, um, it was good. Really good." The entire message struck fear into Ronnie. Maybe it was the whole invasion message. It was a dog whistle. But her friend wasn't racist. No way. She was clearly imagining things. Ronnie was being sensitive, right?

"After this, we'll be able to book any location we want. It's going to be incredible." Caroline grinned, and her teeth looked sharp. Ronnie shivered.

———

"Where's the smoky quartz?" Brit asked. Learning the new organizational system was going to take time.

"Right here, with other protection crystals." Ronnie paused. "If you don't like the way I set it up, tell me! I just wanted to try something new." *Caroline would never cower—suggest more changes. Do it.*

"No, I like it. It's just different. But it makes sense intuitively. I need to get used to it is all." Brit smiled.

"Um, I also had the idea of selling sets of crystals together. For like anyone who needs extra help."

"Like a love set?"

"Yes! In a pretty box or something. And you can charge even more for them."

"I love that idea! Look at you making us better!" Brit's laughter eased the knot inside of Ronnie's chest. She was terrified she had overstepped. That her ideas weren't good. That she sucked at suggesting things.

"Oh, wow, cool. I was worried you'd hate it."

"I could never hate anything you do. I can't wait for Star to see this."

Ronnie felt good. Like, really good. Proud. That was weird. She never felt proud of anything. But this time, she'd done well. She'd done something her new bosses liked. And that made her feel better than anything had in a very long time.

"I bet you have more ideas on how to make us run better. Good, we need them!"

"Uh, sure!" She didn't, but she would. This was the first time anyone had wanted actual ideas from her. Ronnie was determined to not fuck it up.

Ronnie got home and wanted to celebrate, but Marley was out with Caroline doing who knew what. Marley's new video had gone viral, and the news even ran it. Caroline was so cheerful and gloating these days that Ronnie hated being near her. Instead, she fed the birds. None came, but she left the meat out for them all the same.

Chapter 27

THE TOWN

The uproar over Fiona's body made her smile. People were scared. She could feel the fear in the air. It was glorious. They should be scared.

The videos helped. She'd seen them. Of course she'd watched them. Nothing folks here liked more than a hysterical blonde woman spouting off about invaders. She shook her head and laughed. Hey, if it made them behave, she was all for the videos.

She had more to do. With each murder, she came closer and closer to making things perfect. Better than perfect. All the shitty people would flee or be killed. Tourism would dip, but then only good energy would flow in. And the land would be less trashed. The animals would be happy; they'd thrive. That was what most people didn't realize: nature didn't need humans. In fact, nature was better when people weren't around.

The ravens got it. This she knew. She nodded at them. They crowded her yard. They followed her. They watched her constantly.

She had made a pact with them. She'd told them she'd make this place better. And she was living up to that.

"I will keep my word to you," she said to one bird, larger than the others. Its black eyes watched her as if it understood. She was certain it did.

Chapter 28

Marley and Caroline had signs made up: SEDONA SAFETY AND CITIZEN PATROL NOW! They left them at Ronnie's feet while Marley greeted newcomers. Some people were here for her—not many but some. The others were just trying to shop at Whole Foods.

"You got this, babe, don't even worry," Caroline said. She handed a microphone to Marley, who took a deep breath and then smiled. One of the news stations from Phoenix had come for the show. The spectacle.

"Let's do this." Marley cleared her throat. "Everyone, welcome to our rally for a safer Sedona. We're here—" The mic squealed, and Ronnie winced. "We're here to make sure that we don't become prey to this insane killer!"

"Yeah!" Caroline cheered. Ronnie followed her lead.

"So far, two bodies have been found. Two people from our community. And they're dead. Murdered. Their light was taken. And what are the police doing? Nothing. Absolutely nothing."

Caroline booed at that.

Ronnie scanned the small crowd. There were nine people here for Marley, and the customers who were shopping had paused to listen. Not bad for a first rally.

"Well, that's not good enough! We deserve to live in peace and security. If the sheriff won't help us, we'll help ourselves. Who is with me?" Tepid applause. "I have sign-up sheets for our patrols. I want you to join us. Because they won't take us down without a fight! Do you know how Fiona Healer died? She was covered in honey so animals would devour her. Is that what you want for your life? No! We want security! Safety! We want our Sedona back! Join me! Together, we can stay safe from the Sedona Slasher!" Caroline had come up with the name for the killer, of course.

Ronnie held up a clipboard, which some people signed and gave their contact info on. Marley was making the rounds, talking to and shaking the hands of every person who had shown up, regardless of whether they were there for her. The news crew followed, ready to interview her.

"Are you running for office?" a man asked.

"Oh, goddess, no. I just want to make sure there are no more murders." Marley smiled at him. But Ronnie could see it. The glint in her eye. Ambition. That's what it was. Marley was seeing possibilities. A run for mayor perhaps.

"Excuse me, uh, Marley?" It was the sheriff. The same one from that fateful hike where they'd found the head.

"Sheriff—what's your name? I don't think I caught it before." Marley flashed her megawatt smile. She motioned to the news crew to film the interaction.

"Reynolds. Sheriff John Reynolds." He seemed flustered, but maybe it was because of Marley. Gorgeous women and all that. Ronnie watched him. "Listen, I'm all for keeping safe, but you can't do this."

"Why not? We're exercising our freedoms here," Caroline interrupted. She was gunning for a fight.

"And that's fine, but you need a permit. Or be on private property with the approval of the property owner. You've done neither. So y'all have to skedaddle."

Caroline looked annoyed. She had been ready for an epic battle, and it was just a permit issue.

"Oh. That's a bummer. Sorry, I'm new at this whole organizing thing," Marley apologized. It worked; the man softened.

"It's fine, but you're going to have to wrap this up."

"Would you like to sign up for our patrols?"

"No. We do not need you out there, we have increased officers on the trails."

"We're just trying to help. And it seems you need our help. So let me do this for you."

The sheriff blinked, shook his head, and went to his SUV.

"Guess that's that then. The sheriff isn't interested in keeping us safe. So it's on us," Marley said to the camera.

———

When the news segment aired later that same day, they'd cut out the shots of the lot where it looked like only a few people had come. In fact, they'd made it look like a thing. A real, actual protest. One that other people could be a part of. A happening. And once people saw others joining on TV, they wanted in. Ronnie saw herself in the background. She'd tried her best to hide her face—no one needed to see her. She didn't need anyone reporting back that they'd seen her.

Marley's phone rang off the hook. Locals loved her, especially the older ones. The ones who liked to wear guns while grocery shopping. They were ready to act like the police, to get their feelings out. To keep strangers at bay. They were ready to take Sedona back. If they shot people while doing so, even better.

Ronnie watched all this with growing unease. There was no way this wouldn't backfire. Didn't Marley see that? Ronnie could see it unfold— old white locals pulling guns on anyone who looked strange. Anyone like her. But when she brought it up, Marley got angry.

"Stop being such a Debbie Downer! These people are with me, they support me. All I ask is you do too. I don't need anyone who isn't one hundred percent with me on my team."

"I'm with you! I promise!"

"Good. Anyways, I'm so relieved it wasn't a colossal failure. But maybe we can do another one at a better location."

"With a permit!"

"Maybe," Marley demurred. "We'll see." Her phone buzzed. Caroline had texted. "Shit. Caroline said we need to do something about my skin. It looks awful on the screen. She's right, isn't she?"

Ronnie spent the rest of the evening consoling Marley. But it was no use. Caroline had suggested something, and like a devoted servant, Marley listened to her.

Chapter 29

THE TOWN

What the ravens wanted and the humans wanted was similar. They wanted their homes back. They wanted safety, the filth cleaned up. But beyond that, they differed. The birds didn't care who died—if they were glowless humans. They simply wanted the humans gone.

But they watched the small gathering of people, watched their new dark-haired friend Ronnie stand around. She didn't believe any of the things the other woman said. They could tell. She couldn't hide anything from them. She glowed, though. And for that the ravens were thankful.

We should use that, they said to each other. Use her. She will help us. She doesn't lie. Not to them, at least. They didn't care if she lied to other humans. They would, too, if they were human.

They stopped to shit on the red car that had hit and killed their friend. The windshield had been replaced, but their friend was still dead. It was the least they could do.

Chapter 30

July

"What the hell is that?!" Ronnie was staring at what she was certain was an alien or demon. It had to be something not of this world. Things like that simply didn't exist on earth. But here it was, staring at her in the bathroom at the crystal store.

"What's wrong?" Brit heard her yell and knocked.

"Help!"

Ronnie didn't care if she sounded like a baby. There was something monstrous in the bathroom with her. And she needed help.

It was a scorpion. A small, one-and-a-half-inch or so brown scorpion that Ronnie now had to kill. She had nearly stepped on it with her sandaled feet.

Ronnie had never seen a scorpion before. Sure, she'd seen photos. And that old *Clash of the Titans* movie. But in person? Those things didn't exist in New York unless you were a psycho with a weird taste in pets.

The scorpion was standing perfectly still next to the toilet. Its tail was down, and it was smaller than she'd expected. Ronnie had imagined Arizona would be full of the large black ones she saw on TV. She was curious and disgusted and terrified all at once. Would it try to kill her? Could it kill her?

"Oh, it's just a scorpion." Brit laughed. "Don't worry, they mostly leave you alone."

"Oh god, it's awful. You can't have that here!"

"Well, they're not friendly, sure, but it's the season. They come out with the rains. And on new moons. Isn't that freaky?"

"Sure is. Maybe we need a pest-control person to come. They have eco-friendly sprays now."

"Oh, maybe. That's not a bad idea."

"I did see some rats the other night when I was here late. So it's probably a good thing to get someone in." It was a lie. But Ronnie needed this taken care of. She needed the scorpion to disappear back into hell where it belonged.

"If it makes you feel better, we'll get the store sprayed," Brit acquiesced. Ronnie washed her hands and then hugged the twin. Something she hadn't yet done—initiate a hug. "Wow, yes, okay, we'll do it!" Brit laughed. "Oh, also, we need to spray some lavender for now. They hate the smell."

"They do?"

"Yep. You should spray your bed so they don't climb in."

Ronnie had no choice but to do it because images of scorpions stinging her while she slept filled her head. Nope. She wouldn't let that happen. She would buy a bottle of lavender spray and, when she got home, spray every bit of fabric she could find. Until the entire house smelled like a field of flowers.

"Did you see, uh, Marley's rally?" Ronnie was dying to talk about it with someone. Anyone who would listen. "Because of Fiona."

"Oh, Fiona." Brit sighed. "She could have been a great healer, but she was greedy. That's the problem out here. Everyone is trying to make a buck." She shook her head. "It's tragic, though. Anyways, lavender is great."

That was all she said, and Ronnie let it go. Brit didn't enjoy talking about the murders, not like Star. Not that anyone enjoyed it. But Star would at least broach the topic. Brit would change it as quickly as she could. Ronnie wanted to ask her why, but she was overstepping. She had to take it slow.

———

"I have a surprise for you. Don't say no, I want you to try it," Marley said the next morning. "It's to make you feel and look good because you do so much for me."

"Um, okay?" Ronnie laughed. "Another hike?"

"Spa day!" Marley sang out as if she were Oprah.

More massages. She was warming up to the idea of being touched so much. It was still weird. And her feet were ticklish beyond hope. But this was growth, and growth was uncomfortable.

"Sounds awesome!"

She sat in silence as Marley drove to a strip mall and then ushered her into a storefront spa.

"Hi! We're here for facials with DeeDee. A reservation under Dewhurst." Marley handled all the talking.

"We have you down for vampire facials." The woman behind the counter smiled. Incense was burning, and crystals lined the counter. They weren't the twins' crystals, Ronnie could tell. They weren't as nice as what Brit and Star sold.

"For what?" Ronnie asked.

"Oh, Caroline said we had to try these. Because if I'm going to be on camera, I needed to look incredible."

Ronnie nodded. "Cool." Great. Sure. Another wacko Caroline idea. Yet Caroline's vision of the videos was working. More people knew who Marley was, stopped to talk to her on the street.

They changed into robes and sat in a dark room with comfy couches, drinking cucumber water while Enya played. They were taken to separate treatment rooms.

"Now, just relax. First we're going to take some blood."

"Sorry, what? Blood?" Ronnie's heart fluttered with anxiety. She hated needles and blood.

"You signed up for the vampire facial, right? Well, we use your own platelets to turn over new skin. It's amazing. And it won't hurt, I swear."

Tourniquet on, Ronnie wanted to scream. The needle went in, and her ears filled with a horrible shrieking noise. It took her a moment to realize she was the one making the fuss.

"It's okay! Hey, you're done. See?" The skin specialist offered her some tea, the adult version of a lollipop for kids. "Just relax now, okay?"

———

"Oh my god, feel my skin. Feel it!" Marley grabbed Ronnie's hand and made her touch her fresh and dewy skin after they were done. "Oh god, look at you! Your skin is so perfect! Did you get to talk to DeeDee?"

"No, I had some other woman."

"She's beyond. I think we should make this a regular habit. Because wow, your skin is glowing!"

"I didn't know there'd be needles."

"Oh, shoot, sorry about that." But Ronnie saw her smirk. "I'm sorry. I forgot about your needle thing. But you look amazing." Marley offered a lopsided smile. "Really amazing. Wow, your skin is stunning. Caroline suggested this place. She said they'd make my skin look perfect for the new cameras the news uses. But expect some bruising."

"Well, I feel great, so thank you," Ronnie lied. She didn't feel great. She hated needles. Absolutely despised them.

But her skin did feel nice. She was touching her face while lying in bed. The bed had a dream catcher, and there were paintings by local artists on the walls. Her own things took up almost no space. Which was how Ronnie liked it. If you took up too much space, people saw you. This way, she could hide. Not be a pain.

Her face was sore, and it looked a bit beaten up. But it felt soft and smooth, mostly, and that made it worth it. Right?

When she went to work the next day, Star yelped.

"What the hell happened to your face?"

"Oh, just some facial. The bruising should go down soon." Was it that bad? Ronnie had tried her best to cover up the discoloration.

"Does it hurt?" The twin grimaced while staring at Ronnie.

"A bit. Marley really wanted them. Do I look that bad? Should I go home?"

"No, no, don't be silly. You just look like you've had a rough night."

That wasn't what she'd hoped she would look like. But no one else mentioned it, except for one customer who slid a card for a domestic shelter over the counter to her quietly. Ronnie was mortified but touched that she cared.

"Thank you," she said quietly, taking the card.

"You don't have to stay with him, honey," the woman whispered. "Don't let your culture keep you from happiness."

Ronnie bit down to keep from replying. Her culture? Was she serious? "Well, have a nice day," she replied to the woman and then threw the card in the trash.

That night, the ravens came in her dream. This time, they showed her with Marley. And her friend was taking all of Ronnie's blood and smearing it on her own face, until it was a ghastly red mask. The ravens watched. "She'll get to you too," they said.

Chapter 31

Before

Shameem's hair was graying. Ronnie hated this part of her month. She had to dye her aunt's hair for her. She combed it out, sometimes taking care with the knots. Often, not bothering. It made her feel good to make her aunt wince. *How do you like that, Khala?*

"Gently!" Shameem barked.

"Sorry, Khala. It's just tangled." She would also make sure to get dye on her aunt's skin. By accident. Ronnie should have been trying to do a perfect job, but there was no such thing as perfect as far as her aunt was concerned. So why even bother?

"Do it right! You stupid girl!"

"Well, go to a salon then!" Ronnie bit out, her nerves getting the best of her. She saw her aunt tense. "I'm sorry. I shouldn't have spoken to you like that. I'm just stressed with work." That was a lie. She was stressed at the idea of telling her aunt to hit the road. That she was selling the house and moving. She had to do this. She was an empowered woman. She needed to live her own life.

None of which was something she was supposed to do. She was supposed to be good and obedient and listen to her aunt and not want things. But Ronnie wanted. She ached with want. She wanted nice clothes and a circle of friends to have brunch with like on TV. She wanted a social life. She even wanted to go on a date. But none of that was in the cards for her—unless she took control of her life.

"Well, if you aren't capable of doing this, let me know," her aunt said stiffly.

"I got it, I promise. Your hair will be beautiful." Disaster averted, for now. Her aunt wouldn't hit her. Or yell at her. Not yet, at least. Ronnie tried to stay penitent and cheerful so the mood wouldn't get too heavy.

When she finished, Shameem's hair was a gorgeous shade of black. Her aunt nodded at her reflection before she complained of spots Ronnie had missed. Because there was no such thing as a good job in their house.

Chapter 32

No more rallies without a permit. That's what the sheriff had said. But Caroline and Marley—and by default, Ronnie—weren't going to let a silly thing like paperwork get in the way.

"Guess what I did. Just guess!" Caroline was grinning. "You won't guess. So let me tell you. I sent your news segments and videos to Lorraine to see if she'll let you do an event at the Kismet Center!"

"What?! Oh my god! And?"

"You have a meeting with her tomorrow!" Caroline smiled widely. She had delivered the one thing Marley wanted: an in at the Kismet Center.

"Doesn't Lorraine hate you or something?" Ronnie asked. There was a reason Caroline wasn't a member of the Center, and it was the same reason the twins hated her. Ronnie had no idea why, and she was dying to find out.

"No, the twins do. And Lorraine by extension. But I pretended to be your publicist. Fake name and email and everything. 'Hello, I'm Kate Garett. Pleased to meet you.'" She let out a peal of laughter. Caroline had taken a risk—and it had paid off.

"Wow. Imagine a rally at the Center? That would be huge. Huge!" Marley was ecstatic. "You have to help me prepare!"

And off she went with Caroline to go shopping. She had to have the perfect outfit. Ronnie had to go to work, so she didn't feel that excluded. But still, it would have been nice to be invited.

She did bring home a new necklace for Marley. Another idea she had had. Partner with a local jeweler to turn the twins' crystals into jewelry. The tourists loved the pieces, and the markup made the twins happy.

She held on to the quartz pendant and chain until the next morning and presented it to Marley over smoothies. "For you. For your big meeting."

"It's gorgeous!" Marley held it in her hands. "Wow. I love this."

"It's one of Brit's blessed stones. We started selling them as jewelry." Ronnie waited for applause that didn't come. A "Good thinking, Ronnie!" But nothing. "So, uh, what are you going to say to Lorraine?"

"Well, first I'm going to give condolences for Fiona. And then, well, I'm going to suggest we do a safety event. Like with self-defense people and at the shooting range. Really make sure we take being safe seriously."

"The shooting range? We're going to use guns?"

"Ronnie, we live here now. Do as the Romans do."

Ronnie didn't like guns. They were made to kill. They made her nervous. What if she shot everyone who annoyed her? Like Caroline. What then? She'd end up locked up, that's what.

Marley was wearing a new blue caftan that hung on her just so, along with her new crystal necklace.

"Take my pic?" she asked Ronnie, who obliged. They also took a few selfies.

"You're going to kill this," Ronnie said. "I believe in you." Those four words were what she'd wanted to hear her entire life. *I believe in you.*

"Thank you!" Marley hugged her and left.

Ronnie had to go to work but kept her phone in her pocket to hear how it had gone. Brit was with her today, and when Ronnie saw her, the twin gave her a hug. Ronnie's time at the shop was increasing, and she was spending five days a week there now.

"I just like hugging you." Brit grinned.

"I like it too!" And she meant it.

The door chimed as customers came in and out. Ronnie stayed busy all day before pausing to take a breath. And then she saw it.

"Brit. Brit, look!" She pointed.

"Oh, wow!" A raven had wandered in and now stood perched on a shelf. "This is incredible."

Ronnie got a bowl of water and put it near for the bird. Brit talked to it quietly.

"You know, they're very smart birds," she said.

"I feed them. At home. Don't tell Marley."

"So many cultures revere the raven, so that's good. Keep feeding them."

"They do? The cultures, I mean."

The raven cawed as if agreeing with Brit. Ronnie watched as the twin walked over and gently held her hand out. The large bird jumped on her forearm, and Brit carefully took it outside, where it flew off.

"There. Now it can go play with its friends."

———

Ronnie took a deep breath before unlocking the door. "I'm home!"

"We're in here." We. She'd seen Caroline's car outside.

"How'd it go?" she asked.

"Amazing. Caroline was so right," Marley gushed, a glass of wine in one hand. "Oh, also, Lorraine wants to meet you."

"Me?"

"She loves all things Indian."

"I'm Pakistani."

"Same diff!" Marley started rattling off the story of meeting Lorraine. "I mean, the Center is so chic. Have you seen the Rumi quotes everywhere? To die for. And then, when Lorraine found out about you"—she pointed at Ronnie—"she insisted you meet with her."

"Oh. Cool, just let me know when." She'd do it for Marley, of course.

"Tomorrow! Lorraine's having an event, and she wants me to speak at it. You have to come. It's after work, so you'll be fine. You can't say no."

Ronnie nodded. No saying no. "Sounds great!"

"It's all happening, Ron! Everything I wanted, I dreamed about, it's happening!" Marley's eyes were wide, and though she was smiling, there was something solemn about what she said.

"Hell yeah it is!" Caroline cheered. "You manifested this shit!"

"I did, didn't I?"

Manifesting was, as far as Ronnie could tell, a bit like suggesting things. Only instead of whispering it to a person, you had to shout it to the universe. She needed to manifest things too. Later that night, she sat looking out her bedroom window. *Manifest something. Do it.*

"I want a home. A real home, where I feel happy and loved. And friends. Uh, thanks." A home where she could breathe and be herself and be happy.

———

The next evening, Marley picked Ronnie up from the store. "We have an event!" The Lorraine thing. Ronnie had no idea what to expect, just that they were going and needed yoga mats. *Please don't let me get sweaty and fall in front of people.*

"Let's do this!" It was just the two of them. Caroline didn't want to join in. ("It's your show, babe!" But Ronnie thought she was scared of running into the twins.)

Marley half pulled Ronnie with her on the hike to the first plateau point of Bell Rock. Throngs of hikers mingled around them, trash blowing everywhere from the crowd.

"Look, there's Lorraine!" Lorraine was older, somewhere between her fifties and seventies—it was impossible to tell. She wore a flowing dress with several crystal necklaces. "Oh wow, let's move closer so she notices us."

Marley walked over a few mats but ignored the cries of anyone who wasn't Lorraine.

"Sorry, sorry, excuse us," Ronnie said for her. The space was—like everything in Sedona—overcrowded with people.

"It's beginning!" Marley squealed, and Ronnie smiled her awkward smile.

"Hello, everyone! Welcome and thank you for coming!" Lorraine's voice carried without a mic. "So many people! I love seeing that."

Marley clapped her hands.

"Welcome to this session. New moons are about beginnings. Birthing. What do you want to birth into the world?" Marley elbowed Ronnie in the side, eliciting a gasp of pain from her friend. "But before we can manifest good things happening, we have to talk about something heartbreaking." Lorraine took a breath. "We lost one of our own recently. Fiona. And I want you all to know that I will do whatever it takes to find who harmed her and bring them to justice. With that in mind, I'd like to welcome Marley Dewhurst to speak to us."

Marley walked over to her, waving and smiling like she'd just been crowned Miss America. "Thank you, Lorraine. Now, I'm new here. But this is my home. My spiritual home, my physical home. And let me tell you, where I come from, when we have an unwanted guest, we get rid of them." People laughed. Marley was using a twangy accent, and the crowd loved it. "Someone is here, committing these acts. We don't want them here. We need to handle them. So I'm going to ask you to be cautious, look out for your neighbors. We have to stick together to rid ourselves of this evil. We have to make sure Fiona didn't die in vain."

Ronnie squirmed a bit at the language. Caroline had written this one for Marley. Again.

"In the coming weeks, I'll be overseeing self-defense and shooting courses for anyone who needs them. Because you can't achieve true healing if you don't fight for yourself. In the meantime, if you see anything or anyone suspicious, anyone who doesn't belong, call me. I am here to help you stay safe and well!" Marley had set up a new phone and number just for the calls. "We will find the Sedona Slasher and show him just what we think of him!"

Applause and cheers. Ronnie clapped but not loudly. Anyone who didn't belong? That meant her. She didn't belong in this place, and she knew it.

Lorraine took the mic and started a meditation and asked everyone to yell out love to the world.

"Come on, show the world you're full of love! We will overcome all evil with love!" It was a better message than Marley's, but Ronnie would never tell Marley that.

Lorraine started wandering among the group of fifty or so people, all eager to hear from her, touch her. She stopped to hug every person who wanted a hug.

"Hugs are my way of sharing the love with you," Lorraine declared.

Lorraine approached the two of them. She touched Ronnie's head and squatted down next to her.

"You have the best aura I've seen in a long time. So full of love and light." And then she hugged Ronnie.

She had hugged Ronnie—but not Marley.

Chapter 33

THE TOWN

She watched the hugs. The speeches. The mini pep talks to keep everyone focused. "Do this and you won't die!" But they would. They all would if she had her way. Okay, fine, not *all* of them.

She sat through Marley's fake fearmongering and Lorraine's talk. If they were good, people had nothing to worry about. Who was she to judge? Who put her in charge? Nature. She had an order straight from the natural world to put things right. To make shit better. You couldn't go against nature and expect no consequences. That's what had gotten everyone into this mess.

God, these people! Sitting there on their yoga mats made from materials that would never decompose; wearing crystals that had been mined, destroying the earth; drinking from plastic water bottles. They were guilty. All of them were. So was she, though. But she was making a difference. Offsetting whatever damage her being alive caused. That had to count for something, right?

When the crowd dispersed, she went around and picked up all the trash they'd left. Because even when fearing for their lives, humans were the worst. They left garbage everywhere as if nature were one giant landfill to them.

She filled an entire garbage bag with the trash she'd found.

"I hate all of them," she muttered.

Chapter 34

There had been no murders in a month, at least. Ronnie wasn't sure the exact date Fiona had been killed. But it had been a couple of weeks since her honey-covered body had been found. Weeks since she had seen anyone's death. Her own possible one didn't count. Maybe it had been a fluke thing? Someone passing through town? That happened out here, right? Deserts were filled with murderers and their prey. But then why would the ravens show her the murders?

No murders meant she could relax a tiny bit. She wouldn't find a stray body part, she wasn't dreaming about them, she could breathe. She wouldn't be next—she hoped.

Although, right now, she kind of wished someone would kill her. Lorraine wanted Ronnie to come by for tea. It was what had to be done so she'd let Marley host her rally at the Center. Ronnie hated the idea. But she'd go along with it. Unless someone wanted to strike her down dead. Right now. She looked up at the sky. It was blue, of course. The Arizona blue. But there were clouds looming for an afternoon storm.

Ronnie was wearing a green caftan at Marley's insistence. "I look like I'm wearing a tent."

"You look great. Here, add these." Marley piled on some crystals. "Let's braid your hair." And then she took a brush and started attacking Ronnie's wavy-curly hair with abandon. "Do you ever brush your hair?" She yanked as hard as she could. "Damn knots!"

"Ow, no! Stop! That's not what I use!"

"Stop complaining."

Ronnie bit her lip, her eyes watering with each yank of her hair. Marley's face in the mirror was determined and a little amused. Was she enjoying this? "Stop!" Ronnie yelled.

Marley paused, the brush caught on a knot. "I'm trying to help you."

"You don't know how to work with my hair. I'll put it in a braid, just let me do it."

Marley sighed. "Fine."

Ronnie carefully pulled the brush from her tangles and picked up her wide-tooth comb. It did the job without ripping her hair. She combed it out, then added some argan oil, before braiding. Marley watched with fascination. Shameem like Amla oil, but Ronnie had no idea where to get that out here.

"You oil your hair?"

"Well, yeah."

"Is that like a desi thing?" She pronounced it as *deh-zee*.

"Yeah, sort of. My mom would put oil in my hair, and then you sleep with it. But I find it's better to style with it. Especially if it's going to be humid out." The monsoon days were thick and sticky. So much for a dry heat.

"Can we oil mine later?"

"Uh, sure?"

Marley clapped. Ronnie assumed she had been forgiven for having unmanageable hair.

The Kismet Center looked like yet another adobe house. It was red clay colored—like many of the buildings in Sedona. (Even the McDonald's had Sedona colors—red clay and turquoise arches.) It didn't seem like the be-all and end-all to Ronnie, but then, what did she know? She wasn't enlightened like Marley.

"We're here. You ready?" Marley asked.

"As ready as I'll ever be. What does Lorraine want with me?" She had no idea what to expect.

"Hell if I know. Just smile at her."

Smile, she could do that. They walked through the doors, which were surrounded by giant picture windows and columns. Inside, a frazzled woman worked the phones.

"The Kismet Center, please hold," she repeated over and over. Ronnie took in the lobby while they waited. The walls were painted white with quotes on the top. Rumi quotes. Every wall had one. They weren't the real quotes. Westerners had taken Rumi and watered his words down. And now they were as instructive and important as Caroline's **LIVE, LAUGH, LOVE** sign.

"Everything in the universe is within you. Ask all from yourself." "You are not a drop in the ocean. You are the entire ocean, in a drop." "What you seek is seeking you." *Really?* Ronnie thought. *A perfect home is seeking me? Cool.*

Lorraine came out to greet them. Without her adoring fans, the woman seemed smaller. Frailer. An elderly woman in a bold dress— that's all Ronnie could see. She didn't mean it in a cruel way. Elders were to be revered, respected.

"Marley, my dear, so lovely to see you. And this one." Lorraine put her hands together. "Nah-mah-stay. I've spent so much time in India. I love it there."

Ronnie blinked. "Oh. Um. I'm not Indian. I'm Pakistani."

"Is that so?" Lorraine's smile faltered slightly. "Well, we love our subcontinent. I wasn't sure if you're a vegetarian or not, since most Hindus are and—"

"I'm not Hindu," Ronnie said. Marley's eyes went wide. Ronnie could practically feel her friend telling her telepathically to shut up. "I was raised Muslim. Like Rumi." She pointed to the bland quotes on the wall.

Lorraine's nose wrinkled. "Oh dear. Hope you're not one of those crazy Muslims?"

"Uh, no?" What was wrong with this woman?

"Because I don't want any zealots here. Well, we can tell everyone you're Indian."

"She's a Sufi mystic! Tell people that!" Marley interjected, the desperation in her voice obvious to Ronnie. She wanted this conversation to end. "You can tell people that."

"Oh, good idea. Now, let's have some chai tea."

Ronnie didn't correct her or tell her she was saying *tea tea*. Let her sound stupid. It made her smile. Not all elders deserved respect.

———

The meeting was bizarre. Lorraine showed them to her office and picked up every little tchotchke she had bought on her travels to India.

"This marble turtle is my favorite."

"It's made in Pakistan," Ronnie said. She couldn't help it. This woman hated Muslims but wanted Rumi, and the entire thing pissed her off.

"Well, I guess good things are made there. When did you move here?"

"Oh, it's been a few months, back in March with Marley." She smiled at her friend, who sat next to her in front of Lorraine's desk.

"No, I mean the US? Your English is superb."

Ronnie was thankful she wasn't drinking anything because she would have fully choked on it. "I was born in the US."

"That's true, she was!" Marley interrupted, no doubt to save Lorraine from herself. How was anyone this enamored of Lorraine? She was a stupid old woman as far as Ronnie could tell. "So, Lorraine, I want to talk about—"

"Not now, I want to learn more about Ronnie. You're so stunning. Look at that skin. If I could have your skin tone, I'd be so happy."

Ronnie smiled. That was all she had to do, right? Visions of Lorraine skinning her alive and wearing her like a dress filled her head. God, she needed to get away from her.

"You know what, I want to have a party. For you both. But I know so many people who would just love to meet you, Ronnie. Ronnie—what's your given name?"

"Uh, Rania?"

"Rania. Rania. God, that's so musical and beautiful."

"I prefer Ronnie."

"Nonsense!" Lorraine waved her hands as if she'd just decreed Ronnie's new name. "Rania suits you. I'm going to throw a party for you. And you can have your rally there, with everyone. Because that's the only way you'll get the people you want there."

"Sounds great, Lorraine, thank you!" Marley said.

"Fabulous! Now, Rania, tell me everything about yourself."

———

"I owe you big-time for that," Marley said as she drove them home. "I'm sorry, I didn't realize how into the whole Indian thing she is. But thank you. You handled it well."

"Handled it well" was code for not making a scene. You always knew you handled it well when someone white applauded you. Ronnie wanted to scream at Lorraine, call her racist. But being uncivil was worse than calling someone racist. "Here to help!" Ronnie chirped. She didn't like that woman. She was sure Lorraine was perfectly nice, but she didn't want anything to do with her. She didn't like the way she'd looked at Ronnie. As if she'd eat her up if she could. But she'd do what Marley needed of her. For now.

Later, when she was at the shop, she started laughing.

"Whatever's so funny, please share it," Brit urged.

"I just, I met that Lorraine woman, and—"

"Oh, isn't she fabulous?"

Shit, Brit likes her. Ronnie was going to have to be more diplomatic. "I guess. She was so hung up on me not being Indian. It was bizarre."

"Yeah, she loves her travels."

Ronnie opened her mouth but closed it. White people, no matter how well intentioned, never liked hearing that their friends were racist. She had to "handle it well." So she kept her mouth shut. Hopefully, she'd never have to spend time with Lorraine again. Maybe, if she were lucky, the old woman would die next.

"Fuck. I take that back," she said quietly. "I don't wish that on anyone."

"What was that?" Brit asked.

"Oh, just talking to myself."

The door chime tinkled, and a couple of women walked in. Ronnie stood at the register, smiling.

"Welcome, let us know how we can help," Brit said.

"What a darling shop," one said while browsing. Eventually, the two took their crystals to Ronnie. *"Hello, we would like to pay for these."* The woman yelled it at her.

"I'm sorry, you don't need to yell?"

"You speak English! Oh great!"

"Yes . . . ? Why wouldn't I?" Ronnie stared at each of them before the women turned to Brit.

"You know, we'd be more comfortable if you rang us up." They smiled. The customer was always right in their world.

"No thank you," Brit said. "We don't need your patronage. Ronnie is the best there is." Brit walked over and put her arm through Ronnie's. "You can find crystals elsewhere."

Ronnie didn't say a word as she watched the women leave.

"You okay?" Brit asked.

"Sure, that's a usual interaction." She laughed to lighten things. Maybe Brit would care that Lorraine was objectifying her. But still, better not take chances.

"Hey, I have an idea. What are you doing tomorrow morning?"

"Sleeping?" Ronnie laughed.

"No, let's go hiking. So you have a good experience to replace that whole 'finding a head' thing. Don't say no, okay? Besides, I hate going by myself. Star's rule: no hiking alone. You'd be doing me a favor."

Hiking. She would have to hike. Sure, her thighs were getting a good workout, but Ronnie had hiked enough in the few short months she'd been there. Hell, she'd hiked more than she had in her entire life. But a favor for Brit?

"I'd love that." She grinned.

The hike wasn't what Ronnie had expected. There was no breaking a sweat, no being forced to go higher and higher. Instead, Brit led her to a spot that was empty, absolutely no one around. And then they sat down, enjoying the view.

"This place is one of our secrets. Most of the tourists can't find it." Brit pointed in the distance. "That's Cathedral Rock, very cool vortex. Want a snack?" She handed over a piece of chocolate. "I can never stop eating chocolate." She laughed.

"It's so beautiful here. I feel like I can actually breathe."

"Right? That's why I love coming here." They sat, eating the snacks Brit had brought.

"I have a stupid question: What's a vortex? Marley said it was energy."

"Not stupid at all! She's right. It is. It's like everything on the planet has energy. And there are some places where that energy converges and is really strong. The earth has a natural energy and magnetism, and we're lucky enough to feel it. That's what they are."

"Oh." That made sense. "It's like this place is full of secrets, and if you stay long enough, you'll learn them," Ronnie said and then blushed. She wasn't sure where that had come from. She felt stupid just saying it.

"Exactly! I like to tell my secrets to the rocks. To the desert. A lot of things can be hidden out here, you know?" Brit's eyes pierced into Ronnie's, and for a moment, Ronnie again wondered if her new friend was psychic. She shifted uncomfortably.

"I don't tell my secrets to anyone." She laughed to hide her unease.

"You should. See that rock over there?" Brit pointed to a large rock twenty feet away. "Go and whisper your secret to it. You'll feel better."

"You're serious?"

"Oh yes. Nature loves good gossip."

Ronnie pushed herself up onto her feet and wiped her hands on her jeans. And she walked the twenty feet to the rock and stood in front of it.

"You got this!" Brit called.

She put her hands on the rock. It was warm, the morning sun already too hot. "Hi, rock. Oh, wow, I feel stupid. Okay, a secret. I don't like it here. It's weird. But I'm trying."

She turned back to Brit. "Okay?"

"No, tell it more! Tell it something juicy. Look, I'll move away and cover my ears. No one can hear you." Brit walked the other direction, her hands on the sides of her head.

Ronnie gulped. A secret. A real secret. She closed her eyes and pictured her mother's face. She didn't really remember her mom, but she'd had a faded photo she used to keep before her aunt had taken it away.

Ronnie leaned down and whispered, "I had to do it." She gulped and added, "I'm sorry."

Overhead, a raven cawed, and Ronnie was certain it had heard her.

She walked over to Brit. "Can I ask you something? What's with the birds?"

"The birds?"

"The ravens."

"Oh yeah, they're everywhere here. Did you know they're freaky smart? They remember faces, so don't ever cross one." She paused. "They saved my life, you know."

"They did?"

"I was lost in the desert, and they let Star know where to find me. That's why I can't hike alone."

"Whoa, that's so scary. How'd you get lost?"

Brit stared off, her eyes landing on the nearby rock formations. "I was supposed to do a spirit quest. I know it sounds silly. But I felt like I needed it. And I trusted the wrong people. They didn't give me peyote, they gave me jimsonweed. Never ever take jimsonweed. Anyways, Star found me, and I'm so thankful she did. All because of these birds."

Ronnie didn't know what to say to that. *Wow* seemed so lame in response to what Brit had just told her. "I'm glad she found you too."

"Thanks!" Brit reached for her hand, and they both sat, doing nothing. The ravens had saved Ronnie's friend; that meant they were good. "They hold grudges, you know. The ravens. Isn't that crazy? And they definitely have souls. I mean, I read somewhere they have consciousness, so yeah, totally have souls." Brit smiled at the idea of the birds being whole beings.

"Huh. One came into my room once when I slept. I thought it was a dream, but it left a feather for me."

Brit's eyes widened. "Oh wow. That's a message. Some folklore considers ravens to be messengers between this world and the next. Maybe it was someone you lost trying to reach you?"

"Maybe. There's a story I learned when I was little. From the Qur'an. That when Cain killed Abel, a raven taught him how to properly bury the body." Ronnie paused. "That's morbid, I'm sorry."

"No, I love hearing about other cultures! I never knew that about the raven. Our version doesn't have it." And Brit laughed, which put Ronnie at ease. "Well, I'd say pay attention to your dreams because there's a message someone is trying to send you. Or you need to bury a body."

Ronnie laughed. "Yeah, that's it. All my skeletons." She wanted to keep telling Brit everything. Something about her made Ronnie feel safe, trusted. "You know, sometimes they show me things in my dreams."

Brit stared at her before nodding. "I thought there was some higher energy with you. You have psychic dreams, don't you?"

"Sort of? I don't know. It's just weird." She felt foolish for even bringing it up. "I dreamed I was lost in the desert, and a raven came. But maybe it was you?"

Brit stared at her. "Maybe it was. Did you see anything else?"

"No, I woke up. I only ever see bits and pieces. Is it your turn to tell the rock a secret?"

"You know what, I think it is. Excuse me."

Ronnie let a sigh of relief out once she realized no way could Brit have heard her secret when she'd told the rock. She was safe.

Chapter 35

Ronnie flipped through a magazine. It was some local wellness one, complete with ads for Reiki, mediums, and crystals. All about healthy living if you bought just one more thing.

"Ron? You listening?"

"Mmmhmm . . ."

"Put that down. I need help! Please?"

She couldn't say no to that. A *please*. She put the magazine down. Caroline and Marley watched her, expectantly. *Uh-oh, what did I miss?*

"What can I do to help?"

"My hero! Will you stand here in my video?"

"I don't want to be on camera."

"Not even a little?" Marley cajoled.

"Why doesn't Caroline do it?"

"Oh, no, I could never."

Caroline—she had noticed—avoided the spotlight. Just like she did. But why? Did she have a reason? *If there is one, I'm going to find it.*

"What if I hold up cue cards?"

"Oh, that's brilliant. That would help you look more natural." Caroline's accent shifted the more she spoke. Some days, she had hints of that strangely southern-sounding accent white people in Arizona had. Others, her British accent came out strong. How was that even possible? Ronnie wondered yet again who this woman was.

"Caroline, where are you from? Your accent is so hard to place."

"Oh, here and there. I'm a nomad. I travel where the vibes take me." She grinned, but there was something in her eyes that Ronnie didn't like. Something that said, *Stop prying.*

Ugh, you're being jealous and possessive again. Stop it.

"And now you're here! To help me!" Marley clapped her hands.

This video was being filmed in front of the fireplace. Why a house in Arizona needed one, Ronnie didn't know. Maybe it got cold here? The dynamic duo had set candles up and pillows, so it looked serene in tones of gray and soft wellness pink.

"Hello, neighbors. Marley here, with some great news. We'll be having an in-person gathering at the Kismet Center, where you can talk about your concerns with what's happening. We have to stick together now, join forces so we can be safe. New faces come and go here, but we must be vigilant. We must keep an eye out for anything that doesn't belong. Anyone acting strange. Because we are all at risk of being the next victims of the Sedona Slasher." Caroline was proud of the name she'd come up with. The Sedona Slasher. A terrible name but it worked. It got people riled up. The news had even started using the nickname.

"I am here to help you be safe. Details about our gathering will be posted soon. As always, stay safe, and keep your eyes open."

"And cut!"

"Well, what did you think?" Marley asked, watching Ronnie's face.

"It was good! I just, I wonder if we're scaring people though? Like, against strangers?"

"That's the point."

"But—"

"Ronnie, the only way people will stay alive is if they're vigilant."

There was no arguing here. Ronnie closed her mouth and kept it shut. But something about her friend's videos was bugging her. The whole "blonde woman telling people to avoid strangers" thing, in a land where she was herself a stranger, didn't sit well. And she didn't know how to get Marley to see what she was doing was dangerous.

"I think it was marvelous. Now, let's get some shots of you just to edit them in."

Ronnie left them to take photos and went outside. She didn't like this. Not one bit. Marley wasn't wrong—they had to be safe. But how soon before the villagers were knocking down their door with pitchforks?

The video went up not soon after, and Marley had a mailing list viewers could sign up for. Her website was being built. This was becoming a thing. And Ronnie wasn't sure she wanted any part of it.

———

Living out in the desert was a strange experience. Not just because of the critters and heat. But things like gas and water were all set up differently from city life. They had a well; everyone did. And a giant propane tank the size of a small car that heated the hot water and fueled the stove.

Ronnie was watching the propane truck fill their tank.

"Those ever leak?" she asked the man from the gas company.

"Not usually. But sometimes, when there are forest fires—" He made the sound of an explosion. "That's when things explode. If there's a fire here, get out," the man advised.

"You don't have to tell me twice." She glanced down at her right hand. It didn't look strange, but sometimes, she could feel the rougher skin.

———

Before

Shameem was mad at her. That wasn't new. She had burned the roti. It wasn't her fault. Ronnie had put one on the tawa when her aunt had called her away. She couldn't keep Shameem waiting. That would have dire consequences.

"You think roti grows on trees? You can waste it like this?" her aunt yelled.

"I'm sorry, it won't happen again." Ronnie kept her head down. Making eye contact with her aunt when she was upset was a bad idea. Like a wild dog attacking: *don't look.*

Shameem grabbed her hand and held it over the cast iron pan. "How would you like to burn like your roti?" The smell of her burning skin was revolting and what eventually saved Ronnie from getting a worse burn than she did. Because not even Shameem could stomach the scent.

Ronnie was twenty-one when her aunt burned her palm. It didn't look too strange now, but at the time, it had blistered. She slathered cream on it and wore gloves and did what she had to. Now, though, her hand was a little rough, and her palm lines had been ruined. Not that it mattered, but still. Anything fire or burning related was not something she wanted to deal with. Ever.

———

Some days, life working for the twins was awesome. Other times, Ronnie got idiotic tourists she didn't want to deal with. People who would prefer to have their brown people easily labeled and serving them.

"Where are you from?"

"New York."

"No, I mean really."

"Are you dot Indian or feather Indian?" someone else asked. Ronnie stared at them with panic. Who were these strange people? They had no manners whatsoever.

She didn't want to answer. Not because she was ashamed of being Pakistani but because all anyone here had heard about her family's country was bad. It was whatever the TV told them. And she didn't want them to look at her that way.

"Does it matter?" Star interjected. "She's here, she's fabulous. Now are you going to buy something or . . . ?" She muttered something about tourists and snowbirds as the woman left. "You okay? Sorry about that. I hate some of the people we get here."

"I am, thank you." *You don't belong here, no matter what Star says.*

"Brit and I are glad you're here."

That morning, Star rearranged things slightly but left Ronnie's new system in place. "I like it. It's intuitive. Good call."

"Thank you!"

They made four sales the entire day, something Ronnie was shocked by. "How do you guys make enough for rent?"

"Oh, we own the property. And the strip mall. Mom bought it years back." Star grinned at her. "We own other lots too."

"Wow." She would have to tell all this to Marley. But then Caroline had probably told her everything already.

"What's the matter? Your face totally fell."

"It's nothing." *Tell her. You can trust her. You can.* "It's just that Caroline is always around these days."

"Yikes. Marley's still tight with her, huh?" It was Star's turn to make a face.

"Yeah. I can't do anything about it because she's always over."

"You could move out? But then, finding a good rental here is a pain."

"It is?"

"Oh yeah, so many houses are just Airbnbs now. It sucks. There's like no neighborhood anymore. Just party houses. I hate it."

"That sucks."

"I wish we could chase them all out of here."

"I feel that." Ronnie didn't, but she wanted to relate. Maybe she should get her own place. She couldn't live with Marley forever.

"I'm going to go sit with some new crystals in the back. Holler if you need me."

"Sure thing!" She had wanted to ask Star about Lorraine and this great big party she was throwing for Marley and Ronnie. She didn't want to go. But she didn't want to ask Star if her friend was nuts. So instead, she dusted and tried to come up with more suggestions to work on.

Chapter 36

The Town

The patrols were absolutely ridiculous. Just Marley or Caroline interrogating people on the trails or older folks who hated all the tourists. And hated anyone not white.

She could have aligned with them. Shown them that they were ultimately on the same side. But she didn't. Because some of the folks patrolling were on her list. And she didn't want this place to be filled with armed racists. They'd caught her eye, her attention. And now she had to watch them. And eventually, kill them. It wasn't that she wanted to do this (fine, she did), but she had to. This was the only way to make this place whole again.

She herself had been questioned twice by some senior citizens. Her! As if she didn't belong here. She was here. She *was* Sedona. The damn fools.

"Excuse me? Excuse me! Miss? Who are you?" Another old couple was in her face. They weren't even part of the community. They didn't do anything to heal this place; they merely bought up land because it was hot and beautiful and the dry air (in winter) was easy on their arthritis. Every fall they came, and come spring they'd leave. Just like birds flying south. But they were greedy, obnoxious, and rude, not at all like birds. She glared at them.

"Get the fuck out of my way," she snarled.

The woman's jaw dropped as she said it. Good. Be shocked. Fucking snowbirds were as bad as everyone else here. If she had her way, there would be no more part-time living here. All or nothing.

She was getting impatient. Sure, she could take out a patroller or whatever they called themselves. But that was no fun. No, she'd have to move up her targets. Keep things rolling.

She was staring at her next person right now. It was easy when they drank. You could always wrangle a drunk person. Especially the day drinkers.

It was barely evening out; the sun was still bright and blindingly hot. But serendipity struck now and then. A target. A name she wanted. But it wasn't this one's time yet. Unless . . .

She could grab her, and no one would know. She was close enough to her hair to touch it. One quick hit and she'd be down. *Do it, take her. Kill her. Cleanse the world.*

"Excuse me! Who are you? What are you doing here?"

Dammit! The patrollers were everywhere. And for now, it looked like they were succeeding at keeping murders at bay.

Chapter 37

August

Ronnie's phone rang. She had just gotten home from work, and the house was empty.

"Help me!" Marley screamed.

Her stomach sank. Someone was killing her friend—she knew it. The Sedona Slasher was real and killing her Marley. He'd found them; he was going to murder them. Ronnie swallowed.

"What's wrong?" *Stay calm.*

"I'm stuck outside. There are some awful animals. Help me!" she repeated. Ronnie ran to the front door and opened it. There, surrounding Marley's red Mercedes SUV, were what looked like wild pigs.

"What the hell are those?"

"I don't know—just get me out of here!"

"Okay, hold on." She put her phone in her pocket. She had no idea what to do about the animals outside, but she had to do something. She searched the house for something to scare them with. Anything. She grabbed a broom and ran out the door.

"Shoo! Shoo!" Ronnie waved the broom like an idiot, helpless. What were those things? They were like pigs mixed with rats but giant. "Shoo!" The smaller of the herd—there were ten of them in total—scattered. All but one. The largest one stood its ground, watching her. Or rather, smelling her. Its nostrils flared.

Marley mouthed, "Help me!" through the car window.

"Hit the horn!" Ronnie yelled a few times before the loud blare made the herd scatter even more. Except that one. It stood its ground. *Did it just get bigger?*

Shit, what do I even do? Ronnie glanced around their driveway. She had read that you had to make yourself big, huge. So it scared them. Or bears. Was that for bears? Shit. Ronnie lifted her arms and roared. *"Go away!"* She stomped a few times in an attempt to look large. And heavy. She looked absurd—she knew that. But if it worked, then that was what mattered.

The stubborn javelina sniffed in her direction again before retreating.

"Holy cow, it worked!" Ronnie ran to Marley's car and opened the door. "You okay?"

"Whoa, that was so cool. You're my hero! Is it gone?"

Ronnie turned to see the javelina herd down the street. She nodded. "You're safe. I'm here!"

"My protector!"

Ronnie hadn't thought about what would have happened if the javelina had attacked her. She hadn't had time. She'd only known her friend was in trouble and she had to help. She'd had to do something.

"You have got to be in my videos after that!"

Ronnie deflated. "You know how I feel about being on camera. Please, let it go, okay?"

"I'm sorry, sure. Let's have some tea?"

Marley couldn't help but share with the world that Ronnie had saved her. "My hero!" she posted on Instagram. Ronnie hated it. She didn't want her photos out in the world, where anyone could dissect them. She liked privacy and quiet.

Later, when Caroline came over, she made a big fuss over it.

"Hello, hero!"

"Ha." Ronnie hated this.

"So tell me all about it."

"I just chased some animals away, not a big deal."

"It's huge!"

"You saved me," Marley said. "I've never had anyone save my life before. You're my sister for life, Ron."

"Anyways, can we talk about anything else?"

She tuned them out after that. She was no hero. That she knew. She was a chickenshit scaredy-cat and had only acted on impulse. Ronnie was not brave. Nothing was brave about who she was or what she'd done. And no amount of Caroline telling her the opposite would change that.

Marley was working on a new video, changing the script and set design—a.k.a., candles and pillows. Ronnie flipped through the TV channels and hoped no one would make her get on camera.

"I underestimated you," Caroline said.

"Huh?"

"I didn't think you were a fighter. Guess I was wrong."

"Okay." She didn't know what else to say. But there was a look in Caroline's eyes that freaked her out. Like the other woman was about to take the gloves off. "Uh, good luck with the video! I'm going for a walk."

"Now? It's dark?"

"I won't go far." Ronnie smiled.

Chapter 38

THE TOWN

The ravens were fascinated by Ronnie. She'd scared off the javelina. He was a mean son of a bitch too. Normally, the ravens could spook them away, but that one, that one made life difficult. He trounced through the watering holes, acting like he owned the land. He'd even eat all the food left out for the birds. He acted like he was a human. And that was enough to piss the ravens off.

One day, they hoped, a human would kill it. Or a mountain lion would. But, they knew, javelinas were bad meat. They tasted so gamy. They'd still feast on him, but they preferred other meat.

If Ronnie, their dark-haired friend, could scare him off, then she could do other things for them. And the more she did for them, the more they'd like her. Maybe she could join up with their other friend. Together, with two humans helping them, they'd be able to make this place whole again. They'd rid the land of evil. They'd been giving her glimpses of her future. Of all of their futures. Priming her for what had to be done. She'd step up; they knew she would.

One raven left a shiny penny for her as a thank-you.

Chapter 39

If there's a hell, I'm standing in it. Everywhere Ronnie turned, it was like legions of demons were taunting her, their mouths open, laughing at her. She wanted to scream, but she couldn't. She couldn't do anything but watch.

She was in the backyard of the Center, at the gathering Lorraine had insisted on throwing. It was August, and the heat was hotter than anything Ronnie could remember. Arizona didn't have a dry heat in the summer like everyone said. It was humid and 101 degrees out. The monsoon rains threatened to unleash every day, the clouds building up. And if they were lucky, the skies cried. But when they weren't, the sticky, unbearable air was enough to make Ronnie throw up. She was certain she was going to faint as she wiped the sweat beading up from her face. *God, Marley would kill me if I pass out and make a scene.*

Ronnie wanted to stay inside, in air-conditioning. But she couldn't.

She was wearing a cotton caftan, per Marley's request. A white one, to match hers. But Marley had a little something extra on: Ronnie's mother's jewelry.

Ronnie froze when she saw her friend. "That's my jewelry?"

"Yes, thanks for letting me borrow it." Marley hadn't asked her permission. Ronnie didn't know how to ask for it back.

Marley also wore multiple bindis on her forehead and had tried to stick one on Ronnie.

"No. I'm not doing that."

"I'm just trying to help!"

———

"Nah-mah-stay!" Marley greeted every guest. "Welcome, thank you for coming."

This party was everything Ronnie didn't want. Bad versions of Indian food. Bollywood songs playing. Every cliché that Lorraine could think of, she had on display. Including wearing a sari herself. This was supposed to be Marley's big rally, but instead, Ronnie felt like she was at some god-awful mehndi ceremony. Thrown by a white lady.

"Jai Ho" came on as Lorraine was led in by Star. Like she was a bride at her wedding. Ronnie couldn't shake this feeling that she was in some alternate universe.

"I love this song," Marley enthused. It was the only desi song most of them knew, thanks to *Slumdog Millionaire*.

"Everyone, please clap for Lorraine!" Someone had given Marley a microphone. Caroline, no doubt. Even the twins couldn't keep Caroline away from Marley's big moment. Though Ronnie didn't see Marley's friend around yet. "Lorraine, welcome! Everyone, this was Lorraine's brilliant idea to introduce you all to me and Ronnie." Ronnie flinched. Shit, they were all looking at her now. Marley's voice was booming. She was made for this sort of thing, Ronnie thought.

"We'll start soon, but for now, please enjoy some of the amazing food Lorraine had catered for us! And dance a little, shake off some of that nervous energy!" No one was dancing. But they were eating samosas.

"Rania, so lovely to see you. Nah-mah-stay." Lorraine smiled at her.

"Thanks for having me." *Please, someone, kill me.*

"Ronnie, dance!" Marley shouted next. Heads swiveled, pale faces watching her expectantly. Surely, she'd dance. Entertain them all like a dancing monkey they could throw money at. That was her job, to please Marley and her friends. When she was little, she'd had to balance a tea tray for all of Shameem's friends to ooh and ahh over how steady she was. This felt the same. And Ronnie hated it.

"Dance? You want me to dance?" she croaked out.

"Yes, what do you call it? Bhangra?" Marley pronounced it *bonh-grah*.

Ronnie gulped. That feeling of utter panic reached up from her stomach and grabbed her throat until she coughed. She looked for an ally, anyone to help. Her eyes landed on Star, who shook her head as if to say, *Don't do it.*

"I—no. Sorry." Her face felt like it was inflamed. *Please let me burn up into ash and vanish right here and now.*

"Sorry?"

"I-I'm not a dancer." She couldn't have moved if she'd wanted to. Her feet were frozen, stuck to the earth. If she believed enough, would the ground open up and swallow her?

"Well, all good, I'll dance then!" And Marley started lunging in a ridiculous caricature of the dance. "Everyone, join!" A few folks did, but everyone else just watched in amusement.

Marley clapped when she finished. She was out of breath but grinning. She had no sweat on her face thanks to Botoxing her glands.

"Whew, a bit hot to dance!" Marley had fans placed around the garden, blowing hot, moist air on everyone. Sunblock stations had been set up, and streaks of white covered the guests' faces.

"Rania? Come sit with me." Lorraine patted the seat next to her. "Everyone, I'm not sure you had a chance to meet Rania, but she's fabulous and working with the twins. She comes from a long line of Sufi mystics." The grins around her grew wider. A few women nodded their approval. Ronnie had the strange sensation that she was about to be initiated into a cult.

"I—what?" Ronnie whipped her head to Marley, who mouthed the words, "Go with it." She was no Sufi mystic. She wasn't even religious. Her aunt never gave a shit about that sort of thing, except for keeping up appearances. Marley had started that lie. "Uh, yeah. Sufi. Like Rumi." Where was that hole in the ground? It was taking its time getting there.

"We're so lucky to have her here. Now let's toast our new mystic and welcome her!"

I can get through this. It's one day. And it's helping Marley. She exchanged glances with Star, who, in turn, made faces at her. The twin stuck her tongue out; Ronnie smiled and wished Brit had come too.

"Try this!" Lorraine said, shoving some ladoo in Ronnie's mouth, her dry and wrinkled fingers invading her. "I read that's how you do it, you use your hands!"

Ronnie turned her head to move Lorraine's hand and chewed because the other option was to spit it out. The sensation of someone else's fingers in her mouth was not one she would ever get used to. "Yes." She cleared her throat. "Usually from a mother or auntie."

"I'm your auntie! I love it! Call me Auntie Lorraine! You know, when I heard you were Muslim, I got worried. I admit it. But you're one of the good ones, like Rumi!"

She heard someone whisper loudly, "Rumi was Muslim?"

Another woman, an older one who was clearly a friend of Lorraine's, nodded enthusiastically. "We love Sufis. And Indians."

Ronnie choked on her own spit. One of the good ones. She closed her eyes. *Just fake it. Do it for Marley.* When she opened them, she smiled brightly.

"There are more good ones than bad, you just have to turn off the TV news."

"Oh, yes dear, I'm sure there are." Lorraine patted her head.

She sat in silence while Lorraine and her friend—Suzanne—talked about their last trip to India together.

"It was so marvelous. And the children were so delightful! They danced and sang for us. We went to the most luxurious ashram. They waited on us hand and foot." Luxurious ashrams were marketed to Westerners, but Ronnie didn't say anything.

"Do you know what was fabulous? The service. And how everyone called me 'memsahib.' Can you call me that?" Suzanne asked. Ronnie stared at her and didn't answer. Couldn't, to be honest. Whatever she would have said would have ruined the party.

"Remember, Suzy, that divine wedding we stumbled into?"

"Oh, it was glorious. Are you going to have your wedding there? They had elephants!"

"I'm Pakistani, not Indian. You know, Partition, 1947?" They both stared at her with blank looks.

"Why on earth did your family leave India? It's so beautiful there," Suzanne asked.

"They had to." She didn't want to do a history lesson. *Couldn't they google this?*

"Tell me, are Sufis also taught jihad?" Suzanne asked. She had the telltale lisp that came from wearing dentures. Sufis sounded like *Shufis*. *Oh dear god, someone get me out of here.*

"None of us are taught that," Ronnie said through clenched teeth.

"That's not what they said on TV."

Ronnie wanted to leave. To get the hell away, but one look from Marley kept her butt in her seat.

"You should watch less TV then."

Her retort was lost on the women, whose attention had shifted to the entrance of the party, the back door of the Center. There, in white and gold, stood Caroline. She looked stunning, her blonde hair blown out and curled, her lips the perfect glossy pink. The humidity and heat didn't affect her one bit. She looked just like the type of friend Marley wanted, Ronnie thought bitterly. The two women were hugging. They looked like sisters.

The conversation shifted to healing. Everyone had their own take on it. An angle. Not that Ronnie thought it was all a scam, but surely not everyone here was psychic, were they?

"I've been really into astral projection lately."

"I find that sitting with someone before I read them really helps me see into their aura."

"I was doing a past-life regression the other day, and wow, it was intense."

Ronnie had nothing to add. She did none of these things. She wasn't even sure she believed in them. Sure, some people were psychic. That she accepted. But everything else?

"Rania, your aura is a beautiful purple, did you know that?" Lorraine asked her.

"Uh, no I didn't. That's . . . good?"

"Oh yes, very enlightened. Very enlightened."

Ronnie wanted to laugh. She was anything but. And she doubted that Lorraine could see anything, much less auras.

"Everyone, we're going to begin soon!" Marley said on the mic. *Thank god.* Ronnie was sick of these people. The sooner things started, the sooner they would end.

"Is that Brit?" Suzy pointed to Star.

"No, dear, that's Star."

"Oh. What a shame what happened to Brit. Poor girl. She hasn't been the same."

Ronnie leaned in to hear more but was interrupted by Caroline.

"Ronnie, looking fabulous! Oh, Lorraine, great to see you. Having your eat, pray, love moment, are we?" She winked at Ronnie. "Oh, there's Star. Be back!" She mingled with an ease that made Ronnie jealous. Caroline's laugh sounded like the tinkling of champagne glasses.

"She looks so pretty," she said, not realizing she'd said it out loud.

"She's awful, don't get snookered by a pretty face," Lorraine spat out. "You are far more stunning anyways. I wish I had your coloring."

Ronnie didn't answer, but the way the older women looked at her made her uncomfortable, as if they wanted to collect her, add her to the displays of marble from Lorraine's travels. Caroline was intercepted by Star.

"I'll be right back!" Ronnie said, jumping out of her seat and rushing over to the twin.

"How dare you show your face here!" Star yelled, her face so angry Ronnie paused in fear. She had been about to wave and say hi, but the greeting was lost in her throat.

"Oh, come now, Star, let's not let the past get between us." Caroline was smirking. Ronnie felt everyone's eyes on them, but this time it wasn't about her.

"Leave before I make you regret this," Star hissed. The twin then whirled around to face Ronnie before nodding. "Ronnie, stay away from this one. She's a charlatan. A total fraud."

"Aw, that's not nice, Star. Where's Brit today? Under the weather?" Caroline asked.

"Keep her name out of your mouth," Star growled. A few heads swiveled to them, their eyes staring at the commotion. Ronnie was certain a physical fight was about to break out. Would she jump in? No, she knew she wouldn't. She stared, instead, at Caroline's ring: it looked like a human eye.

"Testy. Ronnie, you should spend time with people who will help you evolve." Caroline smiled at her.

"Hey, hey, ladies, let's calm things down." A man Ronnie didn't know was trying to intervene, but he had a smirk on his face the whole time. Like he hoped they'd get physical and have a catfight. "Or you can come fight at my campground." He grinned.

"Peter, shut up. And you, don't talk to Ronnie. Get out. *Get out!*" Star was screaming it, looking entirely insane and unstable. Ronnie took a step back, unsure of what to do. *Why were they fighting?*

Marley rushed over.

"Can you please stop screaming?" she asked, a smile on her face as she hissed the words. "You're ruining the party."

"She ruined it by showing up here."

Caroline merely shrugged. "I was invited. But I can't make everyone love you!"

"Well, she stays to help me. Star, please get over your petty grievances. Rise above, for the good of the community."

Star's jaw dropped. Ronnie jumped in. "Let's all get some snacks and hear the talk, what do you say? Come on!" She pulled Star away before she made an even bigger scene.

"Everyone, thank you again for joining us. For those who don't know me, I'm Marley Dewhurst. And I love living here." Scattered applause. "As you all know, there have been some unsavory events happening lately. And my goal is to keep everyone safe. I've set up a watch for our trails and a hotline if you see anything unusual. I'll also set up self-defense and shooting courses with the Center. We will face evil, and we will win. No outsider, no stranger, is going to scare us from our home. This is our turf, and we will do whatever it takes to keep unsavory elements out."

Never mind that she, too, was an outsider. Her message resonated. Cheers rang out. And Marley officially had a following. The Kismet Center patrons were now hers.

Star and Ronnie watched from afar.

"This is going to backfire," Star said. "Big time."

Chapter 40

THE TOWN

She stood in the yard at the party. She danced. She ate samosas. She even cheered things on. But she knew something that no one else did: some of the people present would die. Not that day, but soon.

Her eyes were on the crowd, on their reactions. They were so stupid. They had no idea that all of them could be next. Her eyes landed on one person. *Oh yes, that's perfect. That will do nicely.*

She drank some water and mango juice and clapped and cheered when she was supposed to. She fit in; she was one of them. Yet she would bring them all down and return things to how they needed to be.

"Isn't this a wonderful gathering?" Lorraine asked her, and she grinned at the woman.

"It sure is."

The Sedona Slasher. What a name. It was hilarious. She wasn't some crazy serial killer—she was just a woman on a mission. And one day they'd all see that and be grateful for her hard work.

Chapter 41

The party had been all anyone talked about. Everyone who came to the store—who was a local—greeted Ronnie with a *nah-mah-stay* now. She wanted to scream.

"Does it bug you?" Star asked. "The *nah-mah-stay*?"

"A bit. I mean, it's what I'd say to my Hindu aunties, you know? It's just weird to hear white people saying it. And they say it wrong."

"They do?"

"Yes." She didn't elaborate.

"They just want to welcome you."

"A simple hello would do."

Star nodded, and Ronnie hoped she hadn't offended her friend. Star and Brit seemed with it, but you never knew how someone would take to being corrected. She wasn't even sure if the twins were white or mixed or what, and she hadn't thought to ask.

"This is a weird question, but what's your heritage?" She fumbled the words.

"We're very mixed-up mutts." Star laughed. "Why?"

"I didn't know shamans could be white. Is that wrong to say?"

"No! It's not wrong. Shamanism spans cultures, including in eastern Europe. But Brit's gift was definitely passed down from our grandmother. That woman could see everything, especially things we wanted to hide." She laughed.

Grandparents. Another thing Ronnie had missed out on. She'd met hers once or twice on trips to Pakistan. But mostly, she was ignored by the family. She was an extra. A reminder that her mother was dead.

Marley's talk had lit a fire underneath folks. Her mailing list had grown, the site was up, and she was setting up even more patrols. This time, the full roster of the Kismet Center was at her disposal. Something Star was dead set against.

"It's such a waste of time," Star said. "Those patrols won't catch this person."

"They won't?"

"Do you really think having elderly women walking around the trails in August is a good idea?"

"Oh. Shit. No, that's stupid." Ronnie hadn't thought of that.

"Exactly."

"Do you think maybe the killer has moved on?" Ronnie asked. There hadn't been a body since Fiona's had been found. It had been quiet, calm. Almost as if the person had come and gone. Maybe they had? What if Sedona were just a stop on a tour of murders?

"I hope so, but I doubt it. Depends on what they're after, you know?" Star sighed. "Listen, I have an appointment, can you watch the store without me?"

It would be Ronnie's first time alone taking care of things during business hours. The thought thrilled and terrified her.

"Of course!"

"Brit will probably be back before me. I appreciate it." She hugged Ronnie tightly. "You're amazing."

————

She was alone! She was in charge! This was everything and terrifying. The twins trusted her, and Ronnie was determined to not let them down. She started tidying up the shop, fixing up her organization. She'd laminated her cheat sheets, and they were throughout the store. Making it easier for people to find what they wanted.

And she had replaced the twins' bulletin board setup with sign-up sheets for appointments with the twins. One for Brit, one for Star. (With spaces for contact info so they could size up the potential clients.)

The door chimed.

"Ronnie!" Marley's perfume enveloped her before her friend did. White Patchouli, by Tom Ford. It was Marley's way of being a hippie.

"Hey! How's it going today?"

"Brilliant. People are dying to sign up for our patrols."

"Are you worried about having elderly people on the trails in this heat?"

Marley shrugged. "They know how to take care of themselves. It's okay. Speaking of, though, can I leave a sign-up sheet next to those?" She motioned to the twins' clipboards.

"Uh, I'll have to ask, but I don't know. The twins don't like the patrols."

"Whatever, the twins can't stop me." Marley reached into her bag and pulled out a display with a clipboard attached. It was a picture of Marley's face, eyes narrow, questioning. In big letters, it read, "Only you can keep us safe. Join us. Marley's Eyes."

"Oh, wow." It was terrifying. Just seeing it gave Ronnie the chills. "That's the new name you're going with?"

"Do you love it? It was Caro's idea."

"It's, uh, eye catching!"

"Perfect. The more people who join, the better."

"Can I ask you something? Why are you so into this? I mean, what happened to healing?"

Marley stared at her.

Fuck, I should have kept my mouth shut.

Then her friend smiled. "Once all this is over, I'll be recognizable. People will know me, trust me. And then I can do the real healing work.

But I can't heal when people are being murdered, right? And besides, getting a following is good. It can only help."

Ronnie blinked a few times. A following. That's all Marley was after. Someone could get hurt because of her, and Marley didn't even care, so long as people subscribed to her newsletter. She didn't even know what to say to her friend.

"No twins today?" Marley asked.

"They're out at appointments."

"You're getting really close with them."

Ronnie shrugged. "I like working for them."

"Well, don't get too attached. Like Caroline said, they're not what they seem."

"Neither is Caroline," Ronnie retorted. And immediately covered her mouth. "Wow, I don't know where that came from."

Marley smiled at her. "It came from being empowered. Imagine what I can do for everyone else. Don't forget, we're learning to shoot next week." She meant guns, not photos.

"Can't wait."

Ronnie had never in her life held a gun, and she wasn't sure she wanted to. But if it meant making Marley happy, she'd do it.

———

Caroline was over at the house, as always. Ronnie wanted to ask what the point of her squatting was when she practically lived with them. But she held her tongue. What if she ended up moving in with them? Would Ronnie have to give up her room? The idea made her heart sink.

They were watching some show about shamans on one of the learning channels when Marley said, "I want to do that. Take peyote. Can you make that happen?" she asked Caroline.

"Of course I can. I can make anything happen for my friends. Ronnie, you want in?"

"Uh, no. I don't like the idea of taking drugs."

"Of course you don't." Caroline laughed, rolling her eyes. "Little miss goody two-shoes."

"I am not! I just, I don't know. I don't think I'd enjoy it."

"Only one way to find out."

Ronnie didn't say more, but she knew the last thing she wanted was to be on drugs near Caroline. The idea of losing control, of letting her inner demons out, was a little too scary for her. And in front of Caroline? No thanks.

"I'm going for a walk," she said.

"You're always out for walks—what do you do on these walks?" Caroline asked.

"Uh, I just walk. It's nice." Ronnie didn't offer an invitation to join her. She wanted to be alone.

Chapter 42

The Town

The ravens were getting antsy. She hadn't lived up to her promise. There'd been no movement on anything since Fiona.

It wasn't her fault. The police and state troopers, park rangers and sheriff, and that stupid citizen patrol had made it all but impossible to do her work. How on earth was she supposed to kill and dump a body if everyone was around? But try explaining that to the birds.

"I promise I'll do something." How could she appease her raven pals? Could they even be reasoned with?

She had to do something. Kill someone soon, something easy. It wouldn't be as fulfilling to her, but it would make the ravens happy. That would ease the pressure on her.

She'd been dreaming about the birds. Every night. They were always there, no matter where she went, whether she was awake or not. You couldn't escape a blood oath; everyone knew that. If she didn't do as she'd promised, the birds would find her. They'd drive her mad.

Think. You have to find a way. She'd tried. Oh, she had. The next person on her list wasn't easy to predict. She would follow them, and they didn't notice or care. They had no set schedule, no routine she could discern. She'd have to get crafty.

The party had been a buffet of potential targets. She'd watched Lorraine's friends harping about, fetishizing Ronnie. White women loved brown and Black cultures, but they didn't love the people. It was infuriating. That was something she could work with. Getting rid of someone like that would make the energy better.

But she couldn't kill Lorraine. The older woman helped so many people. And the ravens, for whatever reason, seemed to like her. Lorraine's friends, however, were fair game. They weren't contributing much to the community, and they were racist: it was kind of a no-brainer.

———

It was too easy to get to Suzy. She simply showed up and knocked, and the woman let her in. Invited death across her doorstep. Really, it was Suzy's own fault.

"Hello, dear!"

"Hi! Do you have time for some tea?"

And she did because Suzy had nothing else to do.

Killing her was a breeze. She shoved her, and the woman fell, hitting her head. So much blood, and then her face went slack.

"Dammit." Head wounds always bled too much. What a mess. She left the pool of red where it was. Before Suzy got stiff, she dressed her in a more appropriate outfit: a red sari. Of course Suzy had a few in her closet from her trips to India.

The red folds were sewn on, so she didn't have to figure out how to make it look right. She sat back to admire her work. It needed more.

"Oooh, I know!" She dipped her fingers in the pool of Suzy's blood and left a mark on her head like a bindi. She then added a henna-like design on Suzy's cold hands, using what blood was left on the floor.

"How's that, Suzy? Feeling more Indian yet?" She couldn't help but laugh. Suzy deserved this. She was the worst.

This had not been a satisfying kill. Not like Matt and Fiona. Those had been cathartic. This was more perfunctory. Something to be done, to buy her time. Sure, she was improving the town by killing her, but her heart just hadn't been in it.

She waited for the right time to dump her, when there was no one around. It had to be late at night or so early in the morning the sky was still dark. That was when the police slept. They'd been lulled into complacency, no bodies showing up. Good. They thought no one was going to dump anything since it had been weeks since Fiona had been found. They were wrong.

She wasn't going to leave this body in the middle of nowhere. No, she wanted Suzy to be seen. She'd made her look so pretty too. She had to make a splash. And then everyone would know they weren't safe. That she was coming for them.

"I'm a genius."

Chapter 43

"You just pull the trigger, gently. Squeeze it." Peter Hughes was teaching her to shoot at the range. He was so close, leaning into Ronnie's ear. It sent shivers down her body and not in a good way. She tried to step away from him, but his hand landed on her hip, pulling her closer.

"You got it," Peter said, grinning. "Don't be shy." He loved his guns almost as much as he loved yoga. His hand fell to Ronnie's butt. She fired and missed the target.

"Ooops! Better luck next time! Who's up next?"

Marley eagerly jumped up, ready. "Me. I want to shoot some assholes." That got a laugh out of everyone. She had set this all up at a range just outside the neighboring town of Cottonwood. They'd driven in caravans, and twenty women had signed up for this.

She held the gun. Ronnie watched her feel the weight. She watched as Marley closed an eye. And when Peter copped a feel, Marley didn't flinch. Instead, she shot the target right through the head.

"Whoa! A natural!" Peter clapped. Marley grinned.

Everyone was, for the most part, cheerful. Even Lorraine was here, and Ronnie was doing her best to avoid another "Colonial India was fabulous" conversation.

"Rania, come sit with me," Lorraine said, thwarting her efforts. The range had chairs set up for them. Peter knew the owner, so he was allowed to take charge.

Ronnie nodded. She went and sat with the older woman, feeling guilty for her dislike of her. One by one, every woman got a turn to shoot, and the ones under sixty got a butt grab for their troubles.

It was as they filed out into the parking lot just off State Route 260 that the news hit. A text came, first to Lorraine. Then to Marley. A body had been found. And it had been left right outside the Kismet Center.

The caravan drove back to Sedona and straight to the Center, where police had tape up. **CRIME SCENE—DO NOT ENTER.** It went well with the Rumi, Ronnie thought. And then felt terrible for thinking that.

Lorraine got out first, followed by Marley and Ronnie. They walked over to Sheriff Reynolds.

"Who is it?" Lorraine demanded. "Who was killed?"

"Lorraine, maybe you should sit down?" the sheriff suggested.

"I just shot up a range, don't tell me to sit down. Who was killed?"

The sheriff sighed. "Suzanne Johnson."

Lorraine gasped.

Suzy. The woman Ronnie had hated at the party. The one who had a lisp and asked her about jihad. She was dead.

"Whoa," she muttered. *Good riddance. Oh shoot, I don't mean that.* And then she realized she hadn't dreamed about Suzy. Maybe her weird dreams were coming to an end?

"I want to see her."

"You don't, trust me, Lorraine."

"Show me."

He led her over to the body, and Ronnie watched the woman fall into him, her body racked with sobs. She felt bad for her. To outlive all your friends would be a curse.

But Ronnie didn't feel bad that Suzy was dead. Rather, she was glad. *Score one for the killer,* she thought. Suzy was not a good person. Ronnie wouldn't say she deserved it but still.

"We are upping patrols!" Marley was yelling. "Everyone, this is dire. We must protect our people! No more letting strangers wander among us!" She was practically frothing at the mouth. Ronnie wanted her to stop. To think about this. You couldn't patrol strangers when strangers were what made the town survive. Without tourists, they'd have nothing. Surely, Marley saw that?

She tried to interrupt quietly, gently. "Don't you think we shouldn't be so anti-tourist right now?"

"Ronnie." Marley put her hands on her friend's shoulders. "This is for the good of *our* community."

Ronnie nodded, swallowing uneasily.

Lorraine was taken inside by someone; she didn't see by whom. And Ronnie moved toward the body, which was covered with a sheet. She wanted to see. She had to. She lifted the sheet, and there Suzy was. Dressed in her sari. A bloody dot on her forehead like a bindi. Ronnie gasped and jumped back. Was this addressed to her? Was this for her? Had someone killed Suzy because of Ronnie?

"No, not possible," she muttered. "I would never have let that happen."

And much to her chagrin, Ronnie turned her head and vomited next to the stretcher.

Maybe Marley was right. Maybe what they needed was to protect each other. She felt a hand on her shoulder. It was Star.

"You okay?"

"Who would do this to a defenseless old woman?" Ronnie asked, tears in her eyes despite herself. Sure, Suzy was annoying. But to die like this? That was beyond.

"Someone horrible," Star replied and enveloped her in a hug.

———

There were people walking in groups, using their phones to snap photos of passersby on the street. They'd stop and question everyone deemed unwelcome or suspicious. They were Marley's patrols, and they were becoming a giant pain in the ass to everyone who had stores and depended on foot traffic. Ronnie watched it happen from the store windows. Ever since Suzy's murder earlier that week, the patrols had gone overboard, flooding the streets.

"What are they doing?"

"Oh, must be the new patrols," Brit said.

"Patrols? Oh shit, that's Marley's patrol?" The citizen patrol, as Marley called it, was made up of elderly white retirees with nothing else to do.

"Yeah, it's not great? But hopefully everything will calm down soon."

Ronnie had a bad feeling about this. Who were the patrols looking for? How could they be on the hunt for anyone who didn't belong when most of the people milling about were tourists?

"I'll talk to Marley about it."

It was a pledge more than anything. She'd help her friend see that the patrols weren't helpful. Or try to. She wasn't sure she could get Marley to see anything she didn't want to.

Ronnie eyed the teams warily—and there were several pairs of people snapping photos and getting in faces and interrogating tourists. Would they question her too?

She texted Marley; they had to talk. Hopefully, without Caroline hovering. Ronnie had had almost no alone time with her friend since Caroline had come into the picture. It was annoying.

Sure babe! Everything ok?

Yep!

No. But no sense hashing it out over text.

———

"So what's up?" Marley sat on the sofa, a glass of wine in hand. They were alone. Thank god.

"I saw your patrols today."

"Really?! Isn't that so cool? Someone is doing what I suggested!"

"That's the thing. I don't know if it's a good idea." Ronnie braced herself. *You can do this. You can stand up to her. She wants you to be empowered. A true friend would be honest with her.*

"What do you mean?"

"Well, like, they're just accosting people on the street. There has to be a better way to stay safe."

Marley stared at her, her smile frozen on her face. "Maybe people need accosting."

"I just think that this could lead to some trouble. Maybe ask them to keep an eye out but tone it down?"

"They're just eager. That's all. No harm."

"Not yet. But they could step over the line."

"So you want me to end the patrols?"

"I want people to be safe." This was not going well.

"Ron, these are my people. My followers. I am going to keep doing what I'm doing. Don't you see, for the first time ever, I am a leader. I have people. You can't take that away from me."

"You've had me," Ronnie offered up. Wasn't she enough for her friend?

"I know, but now I want more."

That was the end of that conversation. Ronnie knew pushing would only irritate her friend. Marley wanted adoration; she wanted submission. Her empowered friend wanted this town to give in to her. This was a disaster waiting to happen.

———

"Uh, want to hear something funny?"

"Obviously!" Brit grinned at her. The twin was getting ready to work with a client, leaving Ronnie in charge of the shop. Something Ronnie loved. They trusted her!

"Caroline is going to set up some drug ritual for Marley."

Brit dropped the crystal she had been holding. The color in her face drained. Ronnie, for a second, thought she may pass out.

"Are you okay? Here, sit! Let me get you water!" She made Brit sit and fetched her a glass. "Just take a few sips. Put your head between your knees."

"I'm fine," Brit said in a monotone. "Just do me a favor. No, promise me something."

"I promise! Anything!"

"Never, ever let Caroline give you any drugs. You need to trust me on this. She will end up killing you. You have to stay away from her. She's evil." Brit's hand shook as she said it.

It was Ronnie's turn to pale. "How do you know this?"

"How do you think?" Brit glared. Brit never glared. "She tried it with me and almost killed me. She's the one who gave me jimsonweed instead of peyote. Star had to save me. Don't let her do that to you."

Ronnie gasped. Caroline really was bad news. "It was just like my dream. All I remember was being in the desert and Caroline laughing. You could have died out there."

Brit shrugged. "She's capable of anything." Ronnie wondered—not for the first time—if Caroline was capable of multiple murders.

And that woman was in her house. Probably. With Marley. Setting up patrols for murders she may have committed. Ronnie felt sick.

"I have to go, you're good to close up?" Brit asked. Her voice was still heavy.

"Yes, of course. I'm so sorry for messing up your evening with my question."

"You didn't. Stay safe. Text me when you get home, okay?"

Hours later, Ronnie locked the front door and started toward her car. There was an insect humming, and moths and various other creatures surrounded any and all lights. Ronnie turned on her phone's flashlight, just in case. No sense stepping on a snake or something. The light landed on a lone tarantula that had parked itself near the store lights to catch bugs. Ronnie found it fascinating; the way it moved was so elegant.

And then she heard it. Footsteps. She whirled around, but no one was there. Not that she could see, at least.

"Hello?" she called out, her phone's light giving her some sense of what was around her. Or who. "Anyone there?" No reply. "Probably some animal. Ugh, get a grip." And then her mind flashed to Caroline. "Caroline, is that you? You can't hide from me." There was no answer. Just the hum of the bugs.

Ronnie hurried to her car and locked the doors. She would never get used to the way the darkness felt here. Like there were eyes on you. Inhuman eyes. Like she was on the menu.

She only relaxed once she got home and locked all the doors.

Chapter 44

The Town

She'd been watching Ronnie last night. She liked her but wasn't entirely trusting of the newcomer. Ronnie had charmed everyone already. But no one was as good as they appeared. She knew that better than anyone. But so far, Ronnie seemed genuine.

She'd almost been caught too. By Ronnie's stupid phone. Never underestimate the power of an anxious person. They planned for all outcomes. Ronnie was safe, for now.

Her last offering had caused an uproar. She'd known it would. But what would they have her do? Those stupid patrols were all over the trails. She couldn't very well leave a body there, now could she? She bet someone had put trail cams up too.

So she'd left Suzy where she'd be found. In an outfit she was sure Suzy loved. She'd done her a favor. She'd done everyone a favor. Didn't they all see that?

"Ungrateful assholes." If it weren't for the ravens, she'd leave. Just give up. *No, you wouldn't. You'd never give up.*

Missions had to be finished, and this one was a request from the universe. To fix up this once-beautiful place. To take it back for the animals and birds. To save her town from shitty assholes.

"New day, new name." She was following her latest target. It was so easy; no one knew she was watching. She could do this all day—and would.

Two elderly people stood in front of her car and snapped her photo. *What the fuck?*

"Excuse me, why are you taking my photo?"

"To make sure you belong here."

Belong here? Were they joking? She would have to take care of them too. No one needed a photo of her while she was staking out a target. Dammit.

"Well, have a blessed day," she said. She'd get that photo. And take care of this public nuisance all at the same time.

———

The ravens acknowledged the latest offering. She wouldn't have been their first choice, but if it helped things improve, all the better. They'd have preferred one of the bigger targets. The ones that really messed things up here. They had a name in mind, but they were waiting. Their human said it would get done in time; they had to trust her.

But the ravens trusted no one.

We could do it ourselves, they said to each other.

Maybe. Maybe. Let's see what she does first. And then we can attack if we have to.

It was agreed upon. No attacks from them, for now. But their human could keep them waiting for only so long.

Chapter 45

Ronnie hadn't told Marley what Brit had said about Caroline. She'd promised her boss and friend that she wouldn't. And Ronnie was determined to keep that promise. But she had to warn Marley.

"Ugh!" she yelled. She was stuck between two people and didn't know what to do. Betraying Brit felt terrible, but what if she saved Marley's life?

It didn't help that Caroline was always over. Always. Ronnie couldn't get time alone with Marley if her life depended on it.

She needed to clear her head. She hadn't told anyone she felt like she was being watched at night. They'd think she was hysterical. Who would watch her? And it was probably an animal anyways.

She put her sneakers on and some sunblock despite it being sunset. And she went for a walk, away from Marley, Caroline, and everything else that was bothering her. Walks cleared her mind. She kept her phone handy, though. Just in case anyone came after her. Or an animal. That almost stopped her in her tracks. What if another javelina was out?

Ugh, it's fine, just walk.

She had no set route planned. Just wanted to walk. To think. How was she supposed to keep her friend safe without betraying her other friend? Ronnie had to find a way.

She was so deep in thought it took a while before she realized there were footsteps behind her. The footfalls matched hers, just slightly echoing each step she took. Step, step half a second later. *Fuck, this is like last night. I didn't imagine it. I know I didn't! What do I do?*

Ronnie tried to casually look over her shoulder but didn't see anyone. Was she hearing things? Was this a trick of the birds or something?

She decided to take a few useless turns and see if the sound continued. Eventually, she'd be on side streets, away from the public. Which wasn't the best idea, but then she'd know if someone was following her. *And then what? Let them kill you?*

She walked closer and closer to the house. It was just a few blocks away. Safety. Freedom. She hadn't been gone more than an hour; Marley would still be there, right? Behind her, Ronnie heard the footsteps speed up. *Okay, killer or mugger, I'm going to fight like hell.*

Ronnie whirled around, her phone in hand. No matter what, she'd get a picture of this person, show it to the police. She would have proof that she was being followed. *Jeez, where are Marley's patrols when I need them?*

Standing in front of her was a woman she didn't recognize. She was older, in her fifties. And she was staring at Ronnie. Ronnie let out a sigh of relief until she saw the gun in the woman's holster.

"What do you want?!" Ronnie asked, her phone ready.

"Excuse me, but do you live here? Are you new in town? Who are you?" The woman was too close—her spit was landing on Ronnie.

"I—um, I—" She got no words in edgewise.

"You don't belong here! Why are you walking around? What's your plan?!" The woman was now yelling at her. Ronnie took a step back to get away from her. "You don't belong here!" she continued to shout.

"Stop, I live here. Stop!"

The woman's hand went to her gun.

Ronnie ran. Just up and ran as fast as she could, away from this nutjob. Away from being shot. She had to get away, escape. She was almost home, and then she'd lock the door. There, it was so close. She could do this. Ronnie heard the woman chasing her still.

Fuck fuck fuck! She ran like her life depended on it because it did. When she saw Marley's house, her house, she felt relief. Her eyes teared up. *Almost home. I'm going to make it.*

She heard the woman running after her still, but she didn't turn around to look at her. She didn't have time to lose.

Ronnie reached the door—which was thankfully unlocked—and slammed it shut.

"Ronnie?" Marley stared at her. "Are you okay?"

Ronnie locked the door before bending over, her hands on her knees. Panting, out of breath. Shit, she was going to have to get better at outrunning people if this kept up.

"No." She panted. "Someone chased me."

Marley gasped. There were too many gasps for just one person. Ronnie shifted her gaze and took in the scene. There were about ten people in their living room, all staring at her. All alarmed. Marley's people. Her followers. They were wearing red shirts that said Marley's Eyes. Were they having a meeting? She couldn't remember.

"Someone chased you?"

"Yes, she had a gun on me and chased me. I was just taking a walk." She was shaking. She couldn't help it. She'd never had anyone almost pull a gun on her before. That was a level of fear she didn't know was possible.

"Dammit, not on our watch," Marley said, sounding like a TV person, Ronnie thought. Like her videos. The group moved en masse to the door and threw it open to find Ronnie's assailant right outside.

"There you are," the woman gasped. "I chased someone down. They're not from here. No way are they from here—" She stopped talking, her eyes landing on Ronnie.

"I live here," Ronnie said slowly, enunciating every syllable.

"I didn't know. I'm sorry. You didn't look like you belonged."

Ronnie was about to retort something, but Marley pulled her away.

"Are you okay?"

"No. No! Look what your little videos have started. She could have shot me! Did you follow me last night too?"

"No, I didn't!" the woman said. She sounded outraged.

"You could have shot me! Why'd you follow me, because I'm not white?"

"How dare you! I'm not a racist!"

"Ronnie, please calm down." Marley was trying to be the peacekeeper.

"You don't get it, do you? A white woman chasing me, screaming I don't belong here. You're okay with that?"

"It wasn't a racial thing—"

"Wasn't it? You need to get a grip on your group, and fast. Before they hurt someone." Ronnie was furious and was letting it all out. How dare Marley and her people do this!

Marley stared at her before glancing at the group. Every person in red was waiting for whatever came out of her mouth. Even Ronnie could see that. And that power, that need, was too much for one person to say no to.

"How dare you! This group is to protect us. And if you had just complied, she wouldn't have had to chase you." Marley was angry at her. At her?! How was that possible? Ronnie was the innocent one here.

"You can't be serious?"

"You're either with us or against us." The red shirts cheered, hugging Marley like she was some savior. Ronnie watched in disbelief and horror. What had happened to her friend? Who had she become?

Ronnie stormed up to her room, her heart racing. That had been the most aggressive she'd ever been with Marley. She wasn't entirely sure she hated that feeling. But that woman downstairs? Ronnie definitely hated her. Ronnie had half a mind to go downstairs and slap her, hard. With a flyswatter.

Before

Ronnie walked to the corner to get milk and paper towels. Her aunt needed both. Or rather, Ronnie did, in order to make Shameem's chai and also clean up. She walked out of the deli and could have sworn someone was watching her.

She walked back to her house—it took a good fifteen minutes. Their little enclave was more of a suburb within the city. They had an actual lawn and everything. But she couldn't shake the feeling that someone was spying on her.

Ronnie glanced around. And then she saw her. Sheedah. Auntie Mahnaz's daughter-in-law. She was staring at Ronnie and typing furiously into her phone. Ronnie waved. Sheedah gasped and ran.

What the hell was that about?

She unlocked the door and greeted her aunt. "Sorry, there was a line at the store."

"Was there?" Shameem asked, looking her up and down. "Or maybe you were meeting someone there you shouldn't?"

"No, I swear I didn't. Wait, is that why Sheedah was watching me? Are you having people spy on me?"

"Don't raise your voice to me, bathameez. Sheedah is helping to keep an eye on you. You can never get away from me or do anything that I won't know about. You and your gora friends. I know you're up to something. Now hurry up and make some chai. Lazy girl."

———

"You should talk to the sheriff, because he can put an end to this citizen patrol," Star said. "This is not normal. No one should chase you with a gun." Star was pacing the store. She was beyond mad. The stupid patrols were chasing customers away and endangering their own lives. "This has to end."

"Someone will get hurt, I know it," Ronnie added. And she was certain that someone would be her.

"I know, and I'm so thankful you weren't." Star texted someone before announcing that the sheriff was on his way over.

"Oh, I didn't know you could text him." Ronnie laughed to hide her discomfort. How tight was her friend with law enforcement?

"I've helped him cleanse some bad energy from his house."

"Oh."

The idea of the sheriff here made her nervous for reasons Ronnie couldn't explain. She was the outsider here. Would he tell her she didn't belong too?

Ronnie busied herself with work, anything to avoid jumping every single time the door chimed. *Get a grip. You've done nothing wrong. You're okay.*

Finally, he showed up.

"Star."

"John. This is Ronnie."

Ronnie waved, a duster in her hand.

"You're the one who lives with Marley, right?" he asked. "We met when you found Matt Ford's body. I'm John Reynolds." He held his hand out. Ronnie was forced to come out from behind the counter and shake his hand. She hated when people did that.

"Ronnie was followed and almost attacked last night by the patrols. Something has to be done," Star said, her voice heavy with fury.

"What happened?" John focused on Ronnie. She felt his eyes on her, and she didn't like it. He wasn't a mean man, but he was the police. And Ronnie didn't trust him. He was tall and white and had the heavily tanned face of someone who eschewed sunscreen out here. He wore a hat, and his badge was stuck to his uniform.

"I was going for a walk, and this woman started following me. I kept trying to shake her. I thought I was being paranoid. Until she came up to me, with her hand on her gun, and questioned me. Like she was the police. And there's more. The other night I was closing up, and I swore someone was following me."

"Here?!" Star swore. "Let me check the cameras."

"Dammit. I was worried this would happen," the sheriff said. "We don't need vigilantes running around. I'll go talk to your roommate and fix this. This isn't the only incident. And two of her patrollers were killed last night in a hit-and-run."

Ronnie and Star both gasped.

"You're kidding!"

"Nope. It was a stolen car, too, as far as we can tell. We're looking for leads on that, but I'm not holding my breath."

"Yikes," Ronnie said. "I don't think Marley knows about that."

"Well, Marley should have come to us before she started this nonsense."

To be a fly on the wall, Ronnie thought. She shouldn't feel this much pleasure at seeing her friend get reprimanded, but Marley's approach was wrong. She was doing this for likes, for followers. There had to be a better way. There just had to be.

Chapter 46

"Can you believe this place?!" Marley shouted. She wasn't shouting at anyone, just out loud. Caroline and Ronnie happened to be the audience of two in her living room. "They said no more patrols. No more! No one has been killed because of us!"

"Well, those two patrollers died." Ronnie regretted it as soon as it was out of her mouth.

"That was an accident." Marley glared at her. "And you! Talking to the sheriff about that little incident." The "little incident" was what Marley called Ronnie getting chased down by an armed woman. "What kind of friend does that?"

"You did screw the pooch on that one, Ron," Caroline said. *Why was she even here? Oh, right, she's always here.* Ronnie hated feeling outnumbered. Ganged up on.

"I did not! He came to the store and asked me. What was I supposed to do? Lie?"

"Yes! For me you should have." Marley's eyes blazed.

Ronnie didn't know what to say. She should have kept her mouth shut for Marley. Don't air dirty laundry, don't tell anyone your secrets. She knew better. And still, she couldn't. When faced with authority, she crumbled.

"Sorry," she said stiffly.

"So now what's the plan?" Caroline asked.

"I guess I should do a video."

"You should, and tell the cops to fuck off."

"I couldn't!" Marley laughed.

"You are our leader. You can do anything you want. Just tell people to be subtler, don't break laws, and look both ways before they cross the street. There, absolved of any guilt."

The two of them devolved into giggles while Ronnie watched. This wasn't the Marley she knew. Her Marley wouldn't do this sort of thing, Ronnie was positive of that. *But how well do you even know her? Dammit.* Maybe this was Marley? So power hungry that she didn't care if people died.

Ronnie stared at Caroline. She was a killer. Her dream had said so. She was possibly *the* killer. She was sure of it. Brit would never lie to her. Caroline had done something awful, and if she were capable of that . . .

"I guess we should delay our fun spiritual quest, huh?" Caroline joked.

"Funny you mention that—I heard you've fucked those up before." Three shocked faces looked at each other. Had those words come out of Ronnie's mouth? "Oh, god! I'm sorry, I didn't mean to accuse you—"

"You've been talking to the twins, I see. Maybe ask them what really happened. Go on. See if they'll tell you the truth. Someone is lying to you, and it's not me."

"I don't have time for these hysterics. Ronnie, apologize, and no more accusing my guests of anything. Okay?"

Her guests. Her house. Ronnie got the distinct feeling that she had worn out her welcome. Maybe she needed to get her own place soon? Wasn't that the goal to begin with? To live on her own, to build her own life? The only issue was, she hadn't a clue how to do that.

Ronnie nodded and went upstairs to her room. She had to find somewhere else to live. She just did. This wasn't home. Home didn't exist.

Maybe her aunt had been right. Maybe she didn't know Marley as well as she thought she did. Maybe all of this had been a mistake.

"No. It's not. It can't be."

———

Before

"What do you mean you're going to move? Where?" Shameem Khala was furious. The Realtor had just finished looking at the house and assured Ronnie they'd get top dollar for it.

"To Arizona," Ronnie said. *You can do this. You can stand up to her. What did Marley say? The rest of your life is waiting for you.*

"Arizona?! With who?"

"My friend Marley."

"Your friend Marley?! You don't even know this Marley-Sharley person!" She was livid. Ronnie had known this part would be hard. Standing up to her. Telling her no, she was leaving. And selling the house.

"I am doing this. Khala, I appreciate everything you've done for me, but it's time for me to live my life."

The slap on her face came as expected.

"What I've done for you? I gave up my life for you! I gave you everything!"

Ronnie just stared at her. She didn't have anything to say to her. Not now. She'd asked for love, for kindness, and it had gotten her nowhere. It was too late to make amends.

Chapter 47

The Town

The ravens followed the woman. They had seen what she'd done to Ronnie. Chasing her like that. That couldn't happen. You didn't do that to their people, human or bird alike. If they wanted their humans to succeed—and they had no doubt that Ronnie would help them too—they had to get rid of these outsiders. The ones getting in the way. Annoying disturbances, nothing more.

They took turns dropping rocks on the woman's car, on her head. They swooped down, coming within inches of her eyes. They could hurt her; they knew that. And they wanted her to know it too. They cawed at her and flew so close she ducked down, screaming.

"Someone, help!"

She wasn't so brave now, was she? The ravens laughed.

The woman screamed and ran inside her apartment. The birds stayed and stood watch. Dozens of them, all over her balcony and the parking garage. There was no way she'd escape without them taking vengeance. They'd get her eventually. They knew her face now.

No one messed with their friends and got away with it.

Chapter 48

September

Ronnie was polishing the crystals with a microfiber cloth. Over and over she rubbed. No dust, no grime. Just rub. Until they shone as brightly as they could.

"Are you okay? Hello?" Brit laughed. "You've been polishing that same crystal for like ten minutes."

"Oh, uh, sorry."

"Spill it. Something's bothering you."

Ronnie was finding it increasingly harder to keep secrets from the twins. Was this what happened when walls came down? When you learned to trust? "It's just . . . this whole thing with Marley. I don't know how to get her to see reason. Like, her patrols aren't helping. And . . ."

"And?"

"What if I made a mistake coming here with her? What if everything she said was wrong? What if . . . I need to move out?"

Brit reached over to grab one of her hands. "Nope. We are not thinking like that. If you had never come here, we never would have met. And that would be terrible because you're our friend. So yes, Marley needs to be reined in a bit. But don't let her make you doubt yourself. Okay? And I will help you find a place if that's what you want."

Ronnie nodded though she wasn't convinced. She'd up and moved here on a whim. Sold everything, lived with a woman she barely knew. Of course things would go wrong. They always did. Why did she think this would be different?

"Hey, why don't we take a break and go have some tea. My treat?"

Ronnie gave in but felt guilty they were locking up the store just for her. "Are you sure I shouldn't stay here and keep working? We could miss a sale."

"So what? They'll come back. Working isn't everything, you know."

Brit took her to the nearest café, the Tree of Life. She ordered two teas and some vegan banana bread and set them down in front of her friend. "Eat. You'll feel better."

"I'm sorry, I shouldn't let this get to me."

They were interrupted by a woman who was watching them. "Brit? Is that you? Goodness, I haven't seen you since—well, since your incident. How are you, dear? I'm Barbara, remember?"

Brit's face was pale, Ronnie noticed. "Hello, I'm fine. This is Ronnie."

Ronnie waved.

"I'm just so glad you're back to your old self and with us. I couldn't believe what had happened to you when I heard it. Not Brit! But here you are, right as rain." The woman went on endlessly, and Ronnie finally had to step in.

"Nice to meet you, Barbara, but we're in the middle of something."

"Oh, of course. Brit, you tell your sister hi for me, okay?"

They watched her walk away. "She's a friend of Lorraine's," Brit answered Ronnie's unasked question.

"Was that about the lost-in-the-desert thing?"

"Yep. Fun thing about small towns is everyone knows your business."

"I'm finding that out. Does it bug you when people bring it up?"

Brit shrugged. "Sometimes. I'm still processing all that happened, you know? It was right before you came to town so not that long ago."

"Oh! I didn't know! Do you want to talk about it?"

"Not right now." Brit smiled. "I want to talk about you. You and Marley. Let it all out."

"All of it?"

"Mmmhmm." Brit grinned at her, her brown eyes wide. "Let it *all* out."

Ronnie took a deep breath. "It's just, Marley's turning into someone I don't recognize. The dog whistles, the whole patrolling, the us-ver-sus-them thing. It's been used against us for so long. And she doesn't see it. I've tried talking to her. The only person she talks to is Caroline." Ronnie grimaced as she said the name. Fucking Caroline. Who she could find no dirt on whatsoever. "And she won't listen to me when I say Caroline sucks."

"Caroline is not a good influence," Brit agreed. "Maybe we need to do an intervention for Marley. Something that helps her see things clearly."

"That's not a bad idea."

They would have kept talking had there not been a commotion. A woman ran into the café, crying. "Oh my god! Oh my god! Someone help me!" She started sobbing.

Brit jumped up to help. "It's okay, you're safe. Tell me what happened. Someone get me water, please." She sat the hysterical stranger down at their table.

"The police. Call the police," she gasped. "They shot my boyfriend!"

"What?! Who did?"

"Some crazy old people with guns! They started questioning us and grilling us about where we were from. I'm from Pasadena! I don't even know how this could happen. I just ran. I saw him get shot. I ran. Oh god, I shouldn't have left him! I didn't know what else to do!" Her wails filled the café until everyone was standing around, trying to figure out what to do.

Ronnie picked up her phone and called 911.

"Where was it?" she asked.

"Just down the road. They were on a trail with us and followed us and . . ."

She gave the info and waited for someone in a uniform to handle this. It didn't take long before Sheriff Reynolds walked in, his face grim.

"Brit. Ronnie. I'll take it from here." The two women nodded and left their table to the woman.

"Her name is Jessica," Ronnie said.

As the two huddled together, Brit looked at Ronnie. "You know, in a way, this takes care of your problem. The patrols will have to stop now."

"But what will take their place?" Ronnie asked. And if she were being honest, she didn't want to find out. The two gave up their plans for a peaceful cup of tea and went back to the shop. They didn't want to be there when Jessica was told her boyfriend was dead.

———

The edict came down swiftly. No more patrols. No more vigilantes. No more of Marley's Helpers, or whatever she called them. The meeting rally slated to be held at the Center was canceled. Brit later told Ronnie that Lorraine was outraged by what had happened and blamed Marley. Everyone, it seemed, blamed her. Ronnie didn't. She blamed Caroline.

When Ronnie got home, Marley was home. Alone. No sign of her followers, her friends. Just her. And she was halfway through a bottle of wine.

"Well, look who's here. Come to yell at me too?" She sniffed, wiping her nose with a tissue to show how upset she was.

"Who yelled at you?" Ronnie sat on the sofa.

"The sheriff. Lorraine. Everyone. I didn't know they were going to kill someone."

"But you had to know it was possible."

"I didn't!" Marley yelled. "I didn't know anything."

"Marley, come on. I warned you." Ronnie said it gently.

"A real friend would be helping me right now. My next rally at the Center is canceled." Marley sobbed. Ronnie wasn't sure what she felt, but it wasn't an urge to comfort her friend.

"Oh. Well, maybe you just need to convince Lorraine that it has to go on?" Ronnie hated saying it. Hated giving advice. But she wanted her friend to be open to her. And right now, Marley was anything but. She doubted Lorraine would give in. What was the harm, then?

"You might be right." Marley wiped her nose. "I'm sorry I've been such a raging bitch." She laughed, so Ronnie joined in. But she watched her like you'd watch a wild animal. Someone unpredictable. Ronnie used to think Marley was being impulsive, but maybe her friend was erratic?

"Caroline says I have to show Lorraine why the patrols are necessary. What do you think?"

"I think Caroline isn't who you think she is and to be careful."

Marley stared at her and shook her head. "I knew it. I knew you weren't with us. How dare you talk about her like that? You know, maybe it's time you did move out. Caroline said you were too close to the twins."

Ronnie's stomach dropped. Her friend wanted her gone. She'd known this was coming, yet it didn't soften the blow any. Another person didn't want her around.

"If that's what you want, I'll start looking for a place." It was her worst fear—to not be wanted.

Marley didn't answer her. Ronnie went upstairs, shut the door, and cried. She didn't want to leave Marley. To strike out on her own. But did she even have a choice now?

Chapter 49

The Town

She hadn't seen the man get killed. But she'd heard about it, even watched the elderly couple who'd shot him get arrested.

What a fucking mess.

But this meant no more patrols. No more people getting in her way. She almost felt bad for the two vigilantes she'd run over. But they had *seen* her. They had photos of her on their phones—which she'd deleted.

With the patrols done, she could get back to work. Which was good. Because the ravens were shitting all over her house right now. She hadn't done her job. They were tired of waiting. She didn't blame them.

She had a new name ready on her list and everything. Just a few more days of spying and she'd take care of it. Of him. And who knew—maybe this patrol fiasco would inspire people to behave better. To be more like animals. Animals cared for their surroundings. Humans didn't.

She could feel something brewing. An energy that said the calm before the storm was here. That something huge was going to come their way, her way. She only had to be open to it. Manifest it. Make it all happen. Everything she wanted would be hers. Soon.

———

Peter didn't realize he had an audience. She was watching. So were the ravens. The birds had made her come here. They'd been so persistent, cawing and throwing things until she'd listened.

Peter Hughes could be forgiven for thinking he had no prying eyes. His camper RV (on which he'd gotten a great deal; the previous owner had died in it) was parked deep in the woods on his lot of land. He was planning on building a house but always got distracted.

He was currently distracted by the very young woman with him.

This was Peter's MO. Targeting tourists, preferably the younger ones, charming them, telling them he'd help with hikes and what have you. And once they slept with him, he dumped them back at their hotels, their credit card numbers already snapped up.

Such a pig, she thought. She was there, behind the dense trees, watching. The forest hid him but also hid her. And she wanted to get that girl out of there. Was she a girl? She looked young enough to be. She shuddered. He was vile.

All around the camper the ravens sat, watching. They didn't like Peter, but he did leave food out. Not for them, just out of laziness. If they didn't eat it, the bears would. Sometimes, they wished the bears would eat people.

"Shit." She paced. How could she help that girl? She wanted to get her away from Peter, but how could she without blowing her cover? "I was just in the neighborhood" didn't work when he lived in the forest, way off main roads.

She debated setting a fire to start things off, but she stopped when she heard screaming. The girl—woman?—young lady was screaming and crying while running away from Peter. It was hard to tell, but it looked like she had red marks on her neck.

"Fuck." She had to hide.

Peter ran after the girl and then stopped, shaking his head. "You get what you ask for, sweetheart!" he yelled, laughing.

The girl was sobbing.

You know what you have to do.

This was not the first time Peter had been caught doing things that should have put him on a sex offenders list. But try as she did, no one would do anything about him. It was up to her.

The ravens cawed and flew near the younger woman, who was running through the trees. She'd help her. It was the right thing to do.

She got up and followed her, and when the girl stopped to catch her breath, she pretended to bump into her.

"Oh! Sorry! Didn't think anyone else would be out here. Are you okay?" She handed her a tissue from her backpack. She had a backpack on because then she looked like she was just out for a hike. Never mind that she had duct tape and a knife in the bag.

"I'm lost!" She was maybe eighteen. At best.

"I can help. Want to follow me? The road is about a mile that way. I have a car and can drive you somewhere?"

The girl looked at her with suspicion.

"Or I can just give you directions? Whatever works for you? Walk that way a mile." She pointed to the road.

"I—I'd like a ride. Thank you."

They walked in silence for a while. "You know, if you were with Peter, he has a reputation. I can take you to the sheriff if you want to press charges." She said it gently. Quietly. No need to scare her.

"I don't know. I just want to get to my hotel."

"Sure! No pressure."

This was her good deed for the day. She was helping this girl. She didn't ask any more questions. Just walked and kept an eye out for her ravens. One day, Peter would get what was coming to him. He would. She would be sure to make that happen.

When they got to her car, she motioned for the girl to get in.

"Listen, even if you don't want to press charges, check your debit and credit cards. He's known for stealing from his guests."

"Seriously? God, wow, I sure know how to pick 'em." The girl slumped in her seat.

"It's not you, it's him. So which hotel?"

"The Hilton."

"You got it."

———

Later, she'd circle back to Peter's. To make sure no one else would be lured in. But it was so difficult to keep him in check. She needed to do something, though. Peter was a scumbag. There was no room here for his kind.

Chapter 50

Every place Ronnie looked at was out of her price range. Renting seemed insane here. Only short-term rentals were available. And there were no houses under a million. She'd sold her house for $1.9 million, but she didn't want to spend all the money. Then she'd have nothing. No safety net, nothing to use in case she had to run. Move away again.

Plus, the idea of buying a place made her anxious. She'd been tied to her Queens house for so long, stuck there. Getting rid of it had freed her. She didn't want to be stuck again.

On a whim, she started googling Marley. Ronnie didn't know why. She was sick of searching for apartments. Shitholes with gorgeous views.

"Marley Dewhurst" got a lot of Google hits. Ronnie searched through them all, trying to figure out who her friend really was. Daughter of socialite Joan Dewhurst, who was famed for marrying for money. Many times over. Marley was rich rich, something she hadn't realized. She'd known Marley was wealthy, but this was beyond that. No wonder she didn't make Ronnie pay rent.

There were blog posts about her friend, photos of her from years earlier, posing at events, her face beaming into the cameras. Marley was made for the attention. And now she was here. With Ronnie.

Photos of an awkward adolescent Marley in braces. Shots of her riding horses. And then the glow-up years.

What did she think she'd find? That Marley was going to start a crazy movement and get people killed?

"Ron, you here?" Marley called. Ronnie slammed her laptop closed. "Yes! Hi!"

"Listen, I'm sorry about our fight. I don't want you to move out. But I can't have you fighting with Caroline, okay?"

Ronnie felt relief course through her. She didn't have to move. She could stay a little while longer. "Okay. Can I tell you something, though? I'm not allowed to go into details, but I heard she almost killed someone with her drug-ritual thing."

Marley stared at her. "I'll take that under advisement. Now, can you get dressed?"

Ronnie looked down at her outfit. Jeans and a T-shirt. "Uh, I am?"

"We're going to the Center. To meet with Lorraine."

"Oh."

"Please, I need you to come with me. You know how much she loves you. Go put on a caftan." Marley pleaded with her to go with her. Ronnie couldn't say no. She just couldn't.

"I'll go like this. I'm not comfortable in caftans." Her voice stayed steady as she said it. (To Ronnie's surprise.)

Marley narrowed her eyes but conceded. "Fine. But let's go." A small victory was still a victory, Ronnie thought.

Ronnie drove while Marley stared at her phone. "Is, uh, Caroline joining us?"

"No, not this time." Her voice was clipped.

"It's going to go great. I know it," Ronnie said with as much optimism as she could muster. She didn't want it to go well, but she kept that to herself.

"I hope so."

She pulled into the lot and parked. Ronnie hadn't been here since the party, and she was bracing for Lorraine to be annoying. To fawn over her while insulting her in the same breath. Fun times!

"Let's get this over with," Marley muttered.

"Hey, remember when I started coming to you and you told me, 'You're Ronnie Khan. There's no one else like you. Remember that.' Because you're Marley Dewhurst. No one is like you."

Marley's lips quirked. "I remember that."

"Good. Now let's go kick some butt. Or something."

———

Star waited for them in the lobby. She hugged Ronnie and nodded at Marley.

"I'm supposed to bring you back."

"That doesn't sound good." Marley laughed; her voice sounded nervous. Ronnie kept quiet. This was Marley's thing—she'd follow her lead. Maybe.

Star led the way back to Lorraine's office. Ronnie took in the marble pieces from India and Pakistan. Just like before.

"Rania, so pleased to see you. Wish the circumstances were better." Lorraine grabbed her hands with both of hers. "Marley."

There were six of them in the room: Lorraine, Star, the sheriff, Peter from the shooting range, and Marley and Ronnie.

"So, with the present information we have, I don't think you can continue your little meetings here. Not after what happened." Lorraine said it like a decree.

"Lorraine, that's not fair. The people involved weren't affiliated with me. And we had just one rally here."

"They weren't?"

"Nope. They took it on themselves to do that. To, uh, shoot. It's a tragedy."

Ronnie knew Marley was lying.

"They claimed otherwise," the sheriff interrupted.

"Of course they did! They want to blame someone else so they don't go to jail." Marley rolled her eyes. "Look, all I'm asking for is a little time. Everyone has goofs in the beginning of any new movement. We'll get it right." She flashed her megawatt smile. No one could resist that smile, Ronnie thought.

"Three people are dead," Peter said. "That's on you."

"The hit-and-run is *not* on me. The patrollers were off duty when it happened."

"Are you going to take responsibility for anything?" Star asked. She was mad—everyone could tell. "People are dead because of you. And you're upset because you want to keep your little following, do more videos. Why? What's your goal here? Because it's not to keep us safe."

The silence that followed made Ronnie squirm. Star was right. She had even used Ronnie's own talking points. Which meant Brit had told her how Ronnie felt.

"Well, I see you've made up your mind. Lorraine, all I ask is you give me time. I'll make it up to everyone, I swear. We need to start the patrols again while the killer is out there. Any one of us could be the next victim. I don't want us to die!"

"We'll see. But for now, no more meetings here. We have to think about the future of the Center. And your vigilantes aren't good for business."

Marley stiffened her back, standing straight, and nodded. "Ronnie, shall we? Thank you, everyone, for taking time to meet with me." She smiled and shook hands like this was some business meeting she had enjoyed. Ronnie didn't know how she did it. But she was slightly in awe of her friend.

When they got to the car, Ronnie sneaked a look at Marley. Her friend was deep in thought. "How are you feeling?"

"Great! Honestly, I have a plan. They'll all want us back there. Soon. You'll see." Marley sat back with a smile on her face. "No one will say no to me after I'm done."

Ronnie wasn't sure why, but the smile made the hair on her neck stand up.

———

Caroline was at the door the next day, knocking and pounding. Ronnie had just gotten home from work.

"Marley's not here," she said.

"Where is she? I've been trying to find her." Caroline came in without an invitation.

Dammit, I wanted to be alone. "No idea, I thought she was with you."

"Huh. No, she's been keeping to herself after everything. I was really hoping to see her."

Ronnie shrugged. "Sorry."

Caroline sat down. "Sit with me, I want to get to know you."

Alarms went off in Ronnie's head. Caroline didn't just want to get to know anyone. She wanted dirt. "No, you want me to tell you about Marley."

"Guilty, okay?" Caroline laughed. "I have to say being here has been great for you."

"It has?"

"Yes. Have you seen and heard yourself? When I first met you, you were like a doormat. And now you're making witty retorts at me. Bravo, Ronnie. You've come so far."

"Oh." Sometimes the changes happened so gradually that Ronnie didn't recognize them. But that was good, right? That's how change happened. "I wish . . . I wish people knew what Marley could really do. She helped me. Changed everything for me. But this . . ."

Caroline nodded. "Maybe the vigilante bit was perhaps too much."

"You think?"

"I just thought it would be a good way to make a splash, get her name out there. I didn't think this would happen."

Ronnie didn't say anything. Just sat there, the silence growing more and more awkward.

"Well, I'll tell—"

"Could I have some wine—are you trying to get rid of me?"

"I just, um, have to be somewhere."

"On one of your walks? Where do you go on these walks?"

The way Caroline looked at her creeped her out. Like she was trying to see inside Ronnie's head. Or worse, she wanted to join her on a walk. "Nowhere, really."

"I'm on to you, Ronnie Khan." Caroline pointed to her eyes and then to Ronnie to show she was serious.

"Uh, I'll tell Marley you came by."

———

Fire. There was fire all around. Ronnie could smell it in her dream. She could practically taste the air. Something was burning.

The ravens told her to calm down. She only had to watch, not taste. She wouldn't burn. So she watched. She saw a man burning. She knew him. How did she know him? Hadn't he been at the Center the other day? The creepy guy who'd groped her ass. Peter.

Ronnie stood back and let him burn. It wasn't as if she could stop it. She couldn't stop any of this from happening. She simply had to witness it. That's all the ravens wanted from her.

Chapter 51

The Town

She'd had to go to his camper, that disgusting, filthy place in the woods. And she'd drugged the wine she'd brought.

Peter had drunk it down, glass after glass. He'd probably thought she was going to sleep with him. The idea made her laugh. She wouldn't let him touch her, ever. Peter went through women like they were tissues. He groped, he groomed. He was, in a word, gross.

He'd fallen asleep quickly. She'd dosed him a lot. This next part was going to be hard. She had to get him into his car. That stupid, ugly car. Black matte with a shining flag on it. Like he cared about patriotism. He just thought it made him look macho. If he could, he'd have set it on big monster-truck-size tires. It wasted so much gas; she hated it. She wanted that car destroyed.

She dragged him to the Mustang, wiping sweat from her brow despite the cool temperatures.

"What's going on?" he slurred. Fuck, had she not given him enough?

"Nothing, just relax." She tried to sound as soothing as possible.

"Wait, why am I . . . ? What are you . . . ?" She thrust him into the front seat of his car. His dazed eyes took in the knife she was holding.

And that's when things got ugly. She climbed on top of him in the driver's seat. *Ugh, gross.*

"Shhh, it's fine, just sleep." But he didn't. He tried to push her off him, but she held on. She was stronger than she looked. *Everyone always underestimates me.*

She stabbed him where she could—chest, arms, stomach. And then, when blood was everywhere, she ran the knife across his throat, watching his eyes as she did it. The fear, the pain, the resignation that this was it—it all filled her with joy. His movements were slow, clumsy, thanks to the wine and pills. He normally would have fought her off with no problem.

"This is karma." She laughed.

He tried to stop the bleeding, but he was too weak, too dazed. She stumbled out of the car and took a look at her bloody clothes. *Dammit.*

She waited for him to die before taking off all her clothes and burning them in the firepit. There was probably something she could wear from his camper though the idea disgusted her. She ended up in a stained T-shirt and sweatpants. It would have to do.

She waited for the fire to go out, to make sure every inch of her clothes was ash. And then she waited some more, until it was so late at night no one would be out. The latest any bar stayed open was two. At three in the morning, she made her move.

She tried to shove Peter's cold body into the passenger seat, but he'd already stiffened up. "Dammit. Next time I'm killing you in the passenger seat."

She left him where he was and went back inside the camper. She came out with bottles of vodka. "Perfect."

If she couldn't dump him, she'd burn him. Before she soaked him and the car with alcohol, she reached into his pocket to find his phone. "Gross." Even when dead, he disgusted her.

She poured the alcohol all over him, the seat, and the car and opened the gas tank. And then before she lit the match, she wiped down the camper and bottles. Though it wouldn't matter. There were so many prints inside from so many women that they'd never be able to find her.

Overhead, a raven cawed.

"It's too early for you, get away from here. It's not safe," she called back. She meant it. She didn't want to burn the forest down, but some parts would get singed. A cleansing.

She set the fire and jumped into her own car. She called 911 from Peter's phone.

"Hi, there's something burning off of Happy Trails Road! Hurry, I can't put it out myself!" She drove the opposite direction the fire trucks would come from and tossed the phone after wiping it for prints and DNA. And then she waited. The explosion from the gas tank was loud enough to make her flinch. She heard the sirens, and she smiled. She drove farther in the wrong direction. She'd sleep in a random campsite—it was fine.

"I'm almost done. Almost."

She would take a hot bath when she got home. And then she'd rest for a bit. Self-care was key in achieving your goals.

———

The ravens were mildly annoyed. One of their favorite spots had burned. Not much, but it had. It was their human. But she'd warned them away; at least that was something.

They'd loved coming by that camper because he left food out for them. They didn't care much for him otherwise. He was so loud, made too much noise. Female humans always ran crying from him. But food was food.

The smell was awful. Humans made everything bad. The birds circled, finding a tree to sit in, one that wasn't singed. The other humans were there, dousing what was left with chemicals.

"Thank god the fire didn't spread."

"Was it intentional?"

"Can't say yet."

The ravens spotted the man they always saw near dead bodies.

"Dammit, at least he's in one piece," the sheriff said.

"One very charred piece," someone joked.

"That's not funny."

"Sorry, boss."

The sheriff just nodded. "Are we sure it's Peter?" he asked.

"Ever seen anyone else in his car? We'll have to use dental records to confirm—the body's too burnt for DNA."

"Dammit."

The man looked ill. He was going to be sick. The ravens took off. They didn't need to see that part. They'd already seen it many times. Before they left the area, they swooped down to taunt one of the humans, aiming for his hat. Just because they could.

The ravens laughed as they flew away.

Chapter 52

October

Ronnie was at the crystal shop when the news broke. They'd just gotten in a new shipment of spherical crystals (which she had chosen), and she was trying to come up with a cool new display. Brit was in the back doing whatever she did; Ronnie didn't ask. Healing was complicated work, and she left that up to the experts.

"Oh my god!" She picked up the paper. "Holy shit."

She ran to the back. "Look!" She thrust the paper at Brit.

"What is it—oh my goddess, nooooo! This is awful." There it was in black and white. Another body found. Not just found but set on fire and nearly burning the forest. It was Peter Hughes. He was dead.

Brit's shocked face matched Ronnie's. They had a new body. That meant the killer—or killers—were still in town. But more importantly, that dream she had had come true. Ronnie had hoped it wouldn't. But she didn't do much other than hope.

"I have to tell Star." Brit ran to the phone. Ronnie wasn't sad that Peter was dead. She had only met the man a couple of times and didn't like him much. She wondered if anyone would actually miss him. She would have felt bad, but it occurred to her that Fiona had also not been well liked. Maybe that's who the killer was going after? Shitty people?

But she didn't say any of that out loud. Nor did she tell Brit she'd dreamed about Peter's death. Ronnie wanted to forget her dreams. "They don't mean anything," she muttered. Instead she focused on the spheres and sent Marley a text to pick up the paper.

"I have to leave," Brit said, running by Ronnie. "Star and Lorraine need me. You have the store?"

She did. In fact, she was almost working full time. Ronnie had become the go-to, opening the shop, closing it. Choosing what they ordered. She was turning the store into something she loved, which seemed to work well for customers. Besides the new layout, jewelry, and spheres, she had stocked room sprays and candles made by locals. A one-stop shop for all things wellness and Sedona.

"Of course! Give Star a hug for me."

Too bad it wasn't Caroline who had died, Ronnie thought. That was someone no one liked, except Marley. Why couldn't she dream about Caroline's death? And then she picked up a black tourmaline to help with her negative thoughts.

———

Caroline's car was out front. She drove a Tesla and loved to show how eco-friendly she was. Ronnie secretly hoped her car would catch fire, like the other electric cars she'd read about in the news.

Ronnie had brought an amethyst sphere home for Marley. She'd love this one. (Amethyst was her favorite.) Ronnie didn't question why she'd bought it for her, just that she wanted to give her friend a present, a pick-me-up.

"Hello!" she called out. "I'm home!"

"Have a good day?" Marley sat on the sofa with Caroline. They were drinking wine, which wasn't strange. But Marley had bruises all over her shoulders and arms. Enough to make Ronnie stop midstep.

"Whoa, what happened to you? Are you okay?"

"I did cupping! Getting rid of my toxins. You should try it, you'd love it!"

Ronnie was certain she wouldn't. The circular marks all over her friend's body were freaking her out. How was that supposed to help with toxins? "I brought this for you." She held out the amethyst. "I ordered spheres and thought this one had to be yours."

"Ooh, how thoughtful! It's gorgeous!" Marley cradled it in her hands. "Stunning."

"Nothing for me?" Caroline asked, smiling.

"Oh, shit, sorry." She wasn't sorry. "I'll bring you one next time?"

"All good, I should get going. Be blessed!" She flashed a weird sign with both hands. Her two index fingers and middle fingers crossed. What did that even mean?

"Uh, yes, blessed!" Ronnie called out.

She watched her leave before holding up her own hands like Caroline had. "What does that mean?"

"Oh, hashtag. As in hashtag blessed," Marley explained.

"Ohhhh. Okay."

"Sit with me. I could use some Ronnie love." Marley patted the sofa.

"Let me just grab a bite to eat. Then it'll be a lovefest!"

Marley followed her. "You know, I was thinking. This Peter thing could be great for us." She'd heard the news. Sedona was a small town despite the tourists. And word traveled fast. She refilled her glass of wine as Ronnie opened a to-go salad she'd picked up.

"Great? You mean him dying?"

"It's not like anyone liked him." Marley shrugged. "But with him dead, now my patrols can continue. My followers need me."

"Have you noticed that the people dying weren't well liked? I mean, there was that first guy, Matt something, who we didn't know. But Fiona. Peter. Suzy." She rolled her eyes at the last name.

Marley whooped out a laugh. "Wow, tell me how you really felt about her."

Ronnie smiled but felt bad about it. "She was just so . . . into me. It was weird. But I wonder if that's like a motive or something?"

Marley shrugged. "I dunno, the police haven't said anything. Or done anything to solve this. But we can help them by being on patrol. I really think with Peter dying there's a new need for Marley's Eyes." She was starting to sound like a crazy person.

"Yeah, uh, great." She was being creepy. Ronnie didn't know how to tell her that.

"I bet we can even get back with Lorraine because of this. I get it, someone is dead. But let's turn it into a positive. What do you think?"

"Maybe? Just, if you do have more patrols, maybe they should all wear those red tees you had made. That way people know they're not random lunatics?" That was the best she could come up with. If they knew the people accosting them on the street were a patrol, maybe there'd be fewer incidents. People would know to avoid them.

"You, my dear, are brilliant." It was the way her friend said it. Laying it on. Being charming. It sent shivers down her back.

———

Before

Shameem elbowed her. "Rania, answer the question." Her smile never wavered. If you didn't know her, you'd absolutely love Shameem. A smile that could melt butter and all that.

Ronnie and her aunt were at dinner with Farrah and her parents. Ronnie's boss. Farrah's parents had been close friends with Ronnie's before the accident. And Shameem insisted on putting on a good face for them. She wanted them to be her friends, but once Ronnie's parents were gone, they only cared for her niece.

Farrah's mother—Lina Auntie—was the type of mother Ronnie dreamed about. She was kind, loving, and gentle and encouraged her daughter to pursue her own life. Farrah never had to scrub the kitchen floor with a toothbrush. Never had to worry about being woken up with a flyswatter. Or that she'd be sent to Pakistan. Seeing them, how they interacted, made Ronnie angry. She hid it, but she was. Her aunt's excuses were always, "That's how we did it in Pakistan." Yet Farrah was proof that wasn't true. Her family treated her with love.

Farrah's father was boisterous and friendly, a college professor. Nothing was more important to Nawaz Uncle than education. And he kept pushing Ronnie to go back to school. Which was the question being posed to her: Why wasn't she going back to university?

"Well, I'd love to, Uncle. But Khala needs me here." There, a perfect answer. Or so she thought. Shameem's sharp elbow dug deeper into her side.

"What she means is, I'd love her to go back to school, but it's so difficult with her schedule. But we absolutely will keep trying to get her back on track."

If Ronnie had a choice, she'd have begged Farrah's parents to take her in. They were nice. She wanted nice. Not everyone had to behave like her aunt.

It also made her angry. Why wasn't her aunt as nice as they were? Was it something Ronnie had done? Had she taken something from her aunt?

The dinner plates were cleared by Farrah and her mother though Ronnie jumped up to help.

"She's very useful," Shameem said. "She'll make a good wife."

"But she's not educated enough. Men today want a smart wife," Nawaz Uncle said.

"She can always take courses. It's no big deal. How's your son doing?"

Their son, Amir, was doing his medical residency. And Shameem wanted a connection between Ronnie and him. A marriage. One that would increase her own bank account and where she'd be taken care of forever. And it would give her bragging rights. "My son-in-law, the doctor." There was nothing an auntie wanted more than that, except grandchildren who grew up to be doctors.

"He's good, busy. He's engaged! Did we tell you?" Lina Auntie said, her face lighting up.

"Oh really? How wonderful!" Shameem's voice sounded fake to Ronnie. Her aunt wasn't happy. She had had a plan and got nothing. It was going to be Ronnie's fault too.

"Excuse me," Ronnie said. "I'm going to go help Farrah in the kitchen."

Farrah didn't need help, but Ronnie needed to escape. She joined her boss/friend, and together they laughed at the idea of her marrying Amir. Like that would ever happen. He was like family to her. "Your khala is delusional," Farrah joked.

"Right?"

It still stung, though. No one thought she was good enough. Not even Farrah.

She walked back out with a tray of chai. She had offered. No sense in Farrah doing this kind of work. It was what Ronnie was good for. Labor. Nokari. A servant.

"Rania will marry one day, inshallah!" Shameem beamed.

Ronnie froze. "No. I'm not." She said it so quietly they almost didn't hear her. "I'm not marrying anyone."

The fury on her aunt's face spoke volumes. She was going to pay for this outburst. But when was Ronnie going to live her own life? Shameem's face contorted back into a benign smile. It was for Farrah's family's benefit—but it meant something bad. Ronnie knew that face. She knew her aunt. And there'd be hell to pay later.

Charming people were liars. And Ronnie hated them.

Chapter 53

The Town

"Is it possible he got drunk and set things on fire?" Star asked Sheriff Reynolds. The two of them were at the Kismet Center with Lorraine, who was inconsolable. One of their own had died. Again. (Though Star didn't count Suzy as one of her own.) Star had never been a big fan of Peter's. But Lorraine loved him, for whatever reason.

"We're still running tests. Did Peter go on benders often?"

"Sometimes? I mean, we weren't close. He was too . . . gropey for my liking."

"He was a kind and generous man!" Lorraine yelled. "We do not speak ill of the dead."

"Sorry, I didn't mean to." Star was properly chastened. "But I'd rather this were a freak accident than a murder, you know?" Star never understood the love for Peter. He was a liability. A lawsuit waiting to happen.

"Yep." John nodded. A drunken idiot in the woods was something they could deal with. A serial killer wasn't.

"What are we going to do?" Lorraine asked. "What if they come after us?"

"Hey, that's never going to happen. I will always have your back." Star hugged the woman. She meant it too. She would do anything for

Lorraine. Well, almost anything. "And we don't know if this was foul play yet."

"Maybe we should let Marley hold her thing here. Since the murders are still happening."

"God. Please don't."

Lorraine was softer on people than Star. She was a de facto mother to the twins, helping them out after theirs had passed a few years earlier. And when Brit had had that awful incident with Caroline in the desert, it was Lorraine who'd pushed the authorities to keep searching. But it was Star who had found her.

Star hated thinking about that day. Those days, plural. Because her sister had been lost in the desert, delirious. Alone. She could have died. All because Caroline had given her the wrong substance. Instead of peyote, she'd given Brit jimsonweed. Devil's snare. A delirium that didn't inspire visions so much as tear your mind up from the inside out for days on end.

"I don't care for her either, but if she can help us until this fiend is caught, then we need to do something."

"I don't know. Don't make any decisions yet. Okay? She and Caroline are too close. You know I hate to have Caroline involved in any way." If anyone deserved to die, it was that woman. She was the reason Star had almost lost her sister. Could the killer take Caroline next?

"You're right. I'm just so upset. I think I'll head home and take it easy."

"Good call."

Star watched her friend leave the office and drive off. Overhead, a couple of ravens warbled at her. She nodded back at them. At least the birds weren't trying to kill anyone.

Chapter 54

The Town

Caroline was oblivious to the eyes on her. She was in Marley's house, but no one was home. She shouldn't have been there. Caroline had taken the spare key and let herself in. She was on a mission. The ravens watched from the windows, from the walls outside, from every perch they could find.

Caroline was searching for something in Ronnie's room. The ravens weren't sure why. But they watched as closely as they could, even perching on Ronnie's bedroom windowsill.

She muttered something about blackmail as she tore the room apart. Black eyes watched her. The raven at the window tapped its beak against the glass over and over.

"You can't get in, so nice try," Caroline taunted.

The raven just watched.

"Birdbrain." Caroline stuck her tongue out at it.

She continued rifling through Ronnie's things. There wasn't much to find. Ronnie didn't have a lot.

The only thing of interest to Caroline was the large black feather Ronnie had kept. A raven's, no doubt. Caroline picked it up. "Pretty."

The raven didn't like that. How dare she touch their gift to Ronnie? Caroline wasn't worthy of a raven's feather. It beat its wings against the glass, making the human laugh.

"Aww, does somebody want to come in?"

The raven cawed, but Caroline had no idea what it had said. Other birds did. Her days were numbered: the raven made that vow.

The raven would show her. Humans never thought anything could hurt them, and the look of surprise on their faces when they realized they were vulnerable always made the birds happy. There was already a small crack in the glass—no doubt from other birds flying into it. The raven flew off and circled around, gaining speed. And then, pulling its wings close to its body, it flew into the window glass, right at the cracked part. At the right angle, it wouldn't hurt the bird. The wrong one, and a broken neck would result. But this raven didn't care. This had to be done.

Glass shattered, and Caroline screamed.

"What the hell?!"

The raven was inside now, in Ronnie's room. It flew to Caroline's face and scratched her until she dropped the feather. And then scratched more, drawing blood. All the while, the human screamed bloody murder.

"Get off of me!" Caroline ran out of the room. The raven didn't follow her. It was protecting Ronnie, not that other human. Let the two glowless women enjoy each other's company. Ronnie was theirs.

The raven picked up the fallen feather and placed it on Ronnie's bed before going back out the window.

No one messed with their humans, no one.

Chapter 55

Ronnie came home to broken glass in her room and the raven's feather on her bed. The birds must have done it, but why? What did they want from her? She cleaned up the mess, put the feather back, and decided she needed to have a talk with the ravens. She would have to find out what they wanted. She'd need to wait until she was asleep, of course. She couldn't very well hold a conversation with them while awake, now could she?

She was home alone and enjoying the quiet. That didn't last. She heard the front door open. Caroline and Marley were home. Ronnie stayed in her room. She wasn't up for dealing with Caroline right now.

"That's a lovely sphere," Caroline said. "Can I hold it?"

"Obviously."

"I want one."

"Let's ask Ronnie?"

The voices were muffled a bit. They mentioned something about a scratch on Caroline's face.

Ronnie had been thinking about Peter. About being set on fire like that. She hoped he hadn't been alive when he'd burned. She didn't like him, but what a horrible way to die. She stared at her palm, where the scars were faint. Burning alive had to be a terrible way to go.

"This would be fun to just chuck at someone's head, wouldn't it?" Caroline laughed. Marley joined her. "Oh, have you emailed Lorraine about setting up rallies now that Peter's dead? If I were the old bag, I'd want extra protection."

"I'm going to."

"Good! Maybe if Lorraine dies next, you'll be able to take over." Caroline laughed louder, a braying noise that Ronnie hated.

"You can't say that!" But Marley laughed too.

"I'm serious! Imagine that useless old biddy out of the way? God, it would be perfect."

"The twins would never let that happen."

"Fine, get rid of them too. Let's kill them all!" And the laughter turned absolutely raucous. The two of them were cackling about killing Ronnie's friends. It was disturbing. How could they joke like that? Ronnie shivered. She hoped they were joking, at least.

She had to go downstairs. She had to and pretend she hadn't just heard what she'd heard. *What if they're not joking? What if they killed everyone?*

"Not possible," Ronnie said to her room. "Marley would never." And besides, they didn't even know that first guy who'd died. Well, Marley didn't. She wasn't sure about Caroline.

She pasted a smile on her face and said hello to both women, nodding politely and being cheerful. That's what made people underestimate her. That smile she wore. Like she'd been lobotomized. She'd learned to smile like that living with Shameem. Her aunt had thought she was simple. Special. Like some cousin of hers back in Pakistan Ronnie had met once. Not all there.

"Hello! Caroline, you look gorgeous today." She grabbed some juice, keeping that smile on herself like she'd die otherwise. "Oh no, what happened to your face?" Caroline's cheek had two deep scratches on it.

"Ugh, a bird attack, can you believe?" Caroline replied.

"How weird. I think the birds broke my bedroom window too. There was glass everywhere. I'll get it fixed." She added the last part for Marley's benefit. She was anything but a bad tenant.

Caroline changed the subject. "I was just reminding Marley that I'd love one of these spheres."

"Well, let me see what I can do about that. Speaking of, I'd better get to work!"

"You sure are working a lot lately," Marley said.

"Yeah, the twins are so busy with their clients. It's good, gives me something to do."

"Ronnie, I have a fabulous waxer," Caroline said, staring at her face.

"Sorry?"

"If you ever want help with the facial hair. She'll get you waxed in no time." Ronnie's face burned. Her facial hair. Caroline had the uncanny ability of zeroing in on someone's flaws, pointing out what was wrong.

"Ha, yeah, we don't have peach fuzz, we have black fuzz," she joked. It was just easier to make a joke than to let Caroline's words hurt her. "Well, have a good day! See you guys later!"

She hummed as she walked out of the house and got into her car. But her heart was racing. She flipped the sun visor down and stared in the mirror. Her mustache was nearly all gone; she was very good at keeping things tidy. But her sideburns were too hairy. Maybe she needed a full-face wax job. She'd done well keeping up Marley's changes to her looks, but every now and again she forgot, and her black fuzz would grow.

Why do I care what Caroline thinks of me? I don't. I look fine.

———

"Wait, what's wrong? You have that panicked smile." Star stared into her face the second she walked into the shop.

"Oh shoot, you can tell?"

"We can, but no one else can. What is it?"

"Caroline was over this morning as I was getting ready. And . . ." *You're really going to say it?* "She said she had a waxer for my face." Ronnie felt stupid for letting it get to her. She'd heard worse her entire life.

"You are perfect and stunning. Do not let her get in your head."

"God, thank you." She squeezed the twin's hand.

"What else did Caroline say today?" Star had a glint in her eye. Ronnie paused. Should she tell her what she'd overheard? Would that be betraying her friend? But what if Caroline was the one they had to be scared of?

"Uh, she was joking this morning about the murders. She said something like who should be next. And to kill them all. I don't know, it was weird. But I'm sure she was just kidding. Also she had a weird scratch on her face she said a bird did. And my window was broken. I don't know."

"Weird. I wouldn't put anything past her. Caroline's got blood on her hands from before all of this started. I wish she weren't at your house so often. Any luck finding a place to move to?" Star looked mad.

"Not yet. And Marley's dropped it. I guess she's forgiven me." She shrugged.

"Oh. That's a shame. I think one of our neighbors is moving, and how fun would it be if you lived near us?"

"That would be so fun!" Ronnie said. And she meant it. Neighbors with the twins? Days upon days of living next to people who accepted her as she was? Maybe she should take a look at the house all the same. Maybe living on her own, near the twins, was just what she needed?

Star nodded, and Ronnie thought that was that. End of conversation, no more Caroline, time to get to work. Until the sheriff walked in thirty minutes later.

"I heard you heard something," he said to Ronnie.

Star had called him. *Dammit.* Ronnie nodded. Told him what she'd overheard that morning. She was ratting out her friend—and Caroline. The conflicting emotions were overwhelming.

John stared at her. "She said, 'Let's kill them all'?"

Ronnie nodded. "But I think she was joking. Or I don't know. I don't want to get anyone in trouble." Oh god, this was bad. Marley would never forgive her. But she had no way out of this. "I'm pretty certain it was just dark humor, you know?"

"Well, I don't know Caroline well, but from what I've heard, she's a troublemaker." He looked at Star as he said it.

"She's the worst and you know it," Star hissed. "Can you at least question her. Maybe put the fear of god into her?"

"I'll see what I can do."

"Can you leave my name out of it? It's . . . complicated." Ronnie made a face but felt relief once John agreed. She didn't want to go around accusing anyone of anything. Her aunt always told her to keep her head down and not rock the boat. That's what she needed to do here.

All day, Ronnie waited for Marley to confront her. For her friend to call and yell at her for betraying them like that. Ronnie didn't think Marley was in on anything. But Caroline? Who knew about her. She had bad vibes. And the twins hated her. That was enough for her.

———

Just open the door. You can do it. You can quietly slip in. No one will even know you're here. Ronnie stood outside the door to the house. She had to do this. She swallowed nervously before stepping inside.

She was alone.

"Oh thank god." The last thing she wanted was a confrontation. But this solitude wouldn't last, and she knew it. Ronnie grabbed a salad she'd picked up on the way home and ran up to her room, where she could eat with no one around. It was a habit she'd picked up from living with Shameem. It was easier to eat in her room than deal with her aunt.

It was hours before she heard the front door open.

"Is she home?" Caroline asked loudly.

"I don't think so. Maybe she went out with the twins."

"Her car's here."

Please don't come upstairs. Just in case, Ronnie quickly shut her door and pretended to be asleep. Surely they wouldn't wake her? She evened her breath and turned her face to the wall.

She heard her bedroom door open and then close.

"She's asleep," Marley said.

"Good."

The voices grew more muffled as they went back downstairs. They were trying to keep things quiet. Ronnie waited for a few minutes before creeping out of her room. She'd eavesdrop from the top of the stairs. They wouldn't even know.

"I can't believe she called the sheriff."

"We don't know that she did."

"Who else would have done it? Maybe it was one of the birds outside." Caroline was angry. Ronnie couldn't blame her. She'd be miffed, too, if someone had told the sheriff she'd threatened to kill anyone. She was going to have to apologize. Again.

Marley defended her. "Ronnie's not like that."

"How well do you even know her?"

"Well enough. She's been through a lot and is a good friend."

"You sure about that?"

"What are you saying?"

"Just that I did some digging on miss goody two-shoes, and she's not what she seems."

"Caroline, come on, that's not fair."

"She doesn't have your back!" Caroline yelled before lowering her voice. "I'm just saying, read through this."

Ronnie heard what sounded like a stack of papers being shifted. "What is all this?"

"I told you, I dug into her. You need to read this. And maybe it'll change what you think of her. Open your eyes. If you can't trust her, she can't be here. Got it?"

"I will take care of Ronnie. Okay? Now, let's have some wine and call it a night."

What had Caroline given Marley? It wasn't like Ronnie could sneak down and look. What could she have dug up? Ronnie's heart raced. *Fuck. Fuck fuck fuck.* What if it said things that Marley didn't know? What if this made Marley hate her? No, she had to do something.

But she had no idea what.

Quietly, she crept back to her room and locked the door. She was safe in here. She was always safe in her room.

———

The next morning, Ronnie went downstairs determined to face her friend. Marley knew her. She knew Ronnie. Marley had to know she didn't want anything bad to happen. That she hadn't meant to tell the sheriff anything.

Marley was already at the breakfast table reading the paper and drinking coffee.

"Morning!" Ronnie said.

"Morning."

"No Caroline today?"

"Not till later. Hey, did you call the sheriff about her?"

Ronnie shook her head, hoping she looked confused. "About . . . Caroline? Nooooo. Why?" *Please let me sound convincing.*

"Someone did and told the sheriff she was making threats."

"Whoa." Was that what the sheriff had told Caroline? That she'd said she made threats? "You know I would never do something like that, not without talking to you first. Here, look at my calls." There were none. Because technically, Star had called him, not Ronnie.

"Well, I hope you would tell me if anything was bothering you. I need you. You tell it to me straight. And I need a friend who can do that." Marley stressed the last part.

"I'm always going to be your friend. Always."

Ronnie went over to hug her friend, which surprised Marley. Ronnie rarely initiated hugs. She was trying new things.

"Wow, a hug! You are making changes, aren't you?"

"I'm so happy I'm here with you."

Ronnie waited to see if she could find the papers Caroline had given to Marley, the ones about her. There couldn't be anything in them. Ronnie was always so careful. No way could Caroline get dirt on her. But she found no papers in the common areas. *Of course not, moron. They're probably in Marley's room.*

"What crystal does Caroline like? She wanted a sphere, and I'll grab her one. So she isn't mad at me."

"She'll love that, thank you. Maybe something really stunning. Like a smoky quartz."

"I'm on the case!" She grinned. A crystal would make Caroline less suspicious of her. She had to make nice with the woman. At least until she knew what was in those papers. Why had she even dug into Ronnie's life?

"Maybe let's all have dinner tonight? As a way of bringing us all closer?"

"Sounds perfect," Ronnie agreed. And kicked herself for not claiming other plans.

Ronnie dreaded dinner all day. A sit-down meal at a restaurant was hard enough. She always felt so stupid when she ate out. What if there were extra forks or something? Another thing to curse her aunt about. She was woefully underprepared for life outside. There had been life inside the house and life outside. And Shameem had made sure Ronnie only knew the former.

Dinner was at one of the fancier places in town in a resort: L'Auberge de Sedona. The sort of place Ronnie had never been. She felt conspicuously underdressed despite Marley choosing her outfit. (A blue caftan and a white crystal.) The tablecloth was white, and everyone looked rich even though they were all in casual clothes.

"It's Caroline's favorite," Marley said of the spot.

"Well, then I'm sure it's great." Ronnie smiled.

Caroline came after them, wearing what could best be described as a goddess gown. All white and folds and she looked like she could have been straight out of Athens.

"Marley! Mwah! And Ronnie! So good to see you!"

"Wow, you look so pretty!" Ronnie said. "Listen, Marley mentioned someone called the sheriff on you, and it wasn't me. I swear. But I wanted to get you something to smooth things over." She handed over the quartz ball.

"Oh, this is lovely! Thank you, Ronnie. So very sweet of you. Let's order, I'm famished."

Marley and Caroline both ordered the steak tartare, while Ronnie got a steak. Had they planned that? Why did she care? Who even ate raw beef? She giggled.

"What's funny?" Caroline asked.

"I was just thinking of my aunt's reaction if she saw you eating raw beef."

"Oh, ha." Caroline's mouth quirked at the corners. "Tell me, any plans to go visit your aunt soon?"

Ronnie dropped her silverware. "What?"

"Are you going to visit your aunt soon?"

Ronnie shook her head. "No. I think she's left New York. She said she was going to Pakistan when we last spoke, and . . ."

"Let's not rehash that. Ronnie's dealt with enough," Marley said, trying to intervene.

"No, it's fine. I'm happy to answer any questions. I know I keep things to myself too much. It's just, you know, when you have someone like Shameem, you learn to keep secrets. To survive."

"Of course. Was it a cultural thing? The way your aunt was with you?" Caroline pressed.

Cultural. Because she was an oppressed person from an oppressive culture. Ronnie hated the stereotype. She hated even more that her aunt made her fit the stereotype. "Shameem? No, it was a *her* thing. There are bad people in every culture. You know, I used to wish my friend Farrah's parents would adopt me. They were just the nicest people. Are. I mean. They're still here. But no, I got Shameem." *Please drop it. Please don't ask me anymore. I don't want to rehash it just to make you like me.*

"Well, you survived. Good on you. Marley, what's the deal with the next rally? Have you talked to Lorraine?"

Ronnie let out a sigh of relief. Caroline was on to the next topic.

"She hasn't replied to my last email. I might go in person to sort it out."

"Good. And in the meantime, we can do a new video. Oh, have you seen DeeDee lately? Because you look a bit tired. Maybe get a facial?"

Marley blanched. "I do?"

"You've been working your butt off, of course you do. Don't worry, I'll set it all up. My treat. For both of you!"

Ronnie watched how Marley gracefully accepted the criticism and followed suit. *Smile, be nice, don't let Caroline suspect you had her questioned. Find out what papers she gave Marley. You can do this.*

"Oh, and I'd love your waxer's number," Ronnie said with a grin she absolutely didn't feel.

Chapter 56

Ronnie hadn't done anything wrong. She knew it. So why did she feel so awful? Maybe she should come clean to Marley. To really show her she had nothing to hide. Fallout be damned. Tell her everything. Keeping secrets was too exhausting.

The next morning, after a few Advil to quell her hangover, Ronnie went downstairs. There Marley was. She looked about as chipper as Ronnie felt.

"Morning. Ummmm . . ."

"Morning. What's up?"

"I need to tell you something. I don't want secrets between us, okay?"

Marley sat up straighter. "I'm listening." Her face was serious.

"I didn't call the sheriff on Caroline. But Star did. I told her what I'd overheard because I was trying to make sense of it, and also I thought it was funny. And she insisted on calling John, and I couldn't stop her. I didn't know that would happen."

Marley blinked a few times. "John? You call him by his first name now?"

"Oh, I don't know, that's what Star calls him," Ronnie stammered.

"Well, I'm glad you told me. But I don't like the influence the twins are having on you. Maybe you need to scale back working there a bit."

"But I love it there! I—"

Marley held up her hand. "You lied to me. And you eavesdropped. That's their influence. Just think about it. For now, we'll keep this between us. I don't want Caroline to get the wrong idea."

"Yeah, okay. Thank you. I'm sorry, it was just eating me up inside. I can't keep secrets from you."

"That's because secrets are bad. Any others you want to spill?" Marley said it with humor, her laugh trilling in the air. But Ronnie felt nothing but panic.

"No. Nothing. I'm good. Thanks."

"Good. I'm going to go see Lorraine. But don't share that with anyone. What we do shouldn't be spread around, understand?"

"Of course. You're right. I was being an awful friend."

Ronnie couldn't believe she had suspected Caroline—and Marley— of anything. They would never kill anyone. In fact, they were trying to make things safer. Maybe Marley was right? Maybe Star's influence was overwhelming her. But the idea of quitting was too much for her. She couldn't give up the twins. Couldn't she have Marley and them too?

Besides, the store was so full of her own ideas that she was loath to leave it.

Marley left before she did, and Ronnie wished her luck with Lorraine. More patrols. More rallies. Just what they didn't need.

Marley's bedroom door was open. Ronnie rarely went in there without permission. A holdover from Shameem's rule. She felt guilty even being there, but she had to find out what Caroline had given her. What did she know?

She went through each drawer, careful to put everything back the way Marley had had it. She found crystals, condoms, and a vibrator that looked like it was made from crystal. Ronnie didn't touch it, just kept looking.

Nothing. "Dammit!" She covered her mouth. She knew she was home alone, but still. And if she didn't get going, she'd be late for work.

Whatever Caroline had on her, it couldn't be anything. There was nothing. No one was after her. No one was tracking her down. No family members were chasing her. She was safe now. Right?

———

Ronnie was jumpy all day. Every time the door chimed—a sound she used to find soothing—she nearly had a heart attack. What if her family was looking for her? Then she laughed. No one was coming for her. No one cared where she was or what happened to her. And that was freedom.

"Deep breaths," she muttered.

"Pardon?" the customer standing before her asked.

"Oh, sorry, I'm just really anxious today. You know?"

"Yeah, I feel that!"

I'm sure you do, random lady on vacation. "Have a great day!"

When Brit came into the shop after lunch, she looked exhausted.

"Rough night?"

"I swear someone is stalking us. I keep finding weird things around the outside of the house. Like, just look what someone threw into one of our windows! They must not like us."

Brit was holding a crystal sphere. Not just any crystal sphere. It was the one Ronnie had given Caroline the night before.

"Oh, shit." *Dammit, this is my fault.*

"What?"

"I know who did that. I gave that crystal to Caroline. I know you hate her, but I'm trying to keep things calm at home, you know? I didn't know she'd do that. I'm so sorry." She had royally screwed up, and the only thing to do was throw herself on Brit's mercy. "Marley made a fuss about telling the sheriff what I overheard, and I panicked and gave her a crystal. That I paid for! I didn't steal it. Oh, god, I'm so sorry. I'm a terrible friend."

Brit nodded before smiling. "Well, at least we can sell it again, right?"

"Right! Is the window broken?"

"Glass everywhere. Caroline, huh? Should have guessed she was the one skulking around our land."

"What else has she done?"

"Stupid things, like putting birdseed all over the outside of our windows. It makes birds fly into them, and I hate that. Our tires were slashed. Someone left piles of sugar out to attract bugs. I thought it was neighborhood kids, but now, well . . ."

"Now you can call the sheriff and have him deal with it."

"Exactly. Ugh, I wish that woman would just disappear." It was as close to cursing anyone that Brit got. Star, on the other hand, would have said far worse.

"I'm sorry, this is my fault."

"No, it's not. You didn't know she was such a psycho."

"But I gave her your crystal! I'm a terrible friend, I'm so sorry." She was repeating herself, but all Ronnie could think was Brit would never have done that to her. It was a betrayal.

"You're not. How could you have known? But now you know she's evil. Just pure evil."

Ronnie nodded and watched the twin call John. If Caroline were arrested and charged, anything she said would be discredited. So Ronnie had nothing to worry about. Absolutely nothing. She was free. That's all that mattered.

For the second time that week, she found herself giving a statement to the sheriff.

"Now, you gave this to her last night?" He asked, holding the crystal with gloved hands.

"Yes, sir. It was a peace offering of sorts. Since she's always over with Marley, I wanted to, you know, stay friendly? But that was before

I knew what she would do. I swear, I never would have given that to her had I known."

She felt awful about it. How could she have been part of something that hurt the twins? And with merchandise from their own store?

John wrote it all down and went to arrest Caroline for criminal damage to property. It wasn't much, and he couldn't charge her with more. They had no proof she was the one messing with the twins. The cameras the twins had put up only caught an outline of a person, not her face.

"Brit, why don't you go home and sort out the window, and I'll watch the store?"

"You don't mind?"

"It's the least I can do. I'll bring you some food later, how's that?"

"You're a dream, Ronnie Khan. Do you know that?" Brit hugged her.

By the time Ronnie got home that night, Marley was asleep. She had stopped to bring dinner to the twins. Only Star had been home. She was furious about everything but had shared the news with her: Caroline had been arrested.

Shit was about to hit the fan, Ronnie thought. And this time, it was her fault.

Chapter 57

The Town

The ravens were watching as the light-haired woman went to the Center first and then to the older woman's house. Their enemy, the one who'd killed one of their own. They followed her from one place to the next. She was up to something, they could tell. Her energy was dark and soulless. More so than usual.

While she was at the woman's house, the ravens sat near windows. They wanted to see what would happen. And what they witnessed scared them. They saw her do something awful. And then hide the evidence in her trunk. She cleaned up all the blood the body had spilled.

Another murder, not one they'd expected. They weren't sure how to react to this. So they flew up en masse, making as much noise as possible. The light-haired woman stared at them before cursing. They knew her. She'd killed before. She'd killed one of their own.

The ravens weren't against killing. But it had to be for a reason. A purpose. A good one, at that. And there was no reason to have done what she did. We have to stop her before she kills anyone else, they said to each other. They'd have to kill her themselves if it came to it.

Chapter 58

"Yessss! Oh my goddess, look!" The next morning, Marley pointed to the email she'd gotten. "Lorraine said yes to the rally! I knew she would!"

"Really?" Ronnie said. She was drinking her coffee before work.

"Yeah, I just had to show her the good we're doing. Sure we had hiccups, but that's okay! Everyone does, right?"

"Right. So, uh, have you heard from Caroline?" She had to be the one to tell her. If Marley heard it from anyone else, she'd flip.

"Not since we had our dinner, which is kind of weird. Why?"

"I have news." Ronnie sat down next to Marley and took a deep breath. "I guess someone has been stalking the twins and damaging property. Anyways, you know that crystal I gave Caroline? The sphere? It was thrown through their window and broke glass. I think Caroline may have been arrested for it."

Marley stared at her. "I'm sorry, what? Caroline did what?" She shook her head as she said it.

"Apparently she's done other things, but they didn't know it was her until we saw the crystal and, well . . ."

"And you told them you gave it to her. Dammit, Ronnie!"

"No one made her go throw it! What was she even thinking! This is her fault!" It was! Ronnie hadn't done anything wrong. She had fought with herself all night about it.

Marley took a deep breath. "You're right. It is. I just, ugh. Why is everyone so nuts?"

"Maybe we need a healing session to bring the town together."

"What'd you say?" Marley stared at her, her eyes bright.

"A healing session?"

"That's genius. Genius!" Marley kissed her on the cheek and ran out of the kitchen while Ronnie sat there wondering what she'd just said that was so inspiring.

———

Star was waiting at the store when Ronnie showed up. "Thanks for dinner last night. I appreciate you."

"I appreciate you! How are you guys today?"

"Better. I'm glad they finally arrested Caroline. It's minor, but it's something. A record. You know?"

"Yeah. Marley was stunned. Guess she wasn't involved."

Star stared at her for a moment. "Good thing. Karma is a bitch."

Ronnie laughed at that and got busy with customers and tidying up. The spheres now felt tainted. She needed to come up with a new plan for them.

"You know, our revenue has gone up twenty percent since you started."

"It has? Wow!"

"Yeah, all your good ideas. Keep them up!"

"Of course!"

The high of that compliment stayed with her all day. She was helping! She was making changes! The twins loved her! Caroline was in jail! All good things. All reasons for Ronnie to relax, take a deep breath, and maybe let her guard down.

———

"Dammit!" Star slammed the phone down. "I haven't been able to get a hold of Lorraine. She's not at the Center and not picking up. I need to go make sure she's okay."

It was closing time, and Ronnie felt her mouth opening on its own. And offering to go with Star. "I can go with you if you like?" *Shit, why did I offer that?*

She didn't want to see Lorraine. But it was that or go home to Marley, who was probably moping about Caroline. The two of them staring at her with accusations in their eyes. No thanks to that.

Ronnie followed Star's Subaru to Lorraine's house, which was on a winding street with an immaculate view of rock formations. Now this was where to live! If Ronnie could ever get rich enough to buy a place in Lorraine's neighborhood, she would. If she could get over her fear of being tied to a place.

"I have a key," Star said and opened the door. "It's for emergencies, but . . ."

"Hopefully this isn't one."

"Right."

They turned on the lights and walked through the empty house. No one was home. "Lorraine? You here?"

"Is it possible she went away? I mean, I know she emailed Marley, so she has to be reachable."

"Emailed her when?" Star asked.

"This morning. About the rally."

"Dammit. Okay. Well, she's not here. I'll check the hospital just in case."

"I'm sure she's fine. Maybe she went to visit family? It's going to be okay." She put her hand on Star's.

"I know, you're probably right."

They locked up the house, leaving a few lights on in case Lorraine came home late. As they went to their cars, a raven cawed. Loudly.

"It's like it's trying to get our attention," Ronnie mused.

"Maybe it is. I wish they could tell us where Lorraine was."

———

Marley was still up when Ronnie got home. It was well after dark.

"Wow, they're making you work late!"

"No, Star couldn't find Lorraine, so we went to her house."

Marley paused, then cleared her throat. "And did you find her?"

"No. Maybe she went out of town. Did she say anything when you talked to her?"

"She did say she had a family thing to deal with? I'm not sure, to be honest. Anyways, I made you dinner."

"You . . . made me dinner?" Marley was many things, but a good cook wasn't one of them.

"Well, I picked it up for you. Close enough." She stuck her tongue out at her.

Ronnie laughed. "Thank you. You're such a good friend to me. I'm sorry things are so crazy." She opened the salad that Marley had bought. It was always a salad.

"Who knew this place was such a font of drama, right?"

"I guess every place is."

"I guess. Caroline is out of jail. She admitted what she'd done. I'm sorry I got you mixed up in all that. I hope it wasn't too awkward at work." Marley sounded sincere.

Ronnie was relieved that her friend knew the truth about Caroline. "It's fine, and the twins know you had nothing to do with it."

"Oh, that's a relief."

Maybe things could go back to normal soon.

Later that night, when Ronnie was about to fall asleep, she thought she heard the front door open. She had to have imagined it, right? That moment between waking and sleep, when dreams danced on the walls. She was just dreaming; she had to be. Where would Marley even go that late? She should have gotten up to check, but she was insanely tired. She couldn't keep her eyes open.

The next morning, Ronnie's head pounded. Her mouth was dry. She felt like she had a hangover even though she hadn't had any wine. She stumbled downstairs for much-needed coffee.

"Wow, you look like shit," Marley said. "You feeling okay?"

"I just feel tired. Coffee will help," Ronnie mumbled. Coffee. Every time she drank some instead of tea, she felt like she was giving a giant fuck-you to her aunt. (Shameem wouldn't let her drink such Amrikan things, never mind that she'd given Ronnie Coke and Pepsi since she was six.)

"Maybe you should stay home today?"

"Nah, the twins need me. I'll be fine." Ronnie's mug fell from her grip. It was as if her hand just decided to stop holding it. And down it went, shattering all over the floor. "Oh shit."

"I got it. I want you to go upstairs and rest. I'll call the twins. Okay? No arguing."

"Yes, Marley." This was what it felt like to be cared for. To be looked after and loved. Ronnie hated being sick but loved that she had someone who cared that she wasn't well.

Later that day she swore she heard voices near, but she was too groggy to figure out if they were real.

———

Before

Ronnie had a fever. She was half-delirious, but still, she was scrubbing the floor. Shameem insisted she finish her chores, even if she was under the weather.

Savita Auntie was over, and the two women were gupshupping on the sofa. Always gossiping, always saying terrible things. Ronnie marveled that anyone could stand them.

She stood up to go clear the tea tray from the coffee table. Her legs shook. Her hands trembled as she lifted everything.

"Be careful. I don't need you breaking my things," Shameem said.

Ronnie didn't reply. She didn't have the energy. She brought the tray to the kitchen counter and managed to not drop it. "Oh thank god," she muttered. And then everything went black as she fainted on the floor.

She woke up with the lights off and her body still lying on the kitchen floor. Her aunt had left her there, passed out. Judging by the new dirty dishes in the sink, she'd even stepped over her to get to the fridge.

Ronnie felt awful. Her head hurt. Her throat was scratchy. Her eyes burned. She pulled herself up—it took a few minutes—and gulped down as much water as she could. She found some Tylenol and took that and slowly went to her room, where she slept for three days.

When the fever finally broke, her aunt only said, "Finally. There's laundry waiting for you."

Chapter 59

THE TOWN

We tried to tell them. That's what the ravens kept saying to each other. They'd tried to tell the humans about what had happened to their friend. They'd tried telling their human, the dark-haired one. But no one would listen. Humans were the stupidest animals. They had to be.

Now they were watching another human. One they didn't like much. She was the one who threw things into houses, who stole. Her face had the marks from their talons. They hadn't faded enough, still healing. This woman was bad. And for whatever reason, still alive. They hoped not for long.

A shot rang out, and the birds scattered.

"Shoo! Get out of here!" She had a shotgun. None of them had been hit. But the woman holding the gun had meant for death. That bitch.

They'd make sure she got what was coming to her. Because nature was a system. And every action caused another action. And she couldn't try to kill them and get away with it.

Chapter 60

Ronnie felt back to normal the following morning. "Whew! That was weird."

"Maybe a minor bug?" Marley suggested.

"Maybe. I just felt so tired. Like drugged, you know?"

"Crazy. Well, take your vitamins."

She did, and she would push to eat something healthy at lunch. Not like it was hard to eat healthy here. But sometimes Ronnie just wanted a cheeseburger.

She drove to the store, where Star was waiting.

"Let's go," the twin said. She was locking up the store.

"Where are we going?"

"To Prescott. Lorraine's son lives there, and I want to see if she's with him."

"Can't we call?"

"I don't have his number. Besides, there's an In-N-Out there, and you haven't had one of their burgers yet." Star grinned at her. It was an offer Ronnie couldn't refuse. "And we can hang out. It'll be fun but useful."

"Whoa, how did you know I wanted a burger?"

"I'm psychic," Star joked.

"Girls' trip! How far is it?"

"Oh, just like an hour."

Ronnie had never been on any sort of road trip with anyone. Even the move out to Sedona had been via a plane. "Do we need snacks? And music?"

"It's an hour, so . . ." Star looked at her eager face. "You know what, sure. Let's get snacks and find a playlist." Ronnie clapped her hands with glee. Her first road trip! She packed bags of chips and granola and made a road playlist that had every woman-themed anthem she could find.

"If I'd known you'd never gone on a road trip, we'd have gone sooner." Star couldn't help laughing. The seriousness of their trip wasn't lost on either of them, but for a moment, they were having fun.

"I've always wanted to do one," Ronnie admitted.

"Maybe, at some point, we can do a real one? Like with motels and rest stops and photos."

"Really?! And like souvenirs? Because I'll need souvenirs."

"Fine. But I'm not wearing a silly shirt."

Ronnie grinned. She'd get her to wear the shirt.

"Didn't your aunt ever take you anywhere?" Star asked.

Ronnie shook her head. "Nope. She hated me. I don't mean that lightly. The woman outright despised me."

Star reached for her hand. "Hey, it's fine. She can't hurt you any-more, right? You're free."

"Right. I just . . . I don't want to look back because so much was out of my own control, you know? Like, I was a kid. But now I'm going to do everything I've always wanted. With you and Brit."

"I like that idea! Count us in!"

———

Lorraine's son, Robert, hadn't heard from her or seen her. The trip was a bust. But the burgers? Delicious.

"Oh god, I could eat these every day," Ronnie said, taking another bite of her double cheeseburger.

"Right? They're the main reason I can't go vegan." Star laughed.

"I'm sorry we didn't find Lorraine. Brit told me what she did, how she helped find her. I hope we can repay that favor."

"That's a very kind thing of you to say."

But Ronnie could see the worry on Star's face. Lorraine had all but vanished. "Maybe you should call the sheriff?"

"I have. He wanted us to check with Robert. And now, I guess he can issue a missing person report."

The words alone sent a chill down Ronnie's back. Missing. Was Lorraine missing? She'd thought she was just away.

"I'm glad you're feeling better, by the way."

"Me too! That was such a weird bug. I felt drugged. Like I couldn't open my eyes."

"Weird." Star tilted her head and looked at her face. "Did you take any sleeping pills?"

"Nope. I never do."

"Maybe you *were* drugged."

"That's impossible, I only ate a salad that night."

"From where?"

"No idea, Marley got it for me . . . no, not possible. I know what you're thinking. And Marley would never."

Star shrugged. "Anything's possible."

Anything was, but her Marley wouldn't do something like that. She just wouldn't.

Ronnie was eager to tell Marley about her first-ever road trip, but when she walked in, her friend was yelling into the phone.

"What is wrong with you? How could you think that was a good idea?"

Ronnie crept into the house quietly. She didn't want to interrupt— and then have the bad mood transferred to her.

"What were you thinking, Caro?" Caroline. Of course. "And now you have an arrest record. What the hell!"

She went to the kitchen and grinned. This was it. Caroline was going to be gone. No way would Marley risk everything for someone who couldn't control themselves. They would finally be free from Caroline and her prying.

"I think Ronnie will take over helping me for now. I just can't risk our patrols because you did something stupid."

What? Ronnie would what? She wanted nothing to do with the patrols. Not one thing.

Marley got off the phone and wandered into the kitchen. "Well, I guess we need to go without Caroline for a while. The whole twins thing is too much. Why'd she have to do that?"

Ronnie poured her a glass of wine. "I'm sorry. I know how much she means to you."

Marley shrugged. "Everyone's gone nuts."

They sat for a while, just talking. Ronnie had missed this. She'd missed her friend.

"How's work?"

"Really good!" Ronnie said. "I'm actually in charge of things! Me!" She laughed. "Did you ever think that would happen?"

"Yes, I did! You have so much potential in you!"

"Whatever." She rolled her eyes, and they laughed. They spent most of the night drinking wine and talking, like old times. Like before Caroline had come into the picture.

The doorbell interrupted them. And then pounding.

"What the hell?"

Ronnie went to open the door, and Caroline pushed past her. She was a mess, her hair disheveled, her clothes ripped. And was that blood?

"I've just been attacked," Caroline said. "The Slasher tried to kill me. But I got away. Oh my god."

She sank onto the sofa, and all Ronnie could think was how she would get any bloodstains out of the fabric.

"What?! Are you okay?" Marley ran over and sat next to Caroline, cradling her. Ronnie shut the door.

"We should call the police," she said.

"No. No!" Caroline shook her head. "Not after what they did, arresting me like that."

"But you can help put this person away."

"Ron's right, we have to call them," Marley insisted.

Ronnie bandaged up Caroline's bleeding arm—it wasn't a deep cut, just enough to make a mess—and then poured wine for them all while they waited for the sheriff. Caroline had been attacked. That meant she couldn't be the killer. Ronnie had been wrong about her. And that made her more confused than ever. If Caroline wasn't the Slasher, who was?

John came pretty quickly and sat with Caroline while Marley and Ronnie waited in the kitchen.

"I should be with her," Marley said.

"Let him do his job and then you will be."

"God, I shouldn't have yelled at her."

"You didn't know!"

They could hear the interview from where they stood.

"It was so dark out. Someone grabbed me from behind. I didn't even see them! I think they must have been in all black? And then I fought like a demon in hell."

She'd seen nothing. She'd recognized no one. And she was alive. Ronnie wasn't sure why, but she didn't believe the story. No one else had escaped the Slasher. Just Caroline. Why was she so special that she'd escaped?

It was a while before John left. "Caroline, I'll need you to come to the station tomorrow to go over all of this. Okay?"

"Sure, whatever you need."

They watched him leave, and Ronnie bolted the door.

"That's it, you have to stay with us from now on. It's not safe for you out there," Marley declared. Ronnie's heart sank. She knew she was about to have to give up her room. Just like before.

"No, I'm okay. I'll stay here tonight, though. I promise, I'm fine." Caroline's eyes were watching her. Ronnie felt them on her.

"Ronnie, can you sleep on the sofa tonight? Just one night."

"Sure." She couldn't say no. This was Marley's house and Marley's friend, and she had no say.

As she was getting pillows and bedding and changing her own sheets, Caroline watched. And then as she was about to go downstairs, the woman hugged her. Tight.

"Thank you, Ronnie. So kind of you." And in a quieter voice only Ronnie could hear, she said, "I always get what I want."

———

The next morning, Ronnie woke up in the worst mood. Her back ached; she had slept poorly. But Caroline looked well rested and cheerful, and she hated her for that.

Star texted her. A missing person report had gone out. It was a silver alert for missing elders. Ronnie found Lorraine deeply irritating and a little racist (okay, maybe a lot), but she hoped they'd find her. If only for the twins' sake. The idea of a confused older woman wandering the trails made her worry.

Marley seemed unconcerned about Lorraine's whereabouts.

"I'm sure Lorraine is just away. She has a life," Marley said, dismissing Ronnie's concerns with a wave of her hand.

"Should you still be planning the rally if she's missing?"

Marley stopped moving and turned to stare at Ronnie as if she had grown three heads. "Yes, of course. My work must go on. My followers need me. We can't abandon them just because Lorraine is off who knows where."

"Marley's right. We need to keep going," Caroline said. "Sorry if I got you into hot water with that crystal, by the way. I don't know what I was thinking. I saw their house, and I couldn't resist. My bad." She said it like it was an oopsie and not a crime. "Your bed is so comfy! I could sleep there forever!"

"Isn't it? Way better than the sofa."

"You're a dear for letting me use your room. I can't believe I was almost killed last night."

Liar. Ronnie knew she was lying. She had to be. The scratch was superficial at best. And now Marley was putty in Caroline's hands.

"I'm just so happy you weren't hurt. Everything else is water under the bridge. Right, Ron?"

"Uh, right."

"You two are the best." And then Caroline got up and hugged them both. Ronnie felt stiff and couldn't relax. This woman was a fraud. Did no one else see that?

"You know what we need?" Marley asked. "Facials. We both look awful. Right, Caro?" Ronnie gritted her teeth every time Marley called her friend that. Caro.

"Right. DeeDee. She's a must."

"Oh." DeeDee. She was the one who did facials with needles. "Well, have fun!" Ronnie was happy to skip this one.

"You're getting one too. She'll be here in the morning. Before work. Easy peasy, and you'll look divine. For me?"

For Marley. Could she ever say no?

———

The next morning, Marley ran to the door while Ronnie was still drinking coffee. Caroline was on her way over. Ronnie, thankfully, had had her own bed to sleep in.

"Welcome, please come in. Let's set up in the kitchen."

"I don't usually do house calls," DeeDee said. "But . . ."

"But I'm paying you for your time, so it'll be great. You'll see." She watched as DeeDee set up everything she needed. There were tubes and syringes and gloves and something that looked a bit like an Easy-Bake Oven.

"For the blood," DeeDee said.

"Wow, that's a lot of equipment." Just seeing it all made Ronnie feel faint. Why did she have to do a blood facial anyways?

"You remember DeeDee, don't you?" Marley gestured to the woman, who was wearing gloves and arranging things just so. Ronnie didn't bother pointing out that she hadn't met DeeDee before; only Marley had met her.

"Do you have to use my blood for the facial?" Ronnie asked. "I hate needles."

"Well yes, of course. That's why we're here, isn't it?" DeeDee smiled at her. "I promise it'll be painless. You won't feel it at all."

Ronnie swallowed nervously. She didn't know how to get herself out of this situation. How to say no. How to walk out. The thought of doing any of that made her nauseous.

"Listen." Marley gripped her wrist so hard Ronnie whimpered. "You will do this for me because you're family. You're my sister. You're loyal to me." She smiled, softly. "I need this. And later we can talk about something Caroline found."

"I . . . fine." There was no way for her to win this. She had to give in. Besides, Marley was her friend. This was good, right? Who hated a facial?

"Okay then. Let's begin."

DeeDee tied a tourniquet around Ronnie's arm, on the fleshy part above her elbow. Ronnie didn't say a word as the woman filled tubes with her blood, placing each one in the warmer. One tube held ten milliliters. DeeDee had ten tubes to fill. She did it patiently, efficiently. She could have been a nurse instead of an aesthetician.

"Are you feeling okay?" she asked Ronnie, who looked a bit pale.

"I guess."

"Nearly done." It had taken mere minutes to fill them all. "There," DeeDee added. "Just gonna put a piece of cotton and a Band-Aid on, and you're all good. Marley, do you have anything with sugar for her? Juice or a cookie?"

"Uh, sure. Here." She poured some organic orange juice for Ronnie. Ronnie gladly took it. She felt faint. She hadn't remembered them needing so many vials for her previous facial. "Ooh, Caro's here." Marley let her friend in.

"Good morning, all!" Caroline sang out.

"You may feel faint, just stay sitting and don't move, okay?" DeeDee nodded at Ronnie and then turned her attention to the other women.

"Finally. Let's do this."

"Normally I'd have to test the blood and—"

"It's fine, Ronnie's clean. Now get to it." Marley was getting impatient.

Ronnie watched as her friend got her facial done. But DeeDee didn't take any blood from Marley. Instead, she used four vials of Ronnie's blood on her friend. That's why Marley had wanted her to do this. To use her blood. But why?

"Why aren't you using her blood?" she asked. Her tongue felt heavy as she said it. Maybe she was just confused?

"Because yours has melanin, and that makes it better and more valuable," Marley said. "It's a theory I'm working on. Your skin is better than mine, so I wanted to even it up a bit. Give my cells a supercharge."

"So . . . you're using my blood? Isn't melanin in the skin?"

"We both are." Caroline grinned at her. "It's fine. It's just a facial. Don't worry so much."

Ronnie wasn't worried. She was mad. How could her friend do that? And without asking her? She stood up, and the room started to swirl around her. A flash of déjà vu hit. This was in her dream. She'd seen this happen already. Marley would wear her blood like a grotesque mask. Was this how Ronnie died? For a beauty treatment?

"I don't—" She meant to say *feel good* but didn't get the words out. Instead, she fainted.

Ronnie woke up on the sofa. Her bandage was still on her arm. DeeDee and Caroline were gone. And Marley was somewhere; she didn't know where.

Her blood. Her friend had used her blood to look good. And Caroline had too. This had to have been her idea. It was all too gruesome for Ronnie to process. She pushed up onto her elbows. She had to get up. She had to go to work.

Chapter 61

November

Marley's event was finally happening. The Kismet Center was full of members, Marley's people, stragglers, anyone who wanted to join. They were here to heal the community and to listen to Marley. There was a sound bath being performed in the garden. Caroline stood next to Marley, beaming. This was the only way she'd ever get into the Center after what she had done to Brit. With Lorraine still missing, no one had stopped Marley from holding her rally.

Ronnie took it all in. She wanted to leave, but after the facial, Marley had made it clear that this was priority number one. Not Ronnie. Not Ronnie's life. This event and her followers were what mattered.

"You're either with me or against me," Marley had said. "And if you were against me . . ." The threat was there. Ronnie didn't know what had happened to Marley, what Caroline had whispered in her ears about her. But this wasn't the Marley she knew. The one who had been so happy whenever Ronnie stood up for herself.

Ronnie hated being manipulated. Shameem constantly twisted things around. If she did X, she could do Y. She hated that her friend was reminding her more and more of her aunt. And she was certain the root cause of all this badness was Caroline. Whose skin looked fucking glowing, to add insult to injury.

The twins weren't there. That didn't surprise her one bit. They were still looking for Lorraine. Search parties had been going over various trails and areas Lorraine liked to visit. No one could find her. And the longer she was missing, the less likely it was she was going to return.

"Everyone, let's all come together and pray for our friend Lorraine," Marley called, and the crowd joined hands. Ronnie held someone's sweaty palm and wished for some Purell to clean her hands.

"Lorraine, we are sending love. We need you, we must find you—alive. Together, we will. This is why we need our patrols. If we were patrolling, we'd find her. So I ask all of you to help me. Sign up for a patrol. Do it for Lorraine."

For Lorraine. Ronnie wanted to scream. All of this wasn't for the community or safety. It was for Marley and her vanity and her need to have followers. Her blood wasn't healing her friend; it had been used to make her face pretty.

Ronnie was used to betrayal. All kinds of betrayal. But this one cut her deep.

Marley continued on, talking about the good of the community, keeping Sedona safe, keeping eyes on those who didn't belong. It was chilling. This woman who'd espoused love and light now wanted to scare people.

"We know who our people are. Who belongs here. And let me tell you, the person doing these heinous crimes is not one of us! There's no way anyone we know could be capable of this." The crowd clapped and cheered her on. They, too, were sick of the murders. The fire that had killed Peter had taken a few popular campgrounds with it.

In the midst of all of it, Star walked in. She cut through the crowd with Sheriff Reynolds behind her. She stood glaring at Marley.

"Sedona needs us. Lorraine needs us . . ." Marley trailed off as all eyes shifted to Star.

"Everyone, I have an announcement," the sheriff said and cleared his throat. "We've found the remains of Lorraine Williams." The remains. The crowd processed his words, and horror started to spread. Lorraine was dead. "It appears she was attacked and then left in the desert between here and Cottonwood."

Gasps surrounded them. Lorraine was dead? Their Lorraine?

"Do you have any leads?" Marley asked, raising her voice so she'd be heard over the crowd.

"It's an ongoing investigation. We are looking at all leads."

"Everyone. Please. Calm yourselves. You see why we need patrols? You see why we must do this? Lorraine would still be here if we'd been patrolling."

"How dare you." Star moved so fast no one could stop her. She slapped Marley. "This is all your fault. Get out of here. And you. You are never welcome on this property," she hissed at Caroline, who so far had remained silent.

"I was attacked by the Slasher a few nights ago," Caroline said, her chin rising to show she wasn't cowed. "I'm a victim here."

"Liar!" Star said.

"Star, she's right. I took her statement," the sheriff interrupted.

"And we have approval to be here," Marley said. "Lorraine said we could do this."

"Lorraine's dead. It's now up to the owners of the property, and that's me. And Brit. And you don't have our permission. Get out!"

Ronnie gasped. They owned the Center? Why hadn't they told her? She saw Marley's face. She shrugged to show she'd had no idea. But she knew Marley. Her friend was about to be so mad.

"Wait, I need to question them. Then they can leave," the sheriff said. Star nodded and walked over to Ronnie.

"I'm sorry," Ronnie said quietly. She put her arm around the twin and waited for the sheriff and his team to question folks. She could feel Marley glaring at her. But Star needed her. And surely Marley would understand that?

The sheriff questioned everyone one by one, making people wait in the garden for hours. Marley and Caroline hovered in a corner together, whispering. People stared at them. Ronnie did; she couldn't help it. Lorraine was dead? And Caroline had wanted that to happen. Caroline had laughed about it.

Ronnie stayed with Star. It felt like the right thing to do. It was clear battle lines had been drawn, and she had to choose even if she didn't want to.

"Star, you holding up okay?" the sheriff asked.

"No. This is the worst. And I know who did it. We all know who did it!" Her voice rose on the last part so everyone heard. "Caroline! You wanted Lorraine dead. You said so. And now she is. Arrest her! She did it!"

"You're not helping," John said. "Ronnie?"

"I got it." She put her arms around her friend, hugging her until Star stopped shouting and instead started sobbing. Slowly, Ronnie led her out and drove her home. There was no need for her friend to deal with this. Ronnie would do whatever was needed; her friend had to rest.

She got Star into the house, which she had only visited a few times. It was small but cozy. And sat on acres of land. The twins could build an entirely new house if they wanted. But they didn't. This was where they'd grown up. This was their home.

She poured some water and handed it to Star.

"I could use something stronger. There's whiskey in that cabinet."

Ronnie dutifully poured some for her friend and watched her drink it.

"I know I shouldn't have said anything, but her being there was infuriating. We all know she's behind this. This is on her!"

"I know, it's okay. Do you want me to call Brit?"

"No, I'm fine. Can you hang out for a while?"

"Of course. Anything you need." Ronnie ignored the buzzing of her phone. She knew it would only be Marley asking why she'd done it. Why she'd helped Star instead of her. And that wasn't a discussion Ronnie wanted to have.

She stayed over with Star awhile before she was sent home.

"Brit's on her way. You should go deal with Marley. I'm sorry if I got you in any hot water."

"It's okay." Ronnie shrugged, sounding braver than she felt. "You needed me. That's what friends do."

"Sisters. You're practically becoming family."

———

Ronnie quietly opened the front door. Marley's car was in the garage. Her friend was home. Hopefully she was asleep.

She tiptoed in, not turning on too many lights. Suddenly a light snapped on.

"You're home." Marley sat on the sofa, her eyes wild. Her hair was a mess. An empty wine bottle sat on the table in front of her. "How's Star?" The way she said the name made Ronnie shiver.

"She's okay. She's taking the news kind of hard—"

"You left me."

"I had to. And you had Caroline. You weren't alone."

"Did you know who owned the Center?"

They were going to do this now. Ronnie groaned. "No. I didn't. The most they ever mentioned was that they owned the land their store is on. And other plots. I didn't ask for details. I'm tired, I'm going to bed."

"No, you're not. You know what I can't figure out? You. You act all sweet and oblivious, but when shit happens, you run to people who haven't done shit for you. Not like I have. I've done everything for you! I moved you here! I helped you leave your shitty family! And this is the thanks I get! You left me when I needed you!"

Ronnie opened and closed her mouth a few times.

"This isn't the Ronnie I know!" Marley shrieked.

Ronnie sighed. "I gave you my blood. Isn't that enough to show you what you mean to me?"

"No, it's not. You're either with me or against me, Ronnie."

"So you've said. What does that mean? Choose you and ditch Star, or else?" She had friends now. Real friends. More than one! Ronnie couldn't give that up.

"It means watch out. If you betray me again, I'll fight back."

Marley stood up and stumbled up the stairs to her room. *She's just drunk, she doesn't mean it. Deal with it tomorrow.* But Ronnie couldn't shake it off. It reminded her too much of her aunt, yelling at how she'd given up her life for Ronnie. Was Ronnie the selfish one? Or had she just replaced Shameem with an Amrikan version of her?

The idea made her nauseous. She threw up before passing out from exhaustion.

Chapter 62

Marley ignored Ronnie the next day. She made breakfast and had her coffee, and all Ronnie heard was the front door slamming as she came down to a messy kitchen.

"Great," she said to the empty house. She cleaned up—leaving bowls and dirty dishes was not something she could do. And then she texted the twins to check on them. Brit said they were staying home, but Ronnie could open up the shop.

Which was fine by her. Ronnie—though she wouldn't admit it—was exhausted. Everything here was so fraught with emotion. Everywhere she stepped, it was as if another person needed something. This was what being a normal adult was—she surmised—but it was still so new to her.

Being at the store was a reprieve. She could relax. She loved it there. And Marley wanted to take that away. Though customers came and went, sales were down that day. And she had a feeling it had to do with the red-shirt-wearing patrols outside, accosting anyone whose looks they didn't like.

"Ugh." She went out with a broom as if to shoo them away. "You can't scare customers away. Get off this corner and go elsewhere. Go on!" She had done it without thinking. Without prepping herself for every possible thing that could go wrong. She had seen what needed to be done and did it. *This is progress! Holy shit, I'm making progress!*

"We work for Marley."

"Well, tell Marley you're on private property, and if you come back, we'll call the cops." We, like she had backup. But Ronnie felt brave. She felt emboldened. Marley was already mad at her. What did it matter if she got even angrier?

The red shirts did as she ordered but glared at her. Ronnie stuck her tongue out at them. It felt amazing.

———

Before

Shameem had been screaming at her all day. It started to sound like background noise.

"Clean up! Why is it so dirty in here? You're so lazy!"

"This chai tastes awful! Make more!"

"Where's my rusk? How can we be out? Go get some!"

At some point, Ronnie was certain she'd be able to tune her aunt out completely. That would be heaven. Instead, she cleaned and went to the store and made more chai. Only to have more yelling ensue. It didn't matter what she did; it was always wrong. So why was she trying?

She got to work late, thanks to Shameem Khala. She apologized to Farrah.

"I'm so sorry. Shameem made me clean the house first thing."

Her boss looked at her, puzzled. "Why do you let her do that? Control you?"

"You know how it is. Besides, it's her house. I should be thankful she lets me stay there."

"No, it's not. I asked my parents, and they're pretty sure your parents left it to you."

To her? It was her house? "I'm sorry, what?"

"That's your house. You need to check on that because if so, you can throw Shameem out."

Ronnie laughed. It was bitter and angry. "You know I'd never be able to do that. Imagine what the aunties would say."

"God, I hate them," Farrah said with a sympathetic smile.

"Me too."

———

Ronnie worked late. They weren't busy; there were no customers. But she dreaded going home. She didn't want to deal with Marley. Maybe she could sleep at the store? There was a bathroom in the back. She could make it work. Worst case. She always had to think out the worst case.

She sneaked into the front door and this time, no Marley. No accusations. No fighting. Ronnie tiptoed up to her room and let out a sigh of relief. Everything was fine. She had nothing to worry about.

That feeling didn't last.

On her bed was an eviction notice. Marley was throwing her out.

Can we talk? Ronnie texted Marley. She had psyched herself up to do this. To discuss what Marley wanted—for her to leave.

If you like. Marley's text was cold. Impersonal. As if Ronnie were a stranger to her.

I'm sorry if it felt like I was choosing Star over you. She had just lost someone important to her. And I wanted to be there for her. But I didn't mean to neglect you either.

But you did neglect me. You turned your back on me. The one person who was there for you. And this is how you thank me?

Ronnie blinked. Déjà vu. All of this was déjà vu. Marley, you mean the world to me. But I can have more than one friend.

You can. But I think it's better if you don't live here anymore. You have thirty days to vacate. And then Caroline is moving in.

Of course. She'd known it was coming. This was what Caroline had wanted. To get closer to Marley, to get rid of Ronnie. It was always going to be like this. Caroline was who Marley was looking for. Not Ronnie.

If that's how you feel, fine.

She wasn't going to beg. She wasn't going to plead and cry, like she'd done when Shameem always threatened her. No, she'd be an adult. She'd move out. This was part of life. She could do this.

Ronnie took being alone as a good opportunity to pack her things. Not like she had a lot of stuff. Two suitcases were all she'd come with, and it was all she'd leave with. Marley hadn't said anything about leaving the clothes she'd bought her, but Ronnie didn't want them. She left the caftans piled on the bed. The only things missing were her mother's gold jewelry, her raven's feather, and the black tourmaline Star had given her months earlier, all of which she found in Marley's room. "Just like Shameem," she muttered. Her words shocked her. Marley—despite her behavior—wasn't like Shameem. Was she?

"Goodbye," she said to the house before locking up and leaving the key under the doormat.

———

The back room at the store wasn't so bad. Ronnie bought an air mattress to sleep on. And during the day, she turned it into a nice break area, the mattress up against the wall. She added a table and a lamp, and with her two suitcases, she was all set. This was temporary. But Ronnie couldn't wait out the thirty days. The idea of living with Marley knowing her friend despised her, well, it was too much for her to handle. Ronnie had already lived that life. She wasn't going to do it again.

And now she could throw herself into work. With Brit and Star dealing with Lorraine's funeral arrangements, Ronnie had free rein of the place. She moved things around some more; she added new products. She even had an area for carbon-neutral crystals—crystals that required no mining and caused no environmental issues. (Customers were shocked to find out their beloved crystals had a human and climate toll.)

"Wow, it looks incredible in here!" Brit said, standing in the shop for the first time in a week.

"Brit!" Ronnie ran over to hug her. "Oh my god, I've missed you."

"I missed you too! Wow, this place looks even better than before." She walked around the new displays Ronnie had made, nodding her approval. "I'm sorry we left you to run things."

"No, it's fine. I'm so sorry about Lorraine."

"Thank you. Wow, seriously, this looks like a whole different store!"

"Is that okay?" Had she fucked up here too?

"Is it okay? Of course it is! I love it!"

Ronnie almost cried from relief. She was running out of places to go. If the twins hated her work, she would have nowhere. Nothing.

Customers came in, interrupting their conversation. Ronnie wanted to tell Brit about her living there. Until she found a place. But she didn't get a chance until they were alone.

"Want to tell me what's up with your new digs?" Brit asked, nodding her head to the back room.

"Marley kicked me out because I comforted Star and not her. And Caroline says she was attacked, so now she's living with her."

"You're kidding. Oh my god, are you okay?" Brit covered her mouth in shock.

"Yeah, I am. This is temporary. I need to find a place, and I will. I'm sorry, I should have asked, but you had so much going on."

"No, it's fine. But you could have asked to stay with us at the house."

"I don't know. I kind of want my own place. I've never lived alone. Though I may borrow your shower soon?"

"Anytime! Are you okay about all of this?"

Ronnie nodded and didn't notice she was crying. "Shit. I'm sorry. I'm putting my problems on you when you're dealing with so much. It stings, but I think this is for the best. But let me tell you, Caroline is lying. She's absolutely lying. If the Slasher had gone after her, she'd be dead."

"She probably is lying. But we're here if and when you need us. Now, why don't you run over to our place and shower." Brit handed her keys over. "I'll hold down the fort."

———

Lorraine's body was released from the morgue later that week. The autopsy concluded she'd died from blunt force trauma. Hit on the head and left to die in the desert. The idea of dying out there, alone, was overwhelmingly sad to Ronnie. After all Lorraine had done for the town, this was how she ended up. Like roadkill.

Star and Brit planned the funeral and memorial service. They handled it all, including a gathering at the Kismet Center, where everyone could pay their respects.

Ronnie went, of course. She had to be there for her friends. She was in charge of receiving and greeting people, which, a few months ago, would have terrified her. But now, she knew a lot of the faces even if she couldn't place their names.

"Nah-mah-stay, Rania," various people said, bowing to her. She let it pass. For Lorraine.

"Should have known you'd be here," Marley said. She and Caroline smirked at her. "You left a bunch of clothes, by the way." Her tone stung. She didn't care about Ronnie.

"Just those caftans you bought that I hated." Ronnie said it with a smile despite wanting her former friend to forgive her. *You can do this. You can stand up for yourself.*

Caroline laughed.

"You two, out. You're not welcome here," Star shouted. "This is a private service."

"We only came to pay our respects."

"Really? Did you now? Get out."

Ronnie was relieved she didn't have to do it. She was also shocked Marley had dared to show up after the last time she'd been here. But Marley wasn't her problem anymore. Or so she kept telling herself.

She watched Caroline and Marley leave, while Star glared at them. *If looks could kill,* she thought. Caroline shot one glance back at Ronnie. It was a knowing smirk. Ronnie had never wanted to wipe a look off someone's face so badly before.

"We're starting soon if you want to come to the back garden," Star said gently to her.

"Sure thing."

The garden had been Lorraine's favorite spot. Her perfect oasis, filled with flowers and birds. The most incredible succulents were here, in all kinds of shapes. And the flowers were stunning. Roses loved the climate, apparently. It was as peaceful a place as any.

Everyone was wearing white and holding candles. They looked like cult members, Ronnie thought. And then chastised herself for being insensitive.

There was a sound bath playing—like at Marley's rally. Only this one was softer, less upbeat but more beautiful. Brit was the one performing it. And for a moment, Ronnie thought she was going to burst into tears, the sound was so beautiful and moving. It was as if Brit had tapped into her very soul. Everyone stood around nodding and then finally, silence. Ronnie caught Brit's eye and smiled at her. And then the speeches began.

"Lorraine was Sedona. We wouldn't be here if it weren't for her."

"She was like a mother to us all."

"This loss will be felt for days to come."

Finally, Brit got up to speak. "Lorraine was family to us. As you all may know, she helped save my life. She made sure to never give up on me. On any of us. And with her help, Star was able to find me after an unscrupulous person took advantage. I wish we had been able to save her. But to the person who did this: We will find you. We will avenge Lorraine. You do not belong in our town."

Everyone was starting to sound more and more like Marley. It made Ronnie queasy.

"Rania, your turn!" someone urged and pushed her to the front.

"What? Oh no." No, she didn't have anything to say. But the microphone was thrust into her hand, and she had no choice. "Um, I'm Ronnie. Rania. And I didn't know Lorraine well. But she welcomed me here, my new home. And I know she'd want us to catch the person who did this but also to stay welcoming. To Lorraine."

"To Lorraine!" echoed back at her.

She handed the mic to anyone who would take it, before walking to a more deserted part of the garden. It was just her in a chair—and a raven. It sat on the grass next to Ronnie's seat and watched her.

"You're still my friend, right?" she asked.

The bird stared at her before cawing and taking off.

Chapter 63

The Town

She went to Lorraine's service. She had to. But she wasn't the one who'd killed Lorraine. Someone else had done the honors, and she needed to find out who.

So she watched the crowd. They said killers always showed up to these. Which was sort of true. She had for Fiona. And Matt. Not so much for Peter because his funeral had been held out of town. Which was fine by her. She didn't have anything nice to say about him.

Everyone was crying for Lorraine. She wasn't. She had a job to do: she had to figure out who'd killed the woman. Because they'd be next on her list. After her current project, of course.

"To Lorraine!" she called out, and everyone cheered. The ravens in the trees watched. They knew what was happening. They, too, mourned. Not Lorraine, but in general.

They were watching too. For the killer. Maybe they knew who it was. She'd have to ask them to show her. But not now. Now, they had to mourn.

Before she left, she stopped in Lorraine's office and offered up a prayer for the woman. "I'll find who did this. So go rest in peace."

Chapter 64

The twins took more time off from the shop to deal with Lorraine's death and the fallout. They had to take over the day-to-day business of the Center, leaving them no time for the store. Ronnie felt awful—for them—and sure, she felt bad the older woman had died. But she relished being in the store. It was becoming hers. A place she could feel herself. She made the decisions; she chatted up customers like she'd always been there, as if the crystals were hers. And she quite literally lived there, though she was hunting for a place to call her own.

"Do you guys ever have events here?" one woman asked.

"No, but we do some with the Kismet Center, but that's on hold. The founder passed."

"Oh, how terrible."

Events at the store—there was a thought. That would bring even more traffic in. More sales. Ronnie brainstormed things they could add on and went around to the neighboring shops to see if they wanted to do an event. A holiday open house of sorts, with food and drinks. People could mill about, buy things. After the summer they'd had, they could all use the sales.

It would be like a fair. Everyone liked fairs.

In between all of this, she saw red shirts everywhere. Marley's Eyes shirts were more prevalent than cowboy hats. *More like Marley's Spies,* she thought. They were standing around, glaring at people, and being a nuisance. Though one did offer directions to a lost tourist, so that was nice.

They didn't say anything to Ronnie, just stared at her and stayed off any property that was the twins'.

Every corner along State Route 89A—which was the main strip for shopping and dining in Sedona—always had two red shirts. This time around, there were more of them. As if with Lorraine's death, they had grown, sprouted new bodies. More had joined their flock, eager to keep Sedona safe. Or their version of safe.

Marley was everywhere, seeing all. The idea of her ex-friend seeing everything made Ronnie nervous. She wanted Marley to either forgive her and move on or to leave her alone. This middle place was hell. Ronnie couldn't move forward with her. She wasn't sure what to do. She hadn't been wrong; she knew that. You could have more than one friend. But Marley didn't agree.

Several red shirts had already done citizen's arrests, forcing the sheriff to come out and deal with them. The arrests were for minor things, like littering or smoking. No one was ever booked. And the sheriff, instead, arrested some of Marley's helpers. Ronnie saw the arrests happen and saw John's tired face. She nodded at him. He, in turn, came into the store.

"The twins around?"

"No, they're dealing with the Center. How are you holding up?" She handed him a bottle of cold water she kept for customers, another new thing. She'd had a fridge installed behind the counter, which also helped her whole living situation.

"Been better. No closer to finding out who killed Lorraine. So we're trying to re-create her final days off her calendar."

"Smart! I hope you find the person. And soon. Maybe then the red shirts will stop."

"They're more trouble than anything else. The mayor loves it, though." He sounded disgusted. "When you see Marley, tell her I'm looking for her. Just to go over her statement about when she last saw Lorraine."

"Oh, um, I don't live with her anymore. I'm looking for a place if you hear of anything."

"Oh, I'm sorry about that. Probably for the best."

"Probably. You know, she had a meeting with Lorraine pretty close to the day she disappeared." She should have felt guilty for telling on Marley. But they weren't friends anymore. Right? This was okay? Ronnie honestly had no idea. "Maybe Lorraine said something to her?"

"Good to know."

At least he wasn't questioning Ronnie. That was a small favor she'd accept. "Oh, before you go, here's a flyer for our open house event. Would love for you to come."

He took it and nodded, thanked her for the water, and left.

———

The twins took turns coming over in the evenings to keep her company. Ronnie didn't want to intrude on their grief, so she gave them space. But she was so glad to see her friends.

"How are you feeling about the whole Marley thing?" Brit asked (it was her night with Ronnie). She'd brought over burgers and fries, and Ronnie was grateful for the company.

"Awful? It feels just like when I left home. She's so angry at me, and I don't know how to get her to see I can have more than one friend."

"I think it's more that she hates us."

"How can anyone hate you guys?"

Brit shrugged, popping a fry into her mouth. "Sometimes people come into your life for a reason. And once they fulfill that, they move on."

"So what was Marley's purpose in my life?"

Brit shrugged. "To bring you here, I think."

"I hadn't thought of it like that," Ronnie admitted. "I like that way of thinking. She had a purpose in my life, and now it's time to move on."

"Exactly! How's the house hunt going?"

"I was thinking of an apartment, to be honest."

"Really? Because there are so many houses you could afford."

Ronnie wasn't sure about buying a place. A permanent home, all hers. Something she wanted and would decorate herself. "Oh. Yeah, I don't know."

"Well, let me know because that house near us is for sale still. It's not a big house, and I feel like you'll love it. Want to go see it tomorrow?"

"Star mentioned that before. And hell yes, I'd love to see it!" Imagine, her next door to the twins? It was perfect.

After Brit left and Ronnie went to sleep on her air mattress, she dreamed another one of those dreams. The ravens came. This death was big. As in a fireball big. Someone would die from fire, again. Ronnie couldn't see who. She could only see blonde hair. Blonde hair that was burning.

She awoke in a panic. "Marley!" She yelled it.

Did that mean Marley? Was she going to die next? She had to do something. Sure, Marley had kicked Ronnie out. But Ronnie didn't want her dead.

When Star came to work in the morning, she found a very agitated Ronnie pacing the store.

"Okay, what's wrong?"

"I . . . I can't tell you."

"You can tell me anything. This is a judgment-free zone."

If anyone could understand these dreams and not think she was nuts, it would be the twins. Ronnie took a deep breath and let it out. "I have these dreams. Just like glimpses of things that happen. Not often, but here, well, it's a lot."

Star nodded. "The energy here does that. Go on."

"I'm dreaming about the murders. I see them happen."

The twin gasped. "Are you sure?"

"I saw Fiona's and Peter's. I don't always see everything, just glimpses of things. I don't know who the killer is, so don't ask."

"And you want to talk to the sheriff?"

"No! Absolutely not. They'll think I did it. No, the dream I had last night—or, well, a few hours ago—was about Marley."

"Ohhhh."

"She's going to die next. What do I do?"

"Can you call her?"

"And say what? 'I've been dreaming about the murders, please be careful'?"

"Well, yeah?"

"She's going to think I'm nuts. Am I nuts?"

Star laughed. "No, you're not. You're just sensitive. It happens living here. There's so much energy that it amplifies any abilities. What do the dreams show you?"

"Promise to not freak out? Okay, so, it's the ravens. They showed me Fiona being hit in the head and Peter's car on fire. And the last dream was a big explosion and a blonde woman. I don't know, I'm officially freaked out."

"Hey, it's okay." Star stroked her arm. "You're safe here. And I believe your dreams. Have you always had them?"

Ronnie grimaced. "Some. I dreamed my parents died. And my aunt hated my dreams, so I just stopped paying attention to them, because I had to."

"Well, I'm sure Marley is safe, but I say text her all the same. If nothing else, you'll stop worrying about it."

"That's a good idea. Okay. What, you're looking at me weird?"

"I'm not. I'm thinking you're more like me and Brit than you realize."

"Oh. Oh! I like that." Ronnie smiled in relief. Her friend didn't think she was crazy. "Okay, let me text her." She didn't even know where to begin, but she kept it short and sweet. Hey, I had a weird dream about you and it's leaving me nervous. Be careful out there, and avoid any fires just in case. Ok?

There, she'd tried to stop it. She didn't know if the ravens would be mad at her for that. She didn't know why they kept showing her the murders. What did they want her to do, exactly? If they wanted her to stop things, they should say so. But also, if they didn't, then why bother with the dreams?

She knew it wasn't them really. It was them plus her dreams. That part of her she'd repressed for decades. But Ronnie couldn't live with herself if she didn't try to stop what was about to happen to her former friend.

———

Before

"My house, my rules. You don't like it, get out. See how you do in the streets. I should have thrown you out years ago, bathameez."

Shameem was on a roll. All because Ronnie had asked a question she'd deemed impertinent. (The question was whether her aunt had tried something Ronnie had made for her.)

"No. It's not your house." Ronnie had had enough. It wasn't her aunt's house. She had the deed from the county office. This was her house, in black and white.

"Excuse me? Talking back will get you a thuppar."

"This is my house. I have the deed. And a copy of my parents' will. And I've been the one paying property taxes, so I guess it's all mine. I dreamed about it." Ronnie said the words that would freak her aunt out the most. Her dreams.

She enjoyed the look on her aunt's face. Just a bit.

"You sneak behind my back and do these things? I don't even know who you are anymore."

Ronnie didn't say more, but she knew she was almost free. She was the one taking control of her life. She felt empowered, finally.

Chapter 65

The Town

She was almost done. Almost. After this, she had one more to go. For now. And if things didn't improve after these two, she'd make a new list and start again. Peter had been dead a couple of weeks, and it was time to move forward.

She had to focus. This one was difficult. The victim was wily. Moving from house to house, never letting anyone know where her next place would be. She stole; she taunted. She didn't care about who she hurt. And then she'd moved into Ronnie's spot. That had been the final straw. But they weren't at that house. No, they were in an empty Airbnb that Caroline had used for a while.

And she'd accused her of attacking her and failing. As if she'd ever fail. Not in this. Caroline's earlier attack had been fake, just like Caroline.

Caroline knew what she'd done. She'd hurt a few people with her scams, taking advantage of them. She didn't care who died in the desert because of her. And that was enough to sign her death warrant. That callousness. Every death mattered. Every soul, every deed. It mattered here. The universe required balance. And with the removal of one person, a void began. Who or what filled that void was a big deal. And her role in Brit's desert situation made her guilty as sin.

"I hope someone good fills yours." She said it out loud and stared at Caroline. Caroline, in return, stared back. It was all she could do. Her hands and mouth were duct taped. She couldn't move; she could only stare and plead with her eyes. "Maybe with you dead, the balance will shift to more positive energy. We can only hope.

"Don't bother crying though it would be fun to see you weep. This has already been ordained. By nature. Now the question is, How do I kill you? Fast? That would be a mercy. Are you deserving of mercy, Caroline?"

Muffled grunts were her only reply.

"Suit yourself."

She had quite enjoyed the whole fire thing with Peter. Fire was cleansing. And if fire spread in these shitty houses they'd torn down wildlife habitat for, then so be it. She was fixing things. Once the fire and debris cleared, there could be new growth. This entire area would be cleansed, only for new life to come. Just like in the forest when things burned. New life grew. New souls came.

It was evening, just after sunset. She'd surprised Caroline. Pretended to be a customer needing guidance, under a fake name. Gave her the address for the Airbnb. There was no one staying there; no one good would get hurt.

The first hit over the head had been enough to knock Caroline out. The moment Caroline had walked into the home, she'd struck. It hadn't been enough to kill her, which was just as well. She'd wanted her alive for the next part. She'd taped Caroline up so there'd be no escaping. She was taking no chances.

She went outside and opened the valve of the propane tank and, using an axe, cut the hose that led to the house. The tank was full. It would make quite a scene. She shivered in anticipation.

Back inside, she placed candles around Caroline and poured alcohol everywhere. It wouldn't take long. Caroline would burn, and then a crisp fireball would take over. It would also cleanse the land of Airbnbs.

Just what they needed. They took over every development, and no one working in town could afford to live in Sedona anymore. They had to branch out to Cottonwood and Clarkdale and Cornville. But soon, they'd all leave. If she had her way, that was.

"Any last words?" she asked the still-taped-up Caroline. "Just kidding, I don't care. I hope this hurts. But remember, fire cleanses. I'm doing you a favor."

She lit the candles and watched as the flames jumped to the floor around Caroline. Her victim squirmed but couldn't move. "I wonder if the tape will melt into your skin," she mused.

And then she left.

It took fifteen minutes for the fire to reach the compromised tank. Fifteen minutes where Caroline burned and writhed. She could see her from the window. She was still there, not moving now.

As she drove away, she felt the searing heat before she heard the noise. And then a huge fireball went up into the sky, devouring the house and a few of its neighbors.

"You're welcome," she muttered.

Chapter 66

The fireball could be seen for miles. The heat was unbearable, despite the fall weather. It felt like they were all burning. The Phoenix news rushed crews out to Sedona. Ronnie watched from the store. She could see it, feel it. This was bad, whatever it was. Her stomach sank.

And then her phone went off. It was Marley. "Uh, thanks? I guess." She was alive! She was okay! Ronnie sighed with relief. But then, who was in the fire?

"I hope no one gets hurt," she offered up to the universe. As close to a prayer as she'd get anymore. The sirens were loud and reminded her of New York.

Ronnie didn't have time to stop and stare at the flames like everyone else. She had a house to look at. The one by the twins. No fire was going to keep her away from that. She only had time to go after work, and the Realtor squeezed her in.

"You must be Ronnie. Star and Brit have told me so much about you. I'm Audra. Let me show you around."

The house was small, only two bedrooms. Possibly three, though Ronnie liked the idea of having a study. Not like she studied. But she could. And maybe she would. A library or home office or something.

It was clean and tidy, no carpeting. The current residents had already moved. The outside was the coral-red clay, and the garden was landscaped but lush. Stonework and a fountain were in the back. It was beautiful. And small. But perfect for her. That's what she felt when she walked in. *This is home.*

"I love it. How much is it?" She held her breath.

The price was shockingly affordable. Less than a fourth of what she'd gotten for her parents' home.

"Whoa. What's the catch?" There was always a catch.

"The sellers are very motivated to sell. To you."

"To me?" It took her a moment to understand. "Oh. Do the twins own this house?"

Audra nodded. "And they want you to be the next owner."

The twins owned this and were willing to sell it at a steal for her. What would they want in return? There was no such thing as a free gift. Everything had strings. But so far, the twins hadn't asked her for anything. Except friendship. Could she trust them?

She had to.

Ronnie did something she never thought she'd do. She bought the house. Or started the process, which took paperwork and inspections and everything else. The twins insisted on it being done by the book so she wouldn't have to worry. Though they let her move in ASAP so she wouldn't have to live in the store anymore.

Ronnie Khan had a home. An actual home that was all hers.

———

The door chimed, and Marley walked in. Ronnie stared at her in surprise. She hadn't spoken to her in over a week, not since she'd texted her about her dream. What was she doing here? Ronnie's mouth was open in shock.

"I have some of your mail," Marley said stiffly.

"Oh. You can leave it on the counter, thanks."

"Do you have a new place yet?"

"Uh, yeah, I bought a house." She couldn't help it—she smiled as she said it.

"You bought a house? Wow."

Ronnie shrugged and went to help a customer. When she came back to the counter, Marley was still standing there, shifting her weight from one leg to the other as if she were nervous. Marley? Nervous? That wasn't like her.

"Listen, I'm sorry about how I acted. I shouldn't have flown off the handle like that," Marley said it quickly. "I just, I don't know. Caroline said so many things, you know? That I couldn't trust you. And . . ."

"It's fine. The twins have helped me realize that some people are in your life for a purpose, and once that purpose is complete, you don't need them anymore."

"Oh. Of course they have."

Ronnie was playing it cool. Inside, her heart was racing, and she was fighting to not cry. She had to do this. She had to show Marley that she was okay without her.

"Oh. Well. Listen, if you ever want to get dinner sometime . . ."

"Oh, maybe. What about Caroline?"

"I haven't seen her in like a week. She's just vanished. I don't know, maybe she's off on one of her trips." Marley sounded angry and sad. But Ronnie wasn't going to comfort her. *Her purpose in your life is done.*

"I'm sorry to hear that. She's a bit flighty."

"Yeah, she is." Marley laughed. "Listen, can we . . . can we start over? Me and you?"

"I don't know. Can I think about it?"

"Sure. Sure. And congrats on the new house. I'm sure you must feel relieved to have your own place. And thanks for, uh, texting me before. You know."

Ronnie nodded and smiled, but she didn't move from her spot. She didn't run to hug her former friend. She stayed still until Marley left. And then she let out a shriek that startled the customers.

"Sorry! I just, whew, ever walk away from something and know it's for the best? I just did that."

"Well, sounds like you need to celebrate," a woman said. She was visiting from LA, she said.

"I think you're right!" And she knew just who to celebrate with.

———

Sheriff John Reynolds came by the twins' house, where Ronnie was having her second glass of champagne. She'd hoped to see both her friends, but only Brit was available. Star was on Center business doing whatever it was they did.

"Champagne? Are you celebrating something?" the sheriff asked.

"I bought a house!" Ronnie grinned.

"Oh, fantastic news. This means you're staying around."

"Guess so!"

"We're so excited she's going to be even closer to us now!" Brit beamed. "She's moved in next door."

"Well, how about that. I think you'll be a good addition to this town."

"You do? I mean, um, thanks, Sheriff." Ronnie grinned and didn't care if she looked like an idiot. A good addition to the town? She'd take it!

"I don't want to rain on your parade here, but we identified the body in that fire last week. The one in the Airbnb." It had made the national news and set off a debate about Airbnbs in tourist towns. The arson investigator had concluded it was human caused and intentional.

"Oh no! I hope it's not someone we know. I can't take much more death," Brit said quietly.

"It's Caroline. The dental records said so."

"Marley did come by earlier and said she hadn't seen Caroline."

"She did?"

"I know, I played it so cool. You would have been proud of me." Brit high-fived her.

"Well, now we know where Caroline is. I'll leave you two to your party."

They waited for him to leave. Ronnie got up and locked the door.

"Let's toast to that," she said, grinning. "No more Caroline." She didn't feel bad one bit about toasting to the end of that woman.

"Hear, hear!" Brit said, holding up her glass.

———

Ronnie's new house had very little furniture. Just the air mattress she'd bought for the store. But that was okay. She was online shopping, and Star said she'd take her to Phoenix to get anything major.

She didn't want to decorate it any old way. She wanted it to be hers. Ronnie had never had a say in how things looked before.

First up, she wanted white walls. Clean. Elegant. So she spent a weekend painting it all by herself. Her muscles were aching and sore, but she was doing it. This was her home. And she'd make it look the way she wanted. No matter what. Between the new house and setting up the open house for the shop, Ronnie barely had time to think. And she liked it that way. Because if she stopped to think, she'd feel the pain of losing her friend. It was a sharp feeling in her chest. No one had told her that friend breakups were a thing, but they were real. And they hurt. Some days she was angry at Marley; others she blamed herself for everything. It was one thing to let go of someone and another to feel the emotions of it all. There was a void where Marley used to be.

No, she didn't want to think about it. Instead, she focused on painting. And at the store, she got everything ready for the holiday fair. She would make this home so perfect for herself that she'd never have to search for a new one. The thought of being a nomad like Caroline, hopping from place to place, never really knowing anyone, was sad. And not what Ronnie wanted. She wanted her home.

———

"Have you checked in on Marley?" Brit asked, her face heavy with concern. "I mean, with Caroline dead, she may need a friend." It had been a few days since the sheriff had come by. Ronnie hadn't heard from or seen Marley since then.

Ronnie blinked a few times. "I guess you're right. I didn't know how to navigate that, to be honest."

"Why don't you text her? I'll help! Say something like, 'Heard the awful news, my sincerest condolences. Please let me know if you need anything?' What do you think?"

"It's a little formal, but sure, why not." She hit send. She had almost deleted Marley's number from her phone. Not out of malice but to prevent herself from calling her. Ronnie didn't know how to handle a friend breakup. Did you just pretend the other person didn't exist? That they hadn't impacted your life?

Was she supposed to pretend Marley hadn't turned on her, accused her of shit, thrown her out? Was she supposed to act normal?

It was all too much, so she hadn't done anything until today, at Brit's urging.

"Oh no, three dots."

"Let's see what it says!"

"'Thanks, Ronnie. Maybe come by later if you're free?' Now what do I do?"

"Do you want to see her?"

"I honestly don't know. I need time."

"Then tell her that. It's okay to put yourself first." Brit said it gently.

Ronnie nodded. Okay, she could do this. She wrote back what Brit suggested.

"I heard John questioned her. About all of Caroline's schemes, the people she messed with," Brit said.

"Wow. I wonder how much she knew about her. I mean, they hid a lot from me."

"Well, he may want to question you too."

"Me? I don't know anything!"

"Don't panic! It's just John."

Just John. The police were the police, no matter how small a town it was. And Ronnie wasn't sure she'd ever not have that feeling of panic when she was near the cops. She had nothing to hide about Caroline, but she didn't want to be involved. *Head down, don't rock the boat.*

Ronnie waited for John to show up. She knew he would. And she'd tell him what she knew. But that still meant going over it all in her head again and again until she felt nothing but panic when he walked in.

"Ronnie, got a minute?"

She yelped but nodded. "Yes, sorry. I'm really anxious about all of this. Caroline, I mean."

"Do you have reason to be?" He asked it with a smile.

"No, but answering questions makes me nervous."

"Let's take a ride. I'll have you back here ASAP. Sound good, Star?"

"Brit." Ronnie said it automatically.

"Dang, I'm usually real good at telling you two apart!"

Ronnie tried to ignore her racing heart as she climbed into John's SUV. At least she was sitting in the front. That had to be something. Right? She held a black tourmaline in her hand. She called it her worry stone. It was the one Star had given her months ago.

"So how well did you know Caroline Landes?"

"Not well." They were sitting in an interview room. It looked nothing like it did on TV. It could have been a conference room if it weren't for the mirror. It wasn't dark or gloomy; light from outside poured in. "She and Marley were tight. Super close."

"But you spent time with her?"

"With Caroline? Um, a little bit? Like if she were over, I'd say hello and all that. And we did all go to dinner now and again. I tried to stay away from her because of the twins." She was talking too much. "Sorry, I don't know what is helpful and what isn't."

"Do you know why Marley said to ask you about Caroline's death?"

Ronnie's face froze. "I'm sorry, she said what?"

"Marley told us to ask you about it," he repeated.

"I didn't even know about it. I mean, I saw the fire. But I was meeting with a Realtor. You can call and ask her." Ronnie was grateful she had a paper trail. An alibi. Why would Marley have told him that?

"So you didn't hate Caroline?"

"No more than anyone else in town."

"Marley also said you had a vendetta against her."

"Against Marley? What?! No! Look. We had a fight. She asked me to move out. I did. And that's that. I have nothing bad against her. I swear." *What the hell, Marley?!*

"She mentioned something about a text you sent her. A threat."

Ronnie stared in confusion. She hadn't threatened anyone. "I had a weird dream about Marley, and I wanted her to be careful. That's all that text was."

John stared at her before nodding. "You have these dreams often?"

"No, just every once in a while. I didn't want anything to happen to her."

"I believe you, but we have to check every lead, dot our i's, so to speak. So did anyone give Caroline a hard time? Besides any dreams you've had?"

"I dunno, the people she tried to kill with her peyote scam? Or the folks whose houses she 'borrowed.' Like, I'd start there."

John nodded, frowning. "Sure, sure. One more thing Marley mentioned. She said you had a past of violent behaviors."

If Ronnie's jaw opened any farther, it would detach itself. She closed it and sighed. She had to tell him. She couldn't keep this secret. "Sheriff, I'll tell you this, but I don't want it getting out. I was raised by a very abusive woman. And any violence was done to me. I would never hurt anyone after what I've been through. I don't like sharing that, but that's the only violence in my history."

He handed her a tissue. She hadn't even realized she was crying. "Shit, sorry, I didn't mean to get emotional."

"Don't apologize. It seems to me Marley is the one with a vendetta against you. Be careful with her. She's likely to escalate." Escalate? More than telling the sheriff that Ronnie was a violent murderer? What could she possibly do next?

"If there are any other accusations, I'd like to clear them up."

"You were raised by your aunt, right?"

"Yes."

"Where is she now?"

Ronnie shrugged. "She won't talk to me. I sold the house, and she was mad. I think she's in Pakistan with other relatives, but I can't be sure."

"Noted. I was just curious. Marley had a whole thing about your aunt. I wouldn't want to be on her bad side. Like a wasp about to attack." He cracked a smile. "Well, thanks for coming down. Let me have someone drive you back to the shop."

Ronnie held herself together until she got to the store. And then she burst into tears.

"What happened?" Brit asked, smoothing Ronnie's hair back.

"Marley's saying the most awful things about me. That I was responsible for Caroline's death. It was just awful. And she said things about my aunt. The sheriff actually asked me if I was violent!"

"That one. She'll get her comeuppance one of these days. Why don't you go home, and I'll handle things here." Brit's jaw was clenched.

She was pissed. Ronnie nodded and left, feeling absolutely miserable. Marley was determined to make sure she wouldn't be welcomed in her new hometown.

Ronnie went to the new house and tried to continue fixing it up. But she was mad. How could Marley turn on her like that? After everything. Had their friendship meant so little? Ronnie was angry and sad and heartbroken all at once and didn't know how to deal with all those emotions crashing in on her.

She went outside, where less work had to be done. The landscape was perfect for her. Ronnie sat down and took a deep breath, trying to calm herself. She wasn't going to let Marley's games get to her. Not now, not ever.

Nearby, two ravens watched her. She had started leaving food for them here, and she hoped they knew she hadn't abandoned them.

"I hope you're not mad at me too," she wailed before sobbing hysterically.

Chapter 67

December

Ronnie was standing in the desert. Near Sedona, red rocks and dirt with green trees making it look like nature was celebrating Christmas. At her feet lay a bundle. She stared at it but didn't move to touch it.

Bury it.

She looked up to see a raven standing near and watching her.

Bury her.

She removed the blanket covering whatever it was. It was Marley, and in this dream they were sisters, and Marley was dead. *Why is she dead?* Ronnie thought.

"Wait, I know this story," Ronnie said. It was like Cain and Abel, Qabil and Habil. One brother burying the other.

You do. Now bury her.

She knelt down and dug a hole with her bare hands, one deep enough for the body. The dirt caked her fingers and nails. When she placed Marley inside the makeshift grave, Ronnie took a step back. Marley was smiling at her.

"We're sisters now, together forever," Marley said, grinning and decaying. Ronnie piled dirt on top of her.

———

She awoke sweating, gasping for air as if she herself had been buried. She glanced at the window, which was closed. No bird visitors. She was fine.

Ronnie got up for a drink of water and tried to shake the feeling that something awful was going to happen, that she was going to do something so bad it wouldn't be forgiven.

She slid back onto her mattress and closed her eyes. She wasn't going to text Marley about her dream this time. Ronnie had learned her lesson.

At her window, a black bird watched her.

Whatever Marley's drama, Ronnie had other things to focus on. The open house event was here, and she wanted it to be perfect. It was just what Sedona needed to cleanse everyone's minds of the recent murders. A winter shopping night, full of a fun time of music, tarot and astro readings, games, hot chocolate, and more. Every store in a ten-block radius was participating, all because of her. The murders and patrols had put a dent in everyone's sales. They needed this to make up for their losses.

Ronnie was jumping out of her skin with excitement. Everyone had a job to do, including the twins. They were going to do readings, trading off with each other whenever one became too tired. .

Ronnie and the twins wore matching dresses, not caftans. They were all in white, so it would be easier to find them in the crowd. The clothes had been Ronnie's idea.

"Star, I know you hate dresses, but I thought it'd be cool if people could see us and know we were with the shop. What do you think?"

To her surprise, Star agreed.

Ronnie had on a new necklace she'd had made. Rose quartz. Come five o'clock, the fun began. With champagne and organic cocktails, readings, sales, and more. Ronnie looked around the crowds, the register ringing up, one twin on duty while the other rested. And she was happy. She was honestly, truly happy.

That should have been her first clue that something was off.

It was Star's turn to do readings. Ronnie did a double take because she looked so much like her sister that night. It was the clothes, she knew it. But still, for a moment she could have sworn Brit was there. Ronnie shook her head. *It's fine, I'm clearly tired. After this night, I can rest.*

The customers came in waves. They were making sale after sale, and Ronnie knew this was going to put them over what they were projected to earn that month. Maybe they'd do one of these nights again, a week or two before Christmas.

"Hey, can I read you? Since it's just us?" Star asked. There was a brief lull as the customers moved to the other shops.

"Sure. Did Brit go home?"

"I think she's around somewhere. Cut the deck." Star pulled cards out one after the other in formations Ronnie didn't understand. "You're about to have big changes. Everything you've been doing is leading to this." Star paused. "The Death card is an ending and new beginning. But with everything going on, it may be literal. Death around you." She reached over to grab Ronnie's hand. "Be careful. Promise me you'll be careful."

"I promise. Does that mean I'm going to die?"

"No, I don't think so. But death is around you. I mean, new beginnings with the house, the death of your friendship with Marley, it's all here. Normally, I wouldn't think it had any deeper meaning, but with everything going on, just be careful. We wouldn't survive losing you too."

"Don't worry, you two are stuck with me." Ronnie grinned, sticking her tongue out.

"Good, because you're family now." Family. The word had never meant so much to her before now. Ronnie glanced away so Star wouldn't see her tear up.

———

Later that night, Brit swapped places with her sister while Ronnie rang up more and more sales. "This was such a brilliant idea. I don't know why we didn't do it sooner!"

"Because you needed me to pull it off!" Ronnie laughed.

"We needed you, period. And still do. Oh, Star asked if you could help her with an errand later. She'll text you?"

"An errand?"

"Yeah, she didn't tell me what." Brit shrugged.

"Sure, happy to help you two with whatever you want." She turned to her customer. "That'll be eighty-five dollars, thank you for shopping BritStar Crystals!" Ronnie was bone tired but also amped, so she'd be up for whatever Star needed. She hoped it was something easy that involved snacks and sitting. Lots of sitting.

John made the rounds, as did his men. They were there to keep an eye on things, and specifically, on Marley's Eyes patrol volunteers. The death of Caroline hadn't stopped Marley from doing what she wanted. But the red shirts were less visible now. Or they just avoided the crystal shop.

"Ladies, looks like this has been a successful night." John smiled at them.

"Ronnie's idea, isn't it great?" Brit said, squeezing Ronnie, who blushed.

"I'm just happy to help after everything you've done for me."

"See, John? Ronnie wouldn't hurt a fly. It's Marley you need to look out for," Brit said, keeping her arm around her friend.

"So it seems. You two have a good night. Tell Star hello for me if you see her." John waved and was gone, and Ronnie relaxed a little bit more.

Chapter 68

The Town

The humans were all in town having a festive night. All of them except this one. It was time. Now or never. They had waited long enough. They'd watched. They'd been patient. It had to be done. The ravens needed revenge. Murderers deserved what they got. And the ravens would make her never want to come back to this place. Their place. Their home. They couldn't wait for their human friend to do it. This was on them.

They'd attack her and take what they needed. It was their turn now. Their time. And anyone who got in their way would suffer too.

They sent one of them to her house. Inside the house. The back window was open. The December weather was warm, too warm. This human was so careless. She thought she was untouchable. Their intrepid spy, the brave one, took note of everything in the house. No food out. Nothing fun to play with. Just her.

"Oh! How the hell did you get in?" The human glanced around and saw the open window. "Of course."

The raven perched on the back of a chair, its head tilted, its cold, black eyes on Marley.

"Shoo! Get out!" Marley waved her hands, and nothing happened. "Dammit." She opened the front door and then walked into the kitchen to get a broom and heard a loud rustling. "Please be gone, please be gone."

The raven gave the sound. The signal. It was now or never.

Marley walked back into the living room, broom in hand, and froze.

"What the fuck?"

There wasn't one raven inside. There were hundreds. Standing on every surface. The couch, the coffee table, even the cushions she kept on the floor. Everywhere she turned, more little black eyes watched her every move. This was their time.

One by one the birds made sounds. Warbles. Caws. Even saying Ronnie's name. It was all meant to frighten her.

Marley took a step back, but that didn't help. They were all around her. Some ruffled their feathers, others screeched, others just stared. The ravens could feel her fear. It was almost intoxicating.

"I-I'm sorry? For whatever you're upset with? I can leave?"

Marley stepped back again, and more wings started rustling. She focused her eyes on the door. She was going to try to run for it.

But the birds moved first. The sound of hundreds of wings, shrieking caws, filled the air as they rose up and flew around the human. They scratched her with their talons, beat at her head with their wings. Marley covered the sides of her head in desperation. But she couldn't move. They made sure of it.

One raven flew for her face and scratched her cheek.

"Ow!" Marley covered it with her hand.

Keep going.

Another bird struck her. And then another. And another. They were taking turns, and she had no break between the attacks.

"Ooof!" One slammed into her mouth hard enough to break her two front teeth. Marley spat, and blood and teeth landed on the floor.

And then they all attacked en masse, pushing her down to the floor. She covered her head and tried to motion them away. There were too many of them to fight, but she tried to inch forward, their claws and beaks digging into her. Eventually she gave up. Marley lay there, her mouth still pooling with blood. They watched her tongue her mouth where her front teeth used to be.

The birds covered her like a shiny, moving blanket, and no matter what she did, she felt their weight on her while they made cuts all over her body. No one could escape them.

The noise was almost too much; the birds were enjoying themselves. This was fun for them. They didn't have to depend on anyone else for their needs. They'd enact their own revenge.

"Help me," Marley whispered.

"I can't," a voice replied. And then laughed.

Chapter 69

"The total sales tonight were $18,433! Wow!" Ronnie was closing out the store. She was alone but talking to herself. Brit had gone home with a headache—too many readings did that to her. Star was doing some errand Ronnie had to help with. But first, first she was going to celebrate this win. This event was all hers. Her idea, her plan, and it had gone off without a hitch. Even Marley's little spies had stayed out of the way. And Marley herself hadn't bothered showing her face.

In all, a win. A perfect night. And Ronnie knew this was only the beginning. She had made this happen. She had manifested this.

She'd stop at the bank for a night drop and then text Star. And then she could go home. To her home. She'd cleaned and scrubbed her bathtub earlier and was going to take a bath. Ronnie never got to do that growing up. She wasn't allowed to waste water. But she wanted to see if she was a bath person. It looked relaxing.

Money deposited, she could let out a worried breath. Ronnie had a fear of being robbed, that she'd somehow lose all the money for the twins. She texted Star. Sorry, had to go to the bank. We made over $18k tonight!

Wow! Can you come meet me? It'd be a huge help. It won't take long?

Sure! Where are you?

She followed Star's instructions, such as they were. Go on 89A, and turn right on a dirt road. *That was helpful.* But if Star needed her, she'd go.

People drove so fast on 89A that it scared her. Ronnie was a slow, cautious driver. She saw the church up ahead that Star had mentioned and then turned right. The dirt road extended behind the church and into the Black Mountains. She hoped that wasn't where she was headed.

She drove for ten minutes, her high beams on. The road was made of the soft red clay. There were no other lights, except the stars. It was pitch black, and Ronnie imagined she was on some distant planet to keep herself from getting too freaked out. Finally, she saw lights up ahead. *That has to be Star, I hope.* She pulled over and got out.

"Star?"

"Over here! Can you give me a hand?"

Ronnie left her headlights on and walked forward, the lights from Star's car blinding her. She held up her hand to shield her eyes. Between the high beams and the blackness around them, Ronnie couldn't see a thing. She really hoped no snakes were around. Or coyotes. Or whatever lingered in the desert at night. She could feel eyes on her, and she didn't know if it was from people or animals. Ronnie shivered.

"What's going on?" she said, her smile already on her lips. She dodged the lights so she could see, her eyes slowly adjusting. That's when she saw Star had a bundle with her. *Was she throwing things away out here? That couldn't be right.* "Star? How's Brit's headache?" Why was she asking about Brit? Ronnie was too confused to know what was going on. She wanted to hurry back to the twins' home, away from this empty, dirty road. She wanted to be in her clean tub in her clean house, relaxing.

"Yeah, Star, tell her how Brit is," Marley taunted, only it came out slightly lispy. The bundle, Ronnie realized, was Marley. And her mouth was bloody, hence the lisp.

"Marley!" Ronnie ran forward. "Oh my god, what happened?" She crouched down to look at her former friend. "Are you okay? Who did this?"

"No, I'm not fucking okay. Your friend is a psycho!" Marley screamed it. Her front two teeth were missing. Ronnie fell backward in shock. Marley had deep scratches all over her face and arms. As if claws had gotten ahold of her.

"Get away from her, Ronnie. The ravens won't like you helping." Star pointed to the cars. Ronnie squinted but finally saw them. Hundreds of ravens stood watching them, on top of Star's car, standing in the lone tree that stood in the dead grass. More were circling. Their eyes gave them away. They shone, reflecting the moonlight. They'd been quiet before, but now they were cawing and calling out. Their wings were rustling. Ronnie had never felt so watched in her life.

"Where did they come from?" she whispered, too scared to raise her voice.

"They've always been here. It's their home."

Ronnie pointed at Marley's face. "Did they do that?"

Star nodded. "They did, and you probably shouldn't interfere."

"But we have to help her!" Ronnie was adamant. "Ravens, come on. We're friends! I feed you! Please?" They just looked at her, their black eyes taking it all in.

Ronnie looked at Star for help, who shrugged.

"She deserved it, though. You know she did. She killed one of theirs. That's why they want her gone." Star was calm. So very calm. That's what Ronnie was distracted by. How could she be this calm? "Ronnie, you need to let her go. She's not your friend. She doesn't care what happens to you or anyone else. You know I'm telling you the truth.

"When Caroline took Brit from me, or tried to—she could never fully take her from me—I thought I'd never feel light again. Until you came. And now, it's like I have my sister with me."

Marley squirmed before shouting, "Brit's dead, you fucking lunatic!"

Ronnie gasped. Brit was dead? Had the killer gotten her? Nothing was sinking into her head; she couldn't make sense of any of this.

"Ask her about it!" Marley continued. "Brit's been dead this whole time!"

"Star?" Ronnie couldn't get the full question out. Brit wasn't dead. There was absolutely no way. Ronnie spent time with her. Hung out with her. She had just seen her hours before.

Star grabbed Ronnie's hands. "I'll never hide anything from you. I promise. Brit is not on this plane anymore. But she's here, in our hearts. She was me. I am her. And now, you're here. You're family.

"Remember that hike we went on? Where we told the rocks our secrets? That was mine."

Star had been with her. The whole time it was Star.

"You tricked me?"

"No, Ronnie, no. I couldn't let Brit go. She was a part of me. Is a part of me. Have you ever lost anyone that was so important to you that you couldn't breathe anymore? How could I live when part of me was dead?

"You're my sister now. I prayed for a sister, you know. After Brit. After what Caroline and Peter and that horrible Matt and Fiona did to her. They lied about what they gave her. They left her in the desert to die. Like she was an animal. They were all in on the scam."

"But you saved her. You both said so."

Star looked Ronnie in the eyes. It was the saddest look Ronnie had ever seen. One of grief, one of pain so intense there was no coming back. Star shook her head. "I couldn't save her. I was too late. Fiona set her up out of jealousy. Peter and Caroline did it out of greed. And Matt, well, who knew why he did it, but they all paid the price."

Ronnie wasn't listening. All she could think about was Brit—why wasn't she there?

"The ravens needed us to clean this place up. It's their home, our home . . . Suzy, well, I did that one for you." Star grinned at her.

"But . . . Brit? I've hung out with her. Stop messing around!" Was this all some elaborate prank they were playing on her? Fool the gullible Ronnie? Because they thought she was stupid. "Where is she? Brit? Hello, joke's over." She wouldn't fall for this.

"It's not a joke. Brit was here, with us. It's time for her to move on. Now I have you. My sister. My new sister, one so pure of heart. I knew you'd come here, I knew you'd make everything better. Don't you see? I had to get rid of them all. I had to kill them. I had to save us, all of us, from people like that. Look, they're happy now!"

Ronnie glanced warily at the birds.

This was too much information all at once. How the hell was her friend dead. "So you're the one who killed everyone?"

Star nodded. "I had to. After what they did to Brit. They all deserved it."

"But Lorraine?"

"I didn't kill her. She did." She nodded at Marley.

If Ronnie could be more shocked, she wasn't sure how.

"Oh, get off your high horse. You killed that Suzy whatever," Marley hissed before turning to Ronnie. "And with Lorraine gone, we can take over. You and me, Ronnie. Come on!"

"I killed them to help this place. You did it to hold your little rallies."

"Like there's a difference. Ron, come on, let's go. Untie me and let's get out of here. You can move back in with me and we'll be like we were—"

"No."

It was one word, but it silenced everyone.

"No. I'm not untying you. I'm not moving back in with you. I have my own home now."

"Fine, you can live in your little house. But come on! She's nuts!"

Ronnie stared at the two women in front of her. Her two friends. One former, one current. And Brit, but Ronnie wasn't sure she counted now. She had a choice to make. She could walk away and let what was going to happen, happen. Or she could do something. Marley had betrayed her over and over. Star loved her. She could do the right thing. She could walk away from this. They all could.

The ravens started getting antsy. They were her friends too. They wanted her to know that. That everything they'd shown Ronnie up until now had been leading to this. It had always been leading up to this.

"I believe in you, Ronnie." Star said it softly. The words Ronnie had wanted someone, anyone to say to her.

"Give me the knife. You're not going to kill her," she said to Star. She couldn't let Star do this.

Ronnie held her hand out, and Star put the knife in her hand. It was her choice. She could decide what happened next. She was the one who had a say in what happened.

"Oh thank god, Ronnie, cut my hands loose. I don't care what you did to your aunt. I'll never turn you in."

Ronnie blinked. There were three murderers out there in the desert.

———

Before

Shameem Khala stared at her. Fury, pure fury. That was all Ronnie could see. Her aunt hated her. Despised her. And now, her aunt was going to stop her.

"This is my house," Shameem hissed. "You don't get to take it away from me."

"It's mine. We've been over this. You need to vacate. Or tell me where to send your things."

"How dare you? After everything I did for you? I'm glad your mother isn't here to see you behave this way."

Ronnie closed her eyes for a moment. Nothing her aunt said would hurt her now. The damage had been done. She'd seen this in her dreams. She knew what was about to happen. "Well, she's dead. So you can leave now. I don't need you here." She sounded cold. She wasn't trying to be callous. But her aunt had ruined her life enough. It was time for a fresh start.

"I won't go. You'll have to take me to court. That'll take months. Months of me being here."

Ronnie expected this. You didn't live with a woman like Shameem and not know she was going to try every trick in the book. She could deal with it. Even delay her move. If it meant she'd be free, she'd do it.

It was the slap that did it. The last slap Shameem ever gave her. The last time she used her hands against her niece. It made her snap. And finally, Ronnie slapped back.

Shameem looked at her in shock. "You hit me?!"

"You started it."

And when her aunt tried again to hit her, Ronnie caught her hand midblow.

"No. No more. You've done nothing but hate me. Beat me. Use me. I'm done. You can leave quietly, or you can make a scene. But either way, you're out of my life after this."

The house was sold. Ronnie had been having it repaired for the new owners. She'd tried to do some herself, but the basement needed new flooring. Ronnie was getting new flooring installed, but the concrete slab needed to be redone. She'd hired workers to pour more concrete later that week. They'd already come and jackhammered the old slab.

She released her aunt's hand and gave her the option to leave. But Shameem refused. Ronnie had tried. She had.

So she did what she had to. She hit Shameem. Over and over. Every insult, every cruel thing her aunt had ever said or done to her fueled her fists. And when her aunt fell to the floor, Ronnie took one look at her and then stomped on her head until there was a bloody mess and her aunt stopped moving.

Ronnie had killed the only family she knew in the world. And she wasn't sorry.

She dragged the body down the stairs to the basement. The basement was a mess, with the old flooring dug up and removed. But now she knew what to do with her aunt. She pulled her into the corner, huffing and panting the entire time. Shameem was not a small woman.

With the old concrete gone, there was actual dirt in the basement, enough to hide what she needed to do. The dirt was a sign from the universe. It told her, "This has to happen."

Ronnie had read about this. A case just like this. Where they'd buried a body in cement. And no one had found it for decades. She was going to do the same. First, bury it under the dirt. Later, the workers would cover it without realizing what they were hiding.

She'd debated using a giant trash can to hide the body but figured that would arouse suspicion. If her aunt didn't want to leave the house, she wouldn't have to.

By the time she was done, it was almost morning. Digging deep enough had taken hours. But Shameem Khala was buried, and soon, no one would ever find her.

Ronnie went upstairs and packed up all her aunt's things. She'd ship them to Pakistan. It would take forever for anyone to realize that her aunt was missing. Would anyone miss her?

Ronnie shrugged.

After she'd finished everything, after the sun came up and she cleaned up and wiped things down with enough bleach to choke on, she lay in bed. She was free. Ronnie was free. And she had no idea what that meant, except she would never again let anyone hurt her the way her aunt had.

The neighbors, the aunties, they'd just think Shameem had gone back home. That she had to get away from her terrible niece. They wouldn't look for her. Brown people disappeared all the time. They would accept that Shameem had gone home to Pakistan, and they'd move on.

The next night, she went to Marley's and told her lie. That her aunt had been awful and she had nowhere to go.

———

"Caroline was right. I did kill my aunt. I had no choice. You don't know what she did to me. What I had to endure. You'll never know." Ronnie said it softly. It was hard to hear her above the feathers rustling.

"And I accept that about you. I love you. I've done so much for you." Marley was begging. "I have the papers she gave me. They're in my car. You can have them! I'll give them to you."

"No! You didn't. You're just like her, holding everything over my damn head."

"Ronnie—"

She shook her head. No questions. No debate. Marley's grotesque grin shone in the moonlight. She was pleased with herself. But with her missing teeth, she looked as ugly on the outside as she was on the inside.

No, Ronnie couldn't let Star do this. No matter what else Star had done, this one wouldn't be on her. The ravens stirred; Ronnie looked up at them.

"They showed me this, you know. Your death. They told me I had to bury you. My sister." She said it quietly. "When you're dead, no one will miss you."

Before Marley could reply, Ronnie buried the knife deep into her old friend's abdomen and aimed it up into her heart. There was no reason to be cruel, to draw it out. No one needed to suffer. Quick and painless—or as painless as being stabbed could be.

Ronnie stepped back, slightly dazed. She let Star take the knife.

"We can leave her on Bell Rock," Star said.

"No. We have to bury her. It's what the ravens would do."

"I have a shovel in the car." Star helped her drag Marley's body as far into the desert as they could go. Until they couldn't see the lights from their cars.

Ronnie buried Marley so deep no one would ever find her. It took hours.

"Want to say anything?" Star asked.

"I had to do it," she whispered. "Give me the knife. I'll keep it."

Chapter 70

The Town

The ravens took flight the second Ronnie stabbed Marley. They flew as high as they could, going in circles and warning everyone to stay away. The work was done, their work. They'd gotten their revenge, and the worst of the worst had been cleansed from their home.

And the other animals listened. Because they trusted the ravens. They could see humans better than anyone else.

There was no screaming coming from below. No crying. Just two humans who were alive and one who wasn't.

Tomorrow, they'd reclaim their land. They'd have it; they'd be free of whatever had come to their town, their home. Tomorrow, the ravens promised everyone. Tomorrow things would be right.

Chapter 71

January

Ronnie felt the sun on her back. It was gorgeous and life affirming. She felt the beauty in the heat, even as sweat started to trickle. *How could it be so hot already?*

She was in her yard. Her yard. Not Marley's. Not anyone else's. And she was making her garden into something spectacular. Digging her hands into the plant soil made her feel connected to everything, dead and alive. Even Marley. She was prepping her garden for planting in a few months.

Poor Marley, she thought.

Marley had vanished. That was the official report. She'd been accused of murder and had disappeared and no one, not even her mother, knew where she'd gone. Joan Dewhurst had come looking, and for the first time, Ronnie understood her old friend at bit more. It all made sense. Joan was more worried about what everyone would think than what Marley really needed. It reminded her of her aunt. The entire state was looking for Marley, and there'd been sightings of her in Tulum and LA. She was an urban legend, hitting every hip wellness spot. It was a way she could live on forever, immortal. It was what Marley wanted in the end.

Videos of Marley threatening to get everyone had been posted online, videos Caroline had filmed. They were jokes, but no one saw them that way now. The town murmured about the obvious guilt, how they'd embraced a crazy woman. Ronnie didn't correct them. She was safer this way—they all were.

The police were still looking for Marley; that was the official story anyways. But not the sheriff. He was retiring, and Ronnie was glad for that.

But no one really vanished. Marley was where she belonged, in the desert. She'd been buried by Ronnie. One sister killed by another, one sister mourned by another. The ravens had watched as she'd done it, and she knew they were happy. Marley was primal now, part of nature. She was on a higher plane. It was Ronnie's gift to her.

Ronnie had taken over the store full time and even hired a staff. It was as good as hers now. Star didn't mind. She got to take it easy, look over the Center. It was her time to rest. She'd done enough for this town.

Sometimes, when Star wasn't around, Ronnie talked to Brit. There was never any reply, but still, she told her how things were going. "I miss you," she'd whisper at night.

Brit's death hit people hard. No one knew she hadn't really been there, that they'd been talking to the other sister. Ronnie had had no idea herself. They were completely different. Every part of them had been different. She'd truly believed Brit was real, and maybe her spirit had taken over Star. Maybe it was just grief and Star losing her mind. Ronnie didn't know the answer, but she didn't press Star either. She was there for her, and that was all Star needed.

The community thought Brit had been another victim of Marley. That in Marley's homicidal craze, she'd killed the other twin and left her somewhere. They didn't know the truth, and Ronnie wanted to keep it that way. Grief could make someone go insane, and now she was here to help Star. She would help her forever if she had to.

A year earlier, Ronnie wouldn't have thought this possible. Any of it. But she wasn't that Ronnie anymore. Old Ronnie was dead. She was New Ronnie now. But still her. She didn't pretend to be a god or a healer. She was just Ronnie.

She lit a fire in the firepit she'd had installed in her yard. It was her job to keep Star safe. She burned a wig first, Star's wig. The one she'd used when she'd dressed as Brit. The smell burned Ronnie's nose. Ronnie had made her hand it all over; there'd be no more Brit. Then she burned one page at a time from the file Caroline had given Marley. It had been hidden in Marley's car, like she'd said. Ronnie burned it all, until nothing remained of anything.

Ronnie knew the truth, though. She knew what had happened to her aunt the day she'd left her. She knew what she had done. She had to live with the guilt of that forever.

She had waited for the police to find her, but no one had. They didn't know there was a missing body in the basement. That Ronnie had shipped her aunt's things to Pakistan, knowing no one would ever claim them. Eventually, someone else would take the boxes.

The dreams had stopped. Or rather, the murder dreams had. The ravens still showed her things, but mostly it was about them. Helping a raven in trouble that she dreamed about or getting them a different food. They stayed close to Star and Ronnie, their homes. This was the ravens' home too.

It was going to be dinner soon. She was going out with Star. That's what they did now. Just her and Star, together. It was the family she had always dreamed about. One that no one could rip apart, because each accepted the other and their bad deeds. That was real family.

Ronnie glanced up and smiled. *New year, new me,* she thought.

ACKNOWLEDGMENTS

Finding one's people is the true reason to write: I found mine and am eternally grateful. This book was Kismet in so many ways. First and foremost, I want to thank my incredible editor Megha Parekh, and Gracie Doyle at Thomas & Mercer. Thank you for letting me get weird with it. And a huge shout-out to the amazing team at T&M: You're all such a pleasure to work with. Truly above and beyond. Major love to my agent, Chris Bucci, without whom this book wouldn't exist. I'm so glad you rep me! Love to Katrina Escudero for being awesome!

I wouldn't be here writing if it weren't for my family (thanks Dad, Ayesha, Omar, and the kids!) and my friends and writing group. Thank-you to Star Akhtar for letting me steal her name for a character! Alex Segura, Kellye Garrett, and Elizabeth Little—where would I even be without you three? You encouraged me when I didn't want to keep going with this book. I give thanks for you every single day! Thank-you to Chantelle Osman and P. J. Vernon for keeping me sane (or reveling in my insanity, either way!); Kelly Ford, John Vercher, Miranda Burgess, and everyone who read and gave me feedback on my little raven tale. Thank-you to Caroline Kepnes, Jess Lourey, Megan Collins, Gigi Pandian, Christopher Golden, and everyone who took the time to read this!

This book is the goth book of my dreams, and I'm so thrilled I can share it with all of you. Thank-you to the ravens for being so incredibly present and special. And with that, a major thank-you to my readers. Without you none of this would be possible.

ABOUT THE AUTHOR

Amina Akhtar is a former fashion writer and editor. Her satirical first novel, *#FashionVictim*, drew critical acclaim and was covered in the *Wall Street Journal*, *Forbes*, *Martha Stewart Living*, *Entertainment Weekly*, *Fashionista*, *Book Riot*, CrimeReads, and more.

Akhtar has worked at *Vogue*, *Elle*, the *New York Times*, and *New York Magazine*, where she was the founding editor of the women's blog *The Cut*. She's written for numerous publications, including Yahoo Style, *Fashionista*, *xoJane*, Refinery29, *Billboard*, and more. She currently lives not too far from the Sedona vortexes.